REBWAR

THE GIPSY

OLS SCHABER

RORSCHACH PRESS

GET YOUR FREE PREQUEL NOVELLA
TO THE REBWAR SERIES

Just visit www.olsschaber.com and sign up. You'll also get news on forthcoming books and deals.

PROLOGUE

He was sitting on the floor of a dark panel van, cramped in-between people, all swaying and sweating. Everyone trying to keep as silent as they could. Suppressing his fear and emotions, taking sharp breaths. They had been transferred from a lorry somewhere in a lay-by which had originally set off in Romania. He'd counted twenty men and women. He was the only one that spoke Persian. A few were Syrians, others he guessed were Libyan. Some spoke English, which was the common language. Their faces were dirty, tired and cautious. He'd tried to strike a conversation, but it was limited and no one was saying anything personal. But they were all in the same situation. Looking for a better life.

The van stopped, car, and engines idled around them. More traffic and stops. Signs that they were getting close. London had been promised to them. He knew they were in England. The van and cars drove on the opposite side of the road. Once they all had realised a series of shy smiles had been exchanged. He'd taken a loan to come over and till he had a job his family were paying the interest. The van broke sharply and honked. He tried to hold on but his body just slid into the man next to him and they all groaned and tried not to shout. Behind the metal divide the driver swore and carried on honking.

The van accelerated away and carried on its journey. He wished it over and his body was numb from sitting. Every position was a repetition of the pain he had been in. The vehicle stopped, and they heard some muffled voices followed by a chain being undone. Someone banged on the metal panel and it moved slowly till someone opened the back door. Light flooded into the cramped space. His eyes adjusted to the bright lights. He could make out a couple of white men waiving them out. He stretched himself, each limb slowly regaining their strength, groggy and tired as he crawled out.

'Come on, over there quick, quick. Haven't got all day.' Said a tall bald man.

He looked around the warehouse, which was filled with cardboard boxes, window frames, industrial blue plastic barrels. At the far end was a metal stair that led to an office with a man standing on the landing watching them. His left arm was tattooed with a snakeskin pattern. The two other men shouted at them to line up against the wall. They all struggled over some more than others. The older man stumbled over, his leg giving way. Without hesitation, he broke ranks and went over to help him. He felt a hand grab his arm. It was the bald man.

'You've been told.'

The tattooed man nodded.

'You're coming with me.' And he pulled him towards a door at the end of warehouse unit.

He tried to protest and fight back. 'I only help what you want? I help.'

But the bald man just carried on dragging him. His

strength too powerful to stop. Another man with a hoodie followed them into a dark office. Lights flickered on and he got shoved into an office chair.

He was too weak to fight back, hadn't properly eaten for weeks or drunk enough. Around was a mess of papers, boxes, filing cabinets and upended office furniture. The dirty carpet had dark stains and cut up cable ties.

The man with a hoodie slipped on brass knuckles and threw a punch into his gut.

He doubled up and felt his lungs empty. Another punch hit his back. Pain exploded whilst he tried to breathe in. His body struggling with a surge of extreme agony. Then another thump, his face jerked to the side with the impact and another. His body fell off the chair and onto the floor. A boot slammed into his back. Pain shot like an electric current and he felt himself spasm.

All he could see that blood dripping and falling onto a concrete floor. He'd passed out and now was being paraded in front of the others, still standing in line by the wall.

'This is what happens when you fall out of line.' Said a voice above him. 'No, silly ideas from any of you. You now belong to us, we own you.'

ONE

Rebwar looked into his cigarette packet. One lonely smoke danced around it. He rested his shaking hand on his leg, took the cigarette and crunched the packet into a ball. He stood up inside the crumbling grey facade of what had been a residential semi-detached. The ground floor was now a car-wash tunnel that led off the street. Next to it was a petrol station and a small café. Rebwar was in red and blue overalls and blue rubber boots. On his breast pocket was an emblem: Matt's Valet Wash. Opposite was a second-hand car dealer. The sound of water jets and whirring fans drowned out the passing traffic.

Rebwar noticed a black Range Rover with a private plate mounting the soapy wet curb outside the entrance. Two men stepped out: the driver was a tall, thin, fair-haired man in a white t-shirt, white trainers and with a tattoo of snakeskin pattern on his arm; the other was shorter, with a shaved head and a teardrop tattoo by his left eye. Both of them wore heavy-looking gold jewellery. They walked to the back of the car-wash using the neighbour's petrol forecourt. A car honked at Rebwar. He turned, picked up a microfiber towel and wiped the car. As he worked his way around the wet panels, he noticed a bunch of kids by the car dealership standing around a cluster of scooters, smoking and laughing. He hadn't seen them before. He bent down to pick up his polystyrene cup off the floor.

'Hey, Rebwar!'

Rebwar sipped his black coffee and looked up. In front of him, stood Matt, the owner of the car wash - medium build, scruffy grey hair, pot belly and faded tattoos.

'Meet Greg, the new guy. Show him the ropes. OK?'

Greg was fresh-faced and had the look of a scared boy who'd come straight from his remote Eastern European village. From his keen smile, he hadn't seen much of this world. Rebwar guessed he was in his early twenties, he appeared skinny but was sinewy and strong in overalls that were a little too short for him. Rebwar could see a glimpse of what looked like a Chelsea football shirt underneath them. Rebwar nodded to Matt, who pushed back his hair and left for his caravan/office, where he liked to hide and play video games.

'Wh-where do I start?' Greg asked above the noise of the car wash.

Rebwar lit a cigarette. 'I'm Rebwar.' He offered his hand. Greg shook it hard, as if he was trying to make an impression.

'N-nice to meet you.'

'My son supports the blues. Done this before?'

Greg smiled. 'Never.'

'Smoke?'

Greg shook his head.

'We'll start with drying. Ever washed a car?'

Greg shook his head again.

'Dishes?'

Greg smiled and squinted as if it was a trick question.

Rebwar handed him a microfiber towel. 'You dry the back of the car, and I'll do the front.' He laid the little towel over the back window, picked up another one, laid that next to it and slowly covered the back window with the towels to soak up the water.

The driver's side window buzzed down and a large round red face appeared. 'Hey mate!' Greg looked up, terrified. 'Yeah you!' Greg went over to the man. 'What the fuck are you doing?'

'Cl-cleaning, I mean d-drying the c-'

'Well get on with it, you idiot! And get those filthy towels off my back window.' As the window slid back up, the man added, 'Chelsea cunt.'

Rebwar raised his eyebrows and took Greg to one side. 'Just, watch me, OK? And do the same on the next car.' The boy nodded as Rebwar removed the towels from the car.

The window slid down again and smoke drifted into the air along with the man's irritated voice. 'Can't get the staff, can you? Country's going to pot.' Realising he wasn't being listened to by anyone, least of all the two men valeting his car, he shouted louder. 'Hey! That's what you get from a Chelsea supporting muppet!' Rebwar carried on polishing the car. A phone ringtone sang out loudly from the car's sound system and the man picked up. Before Rebwar could finish drying the boot he drove off, leaving drips in his wake.

'I need cigarettes.'

Greg nodded his head.

'I'm going to get some. You're doing OK. Just keep doing what I was doing. Got it?'

Greg smiled and carried on. On his way out, Rebwar spotted the two men from the Range Rover again, they were inside Matt's Portakabin now, and angry muffled voices seeped through the closed door and blinds. It was just off the forecourt so Rebwar passed the petrol station and went into the toilets just behind the Portakabin and chose a cubicle. The conversation from Matt's office was just within earshot.

'Mate, you're going to take two more this week.'

'Wayne, I can't. I don't have space for more. And I can't afford them.'

'What don't you understand is what I'm saying.'

'I'll call the police, I will. Look...'

Rebwar heard laughter. 'You're such a dickhead - you've got a fucking record as long as my cock. Go on, do it and see what happens. Twat. Two more and then next week another two... got it?'

'Wayne you can't, people will start to get suspicious and—'

'Matt!' One of the men slammed his fist hard onto the desk or something else solid. 'OK?'

A moment passed and the door slammed shut. Another silence, and then. 'Shit, shit, fuck, fuck.' Rebwar heard Matt let out a huge sigh, open the caravan door and shout out the names Jaz and Will. Rebwar stayed in the cubicle to listen. Two men's footsteps echoed in Matt's caravan.

'Yeah, boss.'

'Right lads. No easy way to say this... so I'm going to make it quick. I'm going to have to let you two go. Not enough work, OK?'

'What?' One of the voices said. 'Seems really busy out there. I'd say you need more men, not less!'

'I'm not in the mood for discussing it, right?' Matt snapped back.

'Boss you can't be serious.' The other man sounded

foreign, and very upset. 'Just been here two weeks. Hey, you just give the job...'

'It's fucking final. I'm not talking about it. Here's your money, now go!'

'What did I do? No, scratch car or nothing.' Rebwar could hear the man's desperation.

'Just take the f'ing cash and piss off, understand?'

'OK, OK...'

Rebwar heard them shuffling to collect their money and leave. Matt sat down in his chair which rolled and hit the partitioning wall. He banged on the table and let out a groan. Rebwar's phone rang and he tried to silence it, but it slipped out of his hands onto the floor. He grabbed it and answered.

'Husband? Husband it's Musa, my little scared baby. The school, he's... he's... had detention. Is like prison for him. And make sure they pay you today. Rent is due...'

Rebwar walked out of the toilet. 'Detention for what? Hourieh take a breath... again?' He heard some slow shuffling heavy footsteps and lowered his voice. 'Burned his homework? The little shi— ...OK well, a detention will toughen him up.'

Matt walked into the toilets as Rebwar stood in front of the wash basins and looked at his boss in the mirror.

'Get back to work - and by the way, this is your last day.'

Rebwar covered the phone. 'Matt, wait I...' Matt slammed the toilet door and left. Rebwar returned to the call. 'Hourieh, listen... I'll be there as soon as I can.' He hung up without waiting for the inevitable abuse from his wife, and chased after Matt. 'Matt, wait!' Rebwar grabbed his arm.

'What?' He looked down at Rebwar's hand.

'Matt, your new boy needs a few more days of training.

He's annoying clients.' Matt's eyes fixed on him. 'You'll lose money and clients. Let me show him the job. Then I'll go.'

Matt looked at him, nodded and grumbled off.

'And I've got a family emergency. I'll be back as soon as.'

'Yeah, whatever. Fucking shits, all of you! Shits. You're all fucking foreign cunting shits.' He shouted at his work-force before returning to his caravan and slamming the door. Rebwar heard him start up a video game as he walked away.

TWO

Geraldine woke to an annoying and very persistent alarm, which was weird as she didn't remember setting one. On further inspection she realised it was her phone and scrabbled to scoop it off the floor before she missed the call.

'Where are you?'

'Sorry? Oh, hi.' Geraldine looked at her phone. It was 10:12 am. Shit. 'I must have slept through my alarm. I'll be there in half an hour.' The call had already been dropped.

Geraldine swung her bare legs onto the floor and knocked over an empty wine bottle which rolled into two crushed beer cans. She was wearing a white tank top and black knickers and scratched at her loose flesh as she yawned and felt her pulsing headache creep towards her eyeballs. Snapshots of a dream suddenly flashed into her vision and she held her chest, looking at her left hand. She remembered holding a bleeding pumping heart. O'Neil taking it away from her and stubbing his cigarette out on it. Geraldine felt a cold shiver run down her spine and trembled. It was over a year since Detective Chief Inspector Richard O'Neil had forced his way into her flat, tied her up and tortured her. She had been working for him as a jobbing DC, when she found out he was involved in an organ smuggling ring they had both been investigating. It had been a strange case, body parts showing up, people disappearing without a trace. Her unofficial partner, Rebwar, brought in for his expertise in the less official side of policing, skills he'd picked up during his time in the police force in Iran, caught the man responsible for doing the dirty work of harvesting the organs. But by then, the actual number of people who had gone missing was hushed up and the murderer, an ex-military medic was handed over to 'Plan B'. This was the secret organisation Geraldine had inadvertently got herself entangled with after a slight error of judgement put her career and freedom in jeopardy. Now they owned her. The problem was, she had no idea whose side they were really on, or even who they were. One thing she did know was that when she was tied up and being punched in the face by O'Neil, she'd never been so pleased to see them. The evidence she needed to prove O'Neil was guilty had finally shown up, thanks to her unusually helpful ex-husband who had got hold of the vital CCTV film, putting O'Neil in the frame. Plan B saw the footage, rescued her and set fire to her flat, with, as far as she could tell, O'Neil still in it. And he'd been tormenting her nightmares ever since. Along with the one image Geraldine would never be able to get out of her mind. In her dreams she saw over and over again the huge gaping hole in her girlfriend Zara, 'Zee's chest, where her heart had once been. Every night she felt herself falling into that deep black void. She shivered again and despite her natural instinct to slump on the sofa and pour herself a large drink whenever she thought of Zee, she resisted the temptation. Her thoughts went to Rebwar and what Plan B had last said to her. 'You make a good team', the big boss had said. They had agreed to get him and his family a permanent Visa, but still hadn't made good on that promise. So they were both beholden to the mysterious organisation, and now they were calling on her again. Where this left her police job she wasn't entirely sure, although being a jobbing DC clearing up all the shit in the office wasn't exactly her idea of police work. But she had no doubt that the meeting she was now over an hour late for would reveal all. Or rather, as much as they were prepared to reveal, which was usually the bare minimum. The sun shone through the blinds and she squinted. The bedroom in her relatively new modern flat was sparse: a black and white framed picture of London's skyline; another two of the Gherkin and the Shard; two large open cardboard boxes in a corner; a smaller one being used as a side table with a lamp on it.

Geraldine checked her phone again. 'Fuck.' She got up and went to the bathroom.

———

In her black bomber jacket, black jeans and DMs Geraldine walked into Starbucks. In the far right corner was her new Plan B contact: a slight woman around 40, mousy brown hair, brown-rimmed glasses, subtle makeup and a grey two-piece suit. Geraldine attempted a smile. She hadn't had her caffeine yet and was still groggy, as if she was under an invisible duvet. She rubbed her face as she collected her coffee and carried the large cup over to the table. The woman made a point of checking her small but expensive looking watch.

'Glad you could make it.' She smiled tightly as Geraldine took a seat in front of her.

'Sorry, my alarm—'

'Yes. You said,' the woman tilted her head. 'Heard of first impressions?'

She took a polite sip of her tea and Geraldine guessed that she might once been some sort of accountant, and probably committed fraud or something to have been enlisted by Plan B. She was thin and wiry, but there was a quiet strength to this woman, even if she looked like a mouse.

Geraldine took a swig of the warming coffee as the mouse took out a grey file and opened it, efficiently swapping her existing eyewear for some light, silver-rimmed reading glasses. It was Geraldine's file: she saw her custody photo stapled onto one of the papers. She felt like everyone in the place was looking at her, prying eyes boring into her back. Obviously that was the point. The woman was trying to put her in a box, one that she could open up and use the contents of at her leisure. 'That's ancient history.'

'Let's start with your timekeeping. Lost time is never found. You need to keep it.' The woman wrote something in the file. Geraldine fiddled with her coffee cup, waiting for the caffeine to hit. 'You need to pass a new assignment to the Robin. Only pay him on completion, I'm not having you waste money.' Geraldine breathed in and was about to complain. 'I make the rules, I run a tight ship, unlike your predecessor.'

'Oh yeah, what happened to Squirrel... sorry, what do I call you?' The woman looked over her reading glasses in silent warning and then carried on reading the file. Tough crowd, Geraldine thought and smiled at the stern schoolmistress look. She crossed her legs, sipped her coffee and looked around the café which was starting to get busier with groups of yummy mummy's. This was the first contact Geraldine had from Plan B since she'd left her burning flat with a hastily packed bag and not much else, under orders from her bosses. She was given keys to a new flat and told to wait for contact. That was over a year ago, until she received a text message yesterday telling her where and when to meet. She still had no real idea what had happened with the rest of the case, aside from the announcement at work that DCI O'Neil had resigned and left the country due to personal reasons. As she glanced idly around, Geraldine suddenly noticed a headline on the front of a folded newspaper on an empty table and sprang up to get it. It was a local rag called the Wimbledon Guardian, not one she'd heard of. She opened it to page eight and read the article that had caught her attention.

'Do you suffer from ADHD?'

'Look.' Geraldine pointed at the paper. 'The inquiry into the fire at my flat... two dead. Romanian migrants? What the fuck I—'

'That's water under the bridge. We feel you're ready to work for us again. She slid a brown envelope out from underneath Geraldine's file. 'Now go and give this to the Robin.' She motioned to the file. 'And remember, any insubordinate behaviour will not be tolerated. You really don't want to get on the wrong side of me. Do we understand each other?'

Geraldine nodded, feeling scolded. The mouse smiled her tight smile again as she got up to leave. 'Now, let's make this a pleasant working relationship.' She picked up her camel coloured coat and soft leather bag. 'When things go well, you are an asset to us. Just don't fuck it up.' She walked off leaving Geraldine momentarily stunned. She wasn't expecting that. She went up to get another coffee and thought again about the news article on her flat. It had been her home, her neighbourhood. She needed closure but, a year on, it seemed like it was back to business and she'd just have to live with it. Move on.

The woman still hadn't told Geraldine what she should call her, it annoyed her that she knew everything about her, and yet wouldn't disclose her own code name. She was like some kind of robot. Maybe she should call her that, although Mouse was probably more apt... or maybe the Rat. Geraldine smiled to herself, but thoughts of the two bodies found at her flat flew back into her mind and she googled for more news coverage on it. As she brought her coffee back to the table she moved the dirty cups out of the way and read the newspaper article again. The inquiry into the flat fire on Elms road had reached a verdict of accidental death. They found the charred remains of a two men suspected of being illegal immigrants from Romania. They believe it may have been a burglary gone wrong. Geraldine looked around her, that's what they always said when they didn't know or care what really happened.

She had found no other articles about the story online, which seemed odd. So, what had happened? When she left her flat, O'Neil, and Plan B's agents - codenamed Fox and the Squirrel respectively - were all still there. They said they were going to deal with O'Neil. So where did any Romanians come into it? That bastard who had left her with PTSD. Maybe something had gone wrong. Why two bodies and not three? And where did Romanians come into it? She had wanted to go back to the crime scene a week or so after it all happened, but she was told in no uncertain times to take a few weeks off and stay away. She went past two weeks later and a neighbour told her the flat had been totally redecorated.

Geraldine sipped her coffee and opened the envelope the woman had left. Inside was an assignment for Rebwar, it was signed the 'Ferret'. Geraldine laughed. How apt. No wonder she hadn't offered up her code name. Geraldine would have had a job trying to keep a straight face. Now she had to find Rebwar to deliver it to him and explain that he'd only get his money on completion. And somehow convince him to go to her flat. She finished her coffee.

THREE

Rebwar walked into the kitchen in an undone grey dressing gown, black boxers and a tank top. He wore a gold coloured medallion with an old Persian poem on it. Hourieh had found it in a market, the actual meaning of the poem had been lost, but it was meant for luck. Hourieh stood at the sink washing plates next to the radio, which was blasting out the news. Musa sat at the small breakfast table.

'They are holding an election!' Musa said. 'She wants to make a hard Brexit.' He frowned. 'Does that mean a war?'

'No, son. Politics. They want to float this island into the middle of the sea. Then we can all sleep soundly.' Musa looked at his father as if trying to work out if that was possible. On the table was a pot of coffee, a plate of cut lavash bread, feta cheese, cherry jam and one last slice of watermelon. The small window behind Hourieh offered a 5th floor view of early spring in north London. The sun was making a brief appearance through the fast moving clouds. Rebwar took a moment to savour the sunlight, nectar for his skin.

'And what about us?' Musa took the last slice of watermelon. 'Does she want to throw all us back to Europe?' Rebwar poured himself a black coffee and lit a cigarette.

'Musa, it's not to do with us.'

'Politics. This country is too proud of its past.' Rebwar sipped his coffee and changed the subject. 'Have you done your homework son?' He listened distractedly to the man being interviewed on the radio.

'Let's not kid ourselves. This election has been called because she wants to do away with the opposition. It's not about Brexit soft or hard. She wants a majority and to crown herself as...'

Rebwar drifted away from the radio and sat down, looking at his son for a reply. He read the slogan on Musa's t-shirt: 5 symptoms of laziness. 'Son, you must study. Life isn't given to you.' Musa looked down at his slice of lavash bread and spoonful of jam.

Hourieh came rushing in followed by an intense wave of heady perfume. 'I have made dinner for you. I'm going out with a friend.'

Rebwar turned and noticed she was all made up and ready to go out.

'It's burgers and chips. You can put them in the oven.'

'Card game?'

'Shopping and coffee. Bijan's new girlfriend, Katerena. She wants to see the sights.'

Rebwar remembered. Katerina was from Ukraine. A prostitute he had thought at first, but at a backgammon game, someone had mentioned that you could 'buy' brides in Ukraine.

'Where is she from again?' Musa asked.

'She's Eastern. A nice and caring girl. Now you call me when you get to school and then at lunchtime. I want to know you have eaten well.'

A gold digger. That was what Rebwar thought. It was rich pickings here in London. He'd heard she had done a lot of work on her appearance. He wanted to find out more about her but had to tread carefully.

'Wife, let him be.' The radio interview in the background droned on.

'... But is this for her to get her Brexit mandate? No deal is better than a bad deal. Is that what she wants? No deal? Where does that leave us? More bad politicians? It seems to me, the mediocre ones have gone to line their pockets in the public sector.'

Hourieh pushed some buttons on the radio to find another station. Rebwar sat down next to Musa. 'Son, I'll be back for dinner, don't worry. Now let me see your homework.'

Hourieh looked at her watch. 'Musa go and get dressed, no silly t-shirts, you have to make a good impression.' He got up, shoulder hunched as if he was carrying the weight of the world and went to his room.

'He'll learn. He needs friends.' Rebwar took a drag of his cigarette.

'Husband, this country is racist. How can he make friends? They mix everybody up and expect everybody to get along?'

Rebwar picked up the local Camden newspaper. There were some circled ads. 'Still looking for a job?'

'Husband, I need something to do.'

Rebwar tutted. 'I'll see what my friends say. Aren't you happy shopping?'

'On car wash money? Anyway, I need stim-u-lation.' Hourieh over-emphasised the word to her husband like a teasing child. She slapped his cheek semi-playfully and wafted out of the flat.

FOUR

Geraldine found Rebwar's car on a little side alley off of Macklin St in Covent Garden. It was lined with small townhouses and a large glass office block and was just off Drury Lane with its theatres and bars lining old cobbled streets. It wasn't a place where Geraldine would hang out. Musicals and plays were for children and retired folk. She had been dragged to a few shows by one of her old flames. She either snored through them or went to the bar. That's where the relationship had ended: in a bottle of wine at the bar. The car was parked on a single yellow by a little tree. It had been a while since she had seen Rebwar. The jobs had dried up since Plan B had changed their contacts. But that was just her assumption, they hadn't actually told her anything officially. She approached the car from behind and opened the rear door. Some Arabic electro music pumped out of the speakers, which didn't seem very Rebwar, but she sat down anyway. She was supposed to see a different pair of eyes in the rearview mirror when the driver looked up.

'Am on break,' said the man. He had the Evening Standard laid out on the steering wheel and there was a headline about the coming election. He was in his thirties, perhaps middle-eastern, thin groomed moustache and handsome. Maybe single, not that that mattered. Since Zara, Geraldine hadn't dated anyone, male or female. No drunken one-night stands either. She hadn't worked out if it was because she was scared of commitment, or the fear of caring about someone, only to have them leave her. Or die. She shook the thought away and noticed that the car smelled of clean laundry, with a hint of minty aftershave.

'I'm looking for Rebwar.'

He smiled and swung his body around to face her. 'Why you look for him?'

'Friend.' She took out a cigarette. He pointed to the no smoking sign. Was this Rebwar's cab?

'He's coming soon. you want a ride?'

Geraldine chuckled at the thought of that possibility. 'This is his cab?'

'Who are you?' His eyes scanned Geraldine as if looking for more clues about her.

'Geraldine. His friend. We have some catching up to do. So, is this now a time-share?'

His face loosened and changed to a surprised look. 'Not police?'

Did she smell that bad? Or had Rebwar mentioned her to him? 'Not your business, mate.' Shit, that kind of gave it away. She smiled to try and soften her tone. 'Is he coming here?' He nodded and stared. Geraldine stepped out to have a cigarette. As she closed the door, the central locking clicked. She dragged on her cigarette, letting the smoke calm her down. She guessed times were tough and Rebwar had to try to get as much money as he could.

She slid the brown manila envelope out of her bomber jacket. She hadn't even looked to see what the assignment was. The newspaper story about her flat had stayed with her. She slid the stapled A4 sheets out.

'Is that for me?' The gruff voice was close to her ear and her heart skipped. She took a step back. 'Shit you... you. Oh, you're such a shit!'

'Nice to see you too.'

She took a moment to look at Rebwar. He wore a white shirt and a loose navy jacket. He'd lost a little weight, a bit too thin, she thought. His thick black hair was neatly combed. 'Who's the guy?'

He smiled, 'Kamal. He's sharing the taxi. So, what's the new job.'

Geraldine shrugged her shoulders and passed him the envelope. 'It's payment on delivery of information. Been some changes.'

He lit a cigarette and scanned the sheets of paper. Now Geraldine wished she had taken a look. But her mind soon shifted to what she really wanted to ask Rebwar. 'I've got a favour...' She nodded over to the car. 'Is he going to leave?'

Rebwar looked up. 'Yes.' He went over and knocked on the driver's window. Kamal stepped out and they talked in what Geraldine guessed was Persian, she watched them talk, exchanging grins and gestures. Then Kamal smiled at her and nodded. He got his newspaper and little burgundy rucksack from the passenger side and walked off, phone in hand, talking English to someone.

'What did you tell him?' said Geraldine from the back seat. It felt like old times; Rebwar's little mobile meeting room. She lit up and Rebwar lowered her window. She smiled. 'And?

'That you were my new girlfriend.'

'Fuck off. Such a shit. Come on, tell me.'

'It's true.'

'Really? But doesn't he... OK.' Clearly, in other words, it was none of her business. She exhaled out of the window. Rebwar handed the envelope back to her.

'Are there some pages missing? Find the Gipsy... a little vague.'

Geraldine shrugged.

'Ferret?'

She sniggered. 'Yeah, she's a piece of work. Where do they get them? Anyway, about this favour.'

'So it's not business, but personal? From a friend to a friend?'

This was the first time he'd used that description. It felt good, like at school when someone called you a mate. 'Yeah, that's it. It's about my old flat. It burned down last year and they found two bodies. I need you to ask a few questions around the neighbourhood. You know... discreetly.'

'Do I need to know anything else? Was it O'Neil?'

Geraldine waited for a moment, she wanted to tell him everything but she couldn't. It was stupid, but she felt that if she held back, it would protect him from Plan B. Also it wasn't fair for him to get involved when she couldn't pay him. 'It's Plan B... so be careful. All I can say. OK?'

'I understand' He took a deep breath as if he was about to ask more questions.

'Can you drop me off by a pub? Need a drink. Any will do.'

Rebwar started the car, drove off, took a few turns then stopped in front of a pub called the White Hart on the corner of Drury Lane and High Holborn. The oldest licensed premises in London was hand painted in gold above the entrance. Geraldine got out of the car, stopped in front of the open double doors and finished her cigarette. As Rebwar drove off she gave him a little salute. 'From a friend to a friend'. She liked that. From the music and laughter seeping out from inside, the pub was busy. Lots of suited office workers letting their hair down. A group of three were outside on the corner. Holding pints and cigarettes. The only girl was listening to the two blokes talking about the upcoming election. A whiff of Chanel No 5 caught Geraldine and it perked her up like a chaser.

'And what about UKIP? Who I am supposed to vote for now? It's a fucking joke, that's what it is.'

'She's going to get away with a landslide. Hey Trudes, what do you think of May?'

Trudes sipped her large glass of white wine. Her face was freckled and little dimples indented her cheeks, round brown eyes were framed with trendy glasses which she pushed back up her nose as she thought about her answer. Geraldine felt like grabbing her. 'I don't like her. She's cold as ice. Leaves me uninspired. And why doesn't she want to go on the TV debates?'

'Where does Corbyn stand on Brexit, that's what I want to know?'

Geraldine flicked her cigarette into a red bucket that was propping open the black door. She went in, hoping the trio would still be there when she came back out to try her luck. There hadn't been much of that lately.

FIVE

It was 9:30 am, sunny with a warm breeze. Rebwar was on a shift at the car wash and stubbed his cigarette out as he watched the new guy Greg. He felt sorry for him, he'd obviously had a tough time with his stammer, being picked on and assumed to be an idiot. Just like freaks were in the middle ages, used for entertainment and never given the chance of an education. Greg would get lost, trying to clean every single drop of water from each car panel. It was like a cat and mouse game. Rebwar started at one end of the car and caught him staring at the drops, almost hypnotised.

Around him, people whistled to the music on the radio. Like a dose of happiness, it made the day easier. The usual nine o'clock crush hadn't yet materialised. They wanted their cars to be even shinier to compete with the sunshine. 'Want to see my fucking face. Not your fucking ugly mug.' Rebwar had been studying them. One of them was Fat Bob, who always wore a creaking black leather jacket. He had slicked back dyed hair and small black eyes that were too close together. They made you uncomfortable, like his dandruff. And he never had anything good to say.

Today Fat Bob had decided upon a thorough valet wash. No one wanted that job. He wouldn't pay for the inside to be cleaned but expected it to be spotless. It was a cheap trick that no one could complain about as Fat Bob seemed to have one over the boss Matt, so the man lorded it over whoever was unlucky enough to serve him. Fat Bob's car arrived at Rebwar's station, and it stank. He lit a cigarette to take the edge off of the pungent stench of stale sweat. It was an old silver Mercedes E class, scratched and potted with rust spots. It had probably been stolen or salvaged from a scrap yard. Rebwar would have to be careful not to take off any more of the flaking paint. For sure, Greg was going to struggle with his very thorough drying technique. Bits of loose bodywork had already been detached during the initial jet wash. Rebwar tried to help by subtly popping them back on while Fat Bob was supervising the washing of the rest of his car. Today this was the unfortunate job of Ajmed, a little thin man from Sri Lanka who would regularly lose control of the powerful jet.

Bob tried to shout over the spraying water and grab the trigger from Ajmed, yelling at him to watch out, pointing a fat finger at the flapping plastic trim. The terrified man tried to push it back into place but ended up taking it off. In a rage, Fat Bob spewed out a stream of racial abuse at the cowering Ajmed. Matt came out of his booth to calm the escalating situation, but it was clear this was not going to end peacefully.

For a couple of days now Rebwar had noticed some scooters hanging around and had asked some of his co-workers if they knew of any local gangs.

Scooters were a favourite with London gangs, used mostly for muggings and robberies. They were easy to steal and could escape quickly through traffic, so the police had little chance of catching them. Today they were back. Four of them. Two with passengers on the back. They all had helmets on so Rebwar could only see their beady eyes. From their slim physiques, he reckoned they were young kids, low down the pecking order. They seemed nervous and kept laughing, twitching and revving their engines. Rebwar was anxious, something was obviously going on, but no one else seemed to have picked up the mood.

Rebwar looked away from the scooters and back to the argument between Bob and Ajmed which had quickly escalated. It seemed that Ajmed didn't feel quite as intimidated as the fat man thought he should be, and Bob suddenly attempted to throw a punch. He missed, losing his balance instead, and his lumbering body fell comically onto the broken concrete. His jeans and cracked leather jacket soaking up the dirty water. His fat face filled with anger as he scrambled to his feet. Ajmed grabbed the jet wash and was ready to defend himself. Greg looked up nervously and stopped drying the car that he and Rebwar had been working on.

'Hey fuckwit you're gonna pay for this. Fire him! Matt, I never want to see that pakki mug here again, did you hear me?'

'Bob, calm down. Let's go to my office and we'll sort this out, OK?'

'I want that cunt to say sorry to me, OK? Now!'

'Sorry mister,' said Ajmed. 'I am.'

Bob was soaking. 'Find him some dry clothes, OK?' Matt said.

Ajmed looked confused. He had no idea even where to start looking for dry clothes, certainly ones that would fit someone that large. As Matt and Bob walked over to the office the four scooters, now all with pillion passengers, pulled into the forecourt and split into two groups. One lot headed for Matt's Portakabin. Baseball bats appeared from their leather jackets. Like a swarm, they dismounted and ran into the car wash forecourt. Greg's eyes were fixed on them. Rebwar felt a shove from behind and his legs gave way. He fell hard onto his knees. Another scooter had parked behind him. Rebwar threw his wet micro towel at the visor of the helmeted thug and tried to get up, but his knees gave way and he fell again. Rebwar reached out and grabbed his assailant's trainer.

The kid fell and his helmet hit the concrete floor. Rebwar kidney-punched him. Muffled cries of pain came out of the helmet. Rebwar grabbed the fallen baseball bat and used it to prop himself up.

He told Greg to run and went to see what was going on. It wasn't clever; running would have been the better option but that was not in Rebwar's nature. By now, the car wash workers were either running away or on the floor, rolling in pain. Another rider came in swinging at him; Rebwar anticipated the move and swung for the man's forearm. The bat connected square on and there was a crack, like he'd hit a dried branch. There was a moment of shock, followed by a piercing scream of pain. The man's arm flopped around like a rag doll. Then the dull thud of a gunshot rang out, and some of the gang started running back to their scooters. Rebwar looked towards the office.

The scooter engines revved and they all left as quickly as they had arrived. When Rebwar looked inside the Portakabin Matt was slumped over his desk. Fat Bob was nowhere to be seen. Blood was spreading over the desk. The bullet had exited through Matt's back and was probably lodged in the back of his chair. Rebwar checked for a pulse but couldn't find one. He could still smell the gunpowder and heard the sound of distant sirens. Someone had called the police so there wasn't much time. He stepped out of the office; in front of him was an Asian kid. Who'd taken off his helmet and was holding his broken arm. They had left him behind.

'Who sent you?'

The kid threw up and yelped with pain. There was no sense going to come out of him. Rebwar spotted a silver gun on the wet floor. He picked it up and put it into his pocket. Again not clever but useful. The sirens were coming closer. It was time to leave. He took the back entrance and went to get his car.

SIX

Rebwar sat in his car and studied the file that Geraldine had given him. He was still sore and troubled by the attack on the car wash and Matt's murder. He thought of returning to the crime scene, but it wasn't anything to do with him. He'd also have to explain why he took the gun. It was pretty stupid, but it might lead him to whoever was behind it. He was also sure someone would come after him, as he'd fought back and injured one of the scooter gang. His police instincts had kicked in and he'd acted without thinking. He dragged on his cigarette and read the file. He and Geraldine hadn't seen each other since she returned his car to him a year ago, after her flat had been gutted by fire. They had texted each other briefly, but it had been more of a cursory check to ensure each other was OK, and to find out if there was any news on the outcome of the case they'd been investigating. There had been none, but now there was a new assignment, so he guessed they both just had to move on.

His job was to find The Gipsy, and that was about as much information as they had given him, apart from ideas of where the name had been mentioned. Which had been around Essex and London. The file included maps of travpeller sites and Romany communities. It wasn't going to be that obvious, Rebwar thought. What they weren't saying in the report was why they wanted to find this Gipsy. That would have helped; it would have at least given him a direction, or some idea of who or what he was up against.

He tapped his cigarette on the half-open window and watched a dog walker collect a treasured pet from a house. The pets seemed to have a better life than most of the low-wage workers here in London. Back in Iran, you'd get lashed for walking a dog. Now Musa was asking for one.

He was parked up just around the corner from Geraldine's old flat in Clapham. Before starting the hunt for the Gipsy, Rebwar had planned to find out more about the fire. From what Geraldine had said, something strange had gone on. He logged into the Uber app to see if any local clients wanted a cab somewhere, maybe a passenger would know something. It wasn't long till he got a job. It was a woman going to the tube station, usually not worth the hassle for a few pounds.

He arrived at the corner of Abbeville Road and Briarwood Road as rain was sweeping in. He stopped at the house, where a woman with a pram was already waiting at the front door. It had a white arched balcony which offered shelter. Rebwar got out of the car and fetched an umbrella.

'Hello,' he said as he walked up to the house.

'Oh, you're a star. Normally I have to do it myself. They stay in their cars.'

'It's no problem.' Rebwar helped to push the pram while holding the umbrella. After a few fiddly moments, they managed to fix the seat into the car and fold the pram. 'Are you sure you only want to go to the tube station?'

'Oh, believe me, it's easier. And with the traffic? It's OK, thanks.' Her voice had a high pitch to it.

From the app, her name was Claire Wood. Her colourful raincoat was adorned with flower prints. She wore glasses and her brown hair was cut into a bob, for practical reasons Rebwar thought.

'Clapham Common? I can go a bit further to the Oval. If you're worried about money, I can set a price?' The intensity of the rain increased and hit the roof like little marbles.

'Oh, I guess so. It's not about the money. I'll pay.'

Rebwar typed in Oval tube station and smiled at her as he drove off.

'What age is your child?'

'Oh, ten months. She's called Rita, but we nicknamed her Nudge.'

'Cute smile.'

'Butter wouldn't melt.'

Rebwar chuckled, he'd heard that phrase before. 'Were you around when that fire happened round here?'

'Sorry?' Claire had been attending to Rita.

'The fire on Elms road, last year? Gridlock it was.'

'Is that what it was? I thought it was some kind of crime. So many police around. They even came knocking on my door.'

'Oh, is that right?' Rebwar followed the traffic up Clapham road.

'They were asking if I I'd seen someone fleeing the scene. A tall guy with his arm in a cast or something'. Rebwar stopped himself from swearing. So, Richard O'Neil could have got away. Aside from being Geraldine's boss on the organ smuggling investigation, O'Neil was a racist with whom Rebwar had had a number of run ins. He'd broken O'Neil's hand in a fight when they first met, and relations between them didn't improve much from then on. But from what Geraldine had said, Plan B had dealt with him.

When they told her to take a few possessions and leave, three men were still there, one of them being O'Neil. 'Oh', Rebwar said fishing a little more, 'so not a flat fire then? I thought it might be one of those faulty tumble dryers that went up in smoke. You know, like the Whirpool ones. You don't have one?'

'Oh no, no, I think ours is a German brand. My husband would have told me.'

'I wonder if they found him.'

'Who?' She smiled. 'Sorry. Got baby brain.'

'That man the police were looking for.'

'Oh, I didn't hear. I don't read the newspapers, no time. Some of the mothers said it was a burglary gone wrong. It's all these immigrants you see. Oh, I mean... not you.'

'Not everyone respects the law.' Rebwar stopped at a traffic light. The rain had eased off and he made a U-turn to drive up to the station. A few upset drivers honked at him. Claire thanked him as he helped her and baby Rita out of the car, and then drove back to Elms Road.

Over the road from Geraldine's old flat, a large house was being renovated so Rebwar parked up a little way down from the skip that was outside and walked up the path to the house. He looked around and went through the gap where the front door should have been. Walls were being plastered so it looked like most of the structural work had been done, hopefully over the last year or more. A workman in a dusty blue denim shirt and ripped black joggers was pushing a battered wheelbarrow.

'I'm looking for the foreman,' Rebwar said to him.

The barrow pusher's head swung back towards the house. 'He back there.'

Rebwar carried on through. The whole bottom floor was open planned, a huge extension had been built including a lavish kitchen. Drills and hammering sounded from the first floor. Three men stood together out the back, drinking tea, smoking and talking. All were similarly dressed in jeans, sweatshirts and high-viz jackets. Rebwar guessed the one with the big belly was the foreman.

'Looking for the foreman.'

It wasn't; a slim, dark-haired man looked up and nodded. He had dark-rimmed glasses and a crooked nose. Tattoos on his arms featured a large pirate galleon.

'I have a few questions, I'm a private investigator doing some work for an insurance company on the flat fire across the street last year.' Rebwar handed over a business card with his name and number on it. The man flicked the card over hoping for more information.

'Yeah? I'm busy, so make it quick. Bloody insurance. You know how much my company premiums have gone up this year? Tripled they have. Probably because of that, huh? More building codes and regulations too.' Rebwar waited for the rant to be over.

'Did you see the fire?' The man took a swig of tea and nodded.

'Who was here?'

'Me and about four others, same guys have been on this job from day one. Bloody mess it was. Lucky no other building went up in smoke.'

'Did you see anyone go in or out?'

He grumbled. 'No, not really'. Rebwar raised an eyebrow. 'Well, yes, if you count the ones in body bags. Jesus, we were stuck here for hours. Can't they just read the police report, the insurance company, who is it...AXA?'

'You didn't see any men going in?'

'Nah, busy working, mate. Which reminds me, I need to make a call.' And he turned away to chat with his colleagues before moving off and digging his phone out of his pocket.

Rebwar had a little look at the mess in the garden they had used as a storage area; slabs, bricks and a cement mixer cluttered what was left of the grass. On the way out he stopped the man pushing the wheelbarrow and asked him for a light. He dug a lighter out of his dirty jeans and Rebwar offered him a cigarette. 'Did you see the fire opposite?'

'Fire crazy, mate. Pops and bangs like fireworks in there and smoke, very black.'

'See anyone go in there?' Rebwar took a drag on his cigarette.

'No. Just two black bags with bodies. Robbery? They say Romanians from my country; I not believe it.'

'Why is that?'

'Lazy police, always us. We are not all Gipsys.'

'Have you heard of someone called the The Gipsy?' The man looked surprised.

'What you make bad joke? Stupid. Who you work for?'

'Insurance company. Investigator.'

The man shook his head and walked back into the house, leaving his wheelbarrow where it was. Rebwar stared at Geraldine's second floor flat, it had been completely renovated, you could almost still smell the fresh paint and new wooden windows. When he came past a week after it had happened the roof had been completely destroyed and a large blue tarpaulin covered what was left. If only he'd done something then. But he assumed it was all sorted, and Geraldine hadn't said anything. He tried to find a way into the back of the flat but there was no side access. Nor were there any obvious routes for someone to escape. He walked around the block. On Abbeville road was a little strip of wall protecting the gardens. By some garages, he noticed broken wooden fencing. A possible exit. There were white scuff marks on the corrugated roof of the three little lock-ups. Plaster from a cast? Surely not after this long. He looked around for any other trails then took a few photos with his phone. He dialled Greg's number and it went to voicemail. For a moment he thought of leaving a message. It would have been the fifth one.

SEVEN

The following day, Rebwar had a taxi fare that took him close to Enfield town train station. He'd tried to make conversation with his passenger, a stern suited man but he just grumbled and tapped on his laptop. This was just down the road from Matt's car wash. Rebwar hadn't planned on going there after he'd dropped his fare, but he was in the area, and his curiosity got the better of him. He drove down to Chase side road. The car wash was shut and taped off, as was the petrol station. There were no parking restrictions, so he found a space down a residential road and parked up.

Opposite the church next to the car wash was a Men's hairdressers 'Hair by George'. Rebwar passed the rotating barbershop pole and walked in to get a trim, and maybe some gossip. He sat down on one of the black plastic chairs. It was a simple set up. There was only room for one or two clients, and it looked like it had been around for decades: yellowing paint, old fashioned sinks and worn lino. Unlike so many other new trendy chains this was about the job and not the experience. He appreciated it when someone was proud about their craft. Glitter and technology hid problems all too well.

He smiled at a trim, white-haired old man with a shiny bald patch. His thick moustache was his pride. He nodded an acknowledgement to Rebwar and carried on trimming. Rebwar sat down and noticed the arm of the man in the barber's chair: it was covered in a snakeskin tattoo. The same man that had come in to bully Matt about his workforce. Wayne. From his reaction, he didn't notice Rebwar, who took a chair immediately behind the barber so that he would block Wayne's view in the mirror. The radio was playing eighties music, Radio 2, Rebwar guessed. A few pictures of men's model haircuts hung around the walls. They were from a few decades ago, which would fit into today's Iran although some of the hipster trend was filtering through to the capital. Style over substance, he thought.

'Were you here when they hit Matt's place, George?' Wayne asked from the barber's chair.

'No, mate. But if I find out I'll be giving them something to think about.' George trimmed around his ears. 'Bunch of little shits. Who do they think they are trying to rob Matt?'

Wayne stood up. 'Sure, I heard he had debts, but I mean why kill the bloke? You're not going to get the money back.'

'Luckily I'm mortgage free and didn't piss my money away down the races like my dad. Every day up to the dogs. Died in front of his bookie. Couldn't have made it up.'

'Did you know Matt?'

Rebwar was pretending to read an old car magazine that he had found on a seat. He glanced at his phone, still no answer from Greg. He was now getting worried about him.

'Just as a neighbour, not much more, seemed to work hard.'

Rebwar studied Wayne from behind the magazine:

clean white Nike trainers; blue jeans; he had a few gold rings on his fingers. Like him, Wayne was fishing for information. George clipped the man's eyebrows.

'Back in five.' Rebwar showed George a cigarette as he got up. George nodded as he picked up a mirror and Rebwar stepped out onto the street. Rebwar lit up just in earshot of what the man was saying. Wayne was getting up and paying.

Rebwar tried Greg again. While the number rang he watched Wayne leave the barbers. The ringing shifted to voicemail and Rebwar dropped the call. With a confident sway, Wayne went to the corner and into the Six Bells, a pub with a dirty white facade, cracking black woodwork and some loose Sky Sports' banners. Rebwar followed him in to where a few men stood at the bar. Blackboards announced weekly karaoke and disco and a colourful fruit machine flickered in a corner. Rebwar felt self-conscious about following Wayne but the man was a person of interest. He had either invested in Matt's business or was blackmailing him. Rebwar had to confront him somehow.

Rebwar ordered a drink, pint of Stella. The barmaid poured it, her white top showing her ample breasts and the outline of her bra. She flicked off the pump, rings on every available finger. She had piercings in her nose, ears and lips. Rebwar made eye contact with Wayne and he registered it. Rebwar sipped his beer. Wayne called the barmaid over and she gave him a cheeky smile. She walked over to him, and he leaned in to whisper something in her ear. She covered her mouth with her hands and giggled.

Rebwar went to find the toilets. The sharp smell of bleach partially masked the stench of stagnant urine. Water dripped out of the old plumbing. Behind him, the rusting hinges screeched. Someone had followed him in. Before he could turn around Rebwar was shoved into a cubicle as Wayne launched into him.

'Don't like snoopers. You were in Georges place just now. What do you want?'

'Hey, hey.' Rebwar tried to get up, but Wayne held him down with his tattooed arm and it looked like he was being held down by a snake. 'I used to work at the car wash.'

'Really? For who?'

'Matt.'

'Were you there when it happened?'

'Yes.'

'Why haven't they arrested you?' His face came closer to Rebwar's.

'Didn't want any trouble. Need the job. You know.'

'And you know nothing about what happened?'

'He was robbed. Kids on scooters.'

'Yeah, that's right... bad men. Scooter's hey?' Wayne let him get up and Rebwar straightened his shirt and jacket. Rebwar wanted to ask about Greg, but the man was on edge and obviously not going to give him information about his business.

'Sorry about that.' Wayne stepped back, light on his feet like a boxer. 'So you need a job, right.'

Rebwar nodded.

'What's your name?'

'Amir.' Rebwar extended his hand.

'Wayne. Take this number and text me, right?' He slapped Rebwar's hand.

Rebwar took out his telephone and typed in the number he gave him.

'What's your skills?' Wayne said. 'Or you got a CV?'

'Have a driving license.'

Wayne went over to the wash basins. Stood in front of

the mirror and leaned in to look at his haircut. He tidied the little quiff and passed his palms over the side of his head. 'You're clean, right? No funny business. Don't want anyone asking about you. Right, Amir?' He looked at Rebwar in the mirror.

'Clean and ready to work.' Rebwar smiled and did a little more fishing. 'I think I saw you before at Matt's? What car do you drive?'

'Silver Beamer. Cab. 330i. M trim. Bird magnet, mate.' Wayne laughed and got out a stick of gum. 'Got any mates that need a job too, come to me. I'll sort it out.'

Rebwar was about to ask about Greg, but Wayne's attention was on another track as he turned towards the exit. 'Where you from?'

'Iran.'

'Came on the raft?' Wayne smiled in the mirror, watching himself.

'Yeah. Something like that.' Rebwar held up the card, 'I'll be in touch' and left the toilet.

EIGHT

Rebwar headed to his local restaurant, Shishawi, on the Edgware road. He'd arranged to meet his old friend Tamar, the exotic dancer who worked in various Soho clubs, to see if she might have heard anything on the grapevine about people smuggling. It was a long shot, but it would be nice to see her again. The place seemed a little shabbier than usual, the owner was on an extended holiday in Turkey. It had been over a month and the manager was letting some things slide. Jokes were flying around from the staff about exactly what he was doing there. Some were saying he was out there for a nip and tuck, others for liposuction. They probably would never know for sure, but things were definitely a little more lapse than usual. The music was veering towards the Mediterranean influence rather than the traditional barbs the owner liked. Prices had gone up, but since the referendum everything had. Most Brexiteers thought it was a conspiracy. Rebwar was reading the Tehran Times, a government-sponsored newspaper, he had bought at Marble Arch News, one of the few newsagents left in the area. He liked to have printed paper in his fingers rather than read the news on a small screen.

Tamar passed by with her sports bag slung over her shoulder, she was dressed in a bright pink tracksuit with the brand, Hollister, over all her available curves. Rebwar called her over. She turned, adjusting her overly large sunglasses and smiled, her lips had had a fresh dose of silicone and were pouting involuntarily.

'Sorry, babe. I'm late.' She kissed him on the cheek.

'Sit, sit, don't worry about it. I have news to amuse you.'

Tamar put her bag on an empty seat and sat on the next one.

'Tea, or something stronger?' said Rebwar.

'I'll have a small beer.'

'I would never have guessed.' Rebwar smiled at her and called over to one of the waiters. They joked back saying that his girlfriend was here.

'I need to know who smuggles people in.' He asked Tamar hoping to find out more on how Wayne got his workforce.

'No chit chat then? How do you like my new hair? Smells good, eh? I managed to burn the last lot of extensions.' Rebwar frowned. 'Argument with a scented candle, I couldn't get rid of that smell for weeks.'

'Nice colour.' He attempted to seem interested. 'What is your natural colour?'

'OK, forget it. You are terrible at chit chat'. She nodded a thank you as her beer and his coffee landed on the table. She took a long drink and leant forward. 'When I was last in that scene the Chinamen ran the racket. No idea who does it now. I'm a free woman, you know.' She put her hand on his and looked around for an audience. 'I'm sure they will have been shut down. Old History. Oh look... telling you how old I am.' She posed for Rebwar.

Rebwar sipped his coffee. 'Any names?'

'Darling it's so long ago... but...' Her long pink fingernails drummed on the table. 'Hang on... you know there was a guy called Kim Dong.' She covered her mouth as she smiled. 'He was a right old character. He had a hand in a lot of the Soho dance clubs. Some of the women belonged to him.'

'Belonged?'

'He was a pimp. But his main business was people smuggling. Last I heard he'd retired and was in the casinos. Genting being one of his faves.'

'What about your friends? The other dancers?'

'They've all changed, I'm the old girl now. They all talk foreign and keep to themselves.'

'I thought you were from Turkey?'

'I was, but that's ancient history. How's the wife and kids? Keeping you married?'

'Can you find out who smuggles people in? I've got a case. There is money...' Rebwar hoped she wasn't going to ask for an advance. He was going to have to find a solution soon. 'Heard of someone called the Gipsy?'

'What, just the Gipsy?'

Rebwar smiled. Her attention span needed a break. 'Are you dancing tonight?'

'Trying a new thing. Have you heard of those internet cams?'

'No, what does it involve?'

'I can do it at my house. Flat actually. I just need a computer, a camera and some lights.' Rebwar looked at her trying to understand what she meant. 'You know?'

Rebwar shook his head.

'I get naked in front of the camera and people watch and tip me. They can chat to me too. I get tips for doing different things.'

'Really? And people pay? To see you?'

'Cheeky,' She slapped his arm. 'Good money, and I get to meet people from all over the world. My friend is making good money from this. She has given up dancing.'

'Just get a computer and you can see girls dancing on the screen.' Rebwar laughed and ordered two beers. 'Crazy world.'

'It was big before, when it was specialised. Now everyone can do it. Like YouTubers but for adults.'

'My son watches loads of them. PewDiePie. I don't get it... why watch someone play a game? Are we turning into voyeurs?'

'It pays. Hell, I'm gonna try it. No pimps or sickos trying to follow you home. Hey, Berker.' She called over to Rebwar's Turkish waiter who from time to time would help him out with information and other things. 'Do you watch these cams?'

He looked around him, checking that no one was listening. 'You mean on the internet? Girls with tits and all that?'

Tamar nodded and smiled.

'My cousin is on them all the time, ahh, he's single and bored. Spends all his money.' He tutted and flicked his chin. 'Don't tell me you are on it too? Tamar, you're too classy a lady. You need a husband, I'll find you one.'

'Get me a nice classy cocktail then.'

Berker moved closer to Rebwar, 'need anything moving?' He winked at him.

'Thanks, not at the moment. Payments have been delayed.' Berker started to head back to the bar, but Rebwar caught him. 'You haven't heard of The Gipsy, have you?'

All of a sudden, the lights went down and the music to happy birthday blared over the restaurant speakers. Everybody looked at a cake with sparkles coming in. For a moment, Rebwar wondered if it was Tamar's. But the cake passed them to a table at the front and a large group of large men and women dressed in black, Arabs he thought.

'Yeah, there is a bloke that comes in and smokes them.'

'No that's Gitannes! Gipsy, Gipsy!' he shouted Berker over the music, which had changed to some Arabic pop.

'Ah, no, then. But I'll keep an ear out.' And he winked again and leaned in. 'Boss is coming back, I'll need to settle that bill. You know, he doesn't like giving credit. To any of us.' He pulled at his thick white moustache.

Rebwar nodded.

Tamar laid another layer of red lipstick on her jelly-like lips. 'What is it with this Gipsy guy?'

'Not even sure myself. Chasing a ghost.'

NINE

Chinatown was only a couple of streets across from Soho. Rebwar had never really driven in there as the main drag, Gerrard Street, was for pedestrians. People tended to be dropped off just outside it on Shaftesbury Avenue, which had a few Chinese restaurants dotted between the coffee chains. Taking the bus into town was a novel experience and he'd fancied a change of scene. The tube would have been quicker, especially as it was past the evening rush hour, as it was, it took the 113 bus an hour to get to Oxford Circus, but he enjoyed the view. He got off and walked down Regent Street to Piccadilly Circus, which was having its crazy light show updated with some new technology. It didn't stop all the tourists from gathering and looking lost, taking selfies and watching street performers. You would have thought it was some kind of theme park with its dubious freak shows. And then there were the overpriced shops, bars and restaurants.

He carried on along Shaftesbury avenue with its slow traffic and colourful theatres, watched a couple of fire engines leave their garages and honk their way through cars and buses. It was there he noticed what he was looking for: Genting Casino on the corner next to the Cambridge theatre. Set on the first floor, the windows promised *card games, slots bar & food*. Written in English and Chinese, it was the one Tamar had mentioned. The entrance was flanked by a wrought iron railing and some fake shrubbery. It felt like you were stepping into a hotel. He walked in and was immediately asked for his passport.

For a moment he thought they were arresting him. The big man standing next to the small pretty Asian girl looked down at him. His suit bulged, not hiding any of his bulk, and large square hands were ready for any trouble. The woman held her smile waiting for Rebwar. It was normal to have your papers with you back in Iran. Here he had gotten out of the habit. Berker had told him to bring his passport, so he pulled it from his inside jacket pocket. It was the first time he'd used it here.

They didn't look at it in any detail, just scanned the photo page and let him go upstairs. He'd seen casinos in the movies but never been in one. He took a moment to look at the different games. House always wins, they said and it seemed from the decor they were right. He wasn't here to gamble; they didn't have his game anyway. Dominoes wasn't known as a high stakes game. He walked around looking at the players. A mix of nationalities, but Asians dominated. He had no idea what Kim Dong looked like and he couldn't just ask any old punter. He had to tread carefully. This was Dong's element.

Rebwar decided that he had to invest something to get some information. That meant playing. The croupiers probably knew their customers like a good bar tender knows their drunks. He looked around for a quiet game where he could ask some questions. The blackjack table looked empty and he went over. It was one he kind of understood. Highest score or twenty-one. He'd forgotten to provide himself with chips and went to get some. Fifty pounds worth was as much as he wanted to get; each pound he lost chipped away at his self-respect and the bills were mounting up. He placed some of his chips on the table. The dealer was a silver-haired man, in his forties he guessed. Had acne scars on his puffy face and his skin was pasty white. Maybe he lived mostly at night?

'Good evening, sir. Fancy a game of blackjack?'

Rebwar looked at the green felt matt. Written in black and red were the basic rules. *Blackjack pays 3 to 2: the dealer must hit on sixteen and stand on all seventeen's, pays two to one, insurance pays two to one.*

'What the minimum bet?'

'Five pounds minimum, and if you're feeling lucky three grand is the maximum the house allows. Want to start with an easy one, sir?'

Rebwar put his stack of chips on the table. He searched for a five pound one and placed it on the felt table. An Asian man sat at the table and put down two hundred-pound chips. The dealer just nodded to him. Rebwar nodded too. The dealer dealt the cards from his dealing shoe. Two cards each. Rebwar had a ten of clubs and three of hearts. The man had a pair: seven of diamonds and seven of clubs. The dealer had three of hearts and a king of clubs. The man split his bet.

'The gentleman would like to split his bet.' The dealer dealt him two more cards. It was a three of clubs and ace of hearts.

'Quiet night?' said Rebwar.

'Comes in waves, sir. Like the winning and losing.'

Rebwar tapped the felt with his index finger and the

dealer dealt him another card. He got a queen of hearts - bust. The dealer took his cards and chips away. Rebwar smiled at his lack of luck. The dealer dealt the Asian man two cards and flipped over. A jack of clubs and three of diamonds. It was the dealer's turn. He flipped an eight of clubs. The Asian man grimaced and sucked his lips in. He snorted some phlegm and said something in Chinese. The look on the dealer's face as he collected up the cards said he heard the snorting all the time, but still wasn't able to block it out. The Asian man decided to go to another blackjack table and look for a better turn. Rebwar put down two five-pound chips.

'I'm looking for Kim Dong. Is he here tonight?'

'Sir, I'm not at the liberty of giving out customer's details. Drink?'

Rebwar looked behind him. A pretty Asian waitress in a tight-fitting top and short skirt was waiting for his order. He smiled. 'Small beer please.' She turned and went to the bar. The dealer dealt him two cards: ace of diamonds and a jack of clubs. Rebwar smiled and the dealer dealt his set. A two of diamonds and five of clubs, and carried on. An ace followed by a queen of hearts. The dealer paid out to Rebwar. He looked around for another game and a high-pitched laughter caught his attention. make up and painted nails. Rebwar tapped the table for him to deal. Rebwar got a seven of spades and an ace of hearts.

'If I was to say that was Kim, would I be right?'

Rebwar noticed the dealer looking over at the laughing man. Rebwar had noticed him too, Long, unbrushed hair tied in a ponytail, thick smudged

The dealer dealt himself two cards. A King of hearts and a Queen of diamonds. He nodded. Rebwar knocked on the table. Dealer slid and flipped a two of hearts. Rebwar knocked the table again and got a king of spades. The dealer collected his cards and chips. Rebwar got up and walked over to Dong. He could tell immediately that the man liked to be the centre of attention. Around him were a few young men who looked barely eighteen. They hung on to every word or gesture that Dong made. All were dressed similarly: jeans and tight t-shirts showing any piercing or tattoos they might have. Rebwar could see that it made some people feel uncomfortable; then the group moved to another game.

The little gang went over to the roulette table where a few couples and some men were playing. As soon as Dong and his entourage moved in, they took over the table. The original players all stared at them. Dong made some jokes, to which his gang of boys laughed excessively at, like they were being paid to do it. Rebwar sat opposite the croupier, who had a thick black moustache and an ill-fitting light brown wig. He looked nervous at Dong's arrival as the man slid a large stack of chips across to black six.

'Sir, £200 maximum bet.'

'Don't insult me. I have credit here. Throw that little ball and let me hear its cute little bounce.' He grabbed one of the men and kissed his lips. The croupier looked around for someone. Rebwar couldn't tell who, but he must have found them as he got the go-ahead to let them play. Les jeux son fais, He threw the ball into the spinning roulette. The little black ball bounced around, everyone watching it make its little dance between the passing numbers and finish on the number thirty-six. Dong made a high-pitched cry and his entourage added to the drama. Rebwar felt like he was watching some kind of pantomime.

He put a stack of six red and white chips on red. One of the Asian men from Dong's entourage looked at him like he had done something wrong. His cheeks were highlighted with blusher. He puffed his chest at Rebwar and wiggled like he had an itch around his crotch. Rebwar couldn't work it out.

'Faites vos jeux,' said the croupier.

Dong put down five twenty pound red and white chips on a few numbers. The other players placed their chips on individual numbers. Rebwar decided to put a yellow and white five-pound chip next to Dong's number twenty-two. The man who had been checking him out whispered something into Dong's ear. He just nodded and looked on.

'Les jeux sons fait,' and the ball made its dance into the spinning wheel. Some of Dong's boys were now shouting at it, trying to encourage it. The little ball bounced and stopped on twenty-two. They all jumped around like they had won the world cup. Each of his boys kissed him. One put his hand down his swirly shimmering shirt. Rebwar spotted a red bra. As the croupier dished out the chips onto the winning square and colours, the boy took Rebwar's winnings.

For a moment, Rebwar wasn't too sure what to do. His instinct was to grab it back. 'Hey you, hey! You!' But they were still celebrating. Rebwar walked around the table to confront him about the mistake, which he well knew wasn't. He grabbed the boy's thin, soft arm. The boy jerked around like he'd been bitten. 'Watch it man. You try to hurt me, man!' And lifted his arms away from him as if Rebwar had tried to hit him.

'You've taken my winnings.' Rebwar said calmly.

'What? No, no it was mine, you thief! Get this man off me!'

Dong squeezed between Rebwar and the table. The waft of a cheap aftershave washed over him, it was like he had been bathed in it. There was a hint of sweat mixed in with the Jasmine. 'You leave, thief!' He looked at the Croupier 'Call management and get this man out. Or I call police. Understand?'

'It's just a simple mistake.' I put a five-pound chip on the same square.'

'He lie, he lie!' said one of the men.

'I didn't see him put anything. You trying to steal from Kim, thief?' Another one screamed.

The croupier tried to say something but was drowned out by the boys' shrill voices. Two men in black suits came.

'He just tried to steal from me.' Dong said. 'Take him away!'

'Let's watch the CCTV,' said Rebwar.

'Sir, calm down. You step back from the gentleman here and come with us.'

'I'm owed money, I put a five pound chip on twenty-two. Ask the croupier.'

'Get the dirty fucking foreign thief out of here. I won fair and square!' Dong shouted theatrically, and his entourage joined in again. The security men grabbed Rebwar's arms. He gave a token struggle but thought it better to go with them. People around stared at him as if he was clearly guilty.

'I want to see the manager. Who is he?'

They pushed an emergency exit and took him onto a bare concrete staircase. Strip lights made it feel like a sterile cold box. One of the men snatched his wallet from his jacket.

'Hey, that's mine. You have no right.'

'Mate, we can do what we want. You're on private property. Were you trying to steal?' He took out all of Rebwar's money and his driving license. 'We're taking this, right? And if I ever see you here again, you won't be walking again. Understand?'

'No, no I want the police. This is theft, I won on the roulette. Watch the CCTV.'

'Well, it's too bad, there is no CCTV here.' Rebwar had to act quickly.

As one of them continued to rifle through his wallet, he kneed the other one in the crotch. It took a moment for his face to register the pain, but it got there soon enough. Rebwar decided to send a message to these people, whoever they were. He undercut the other man with his fist and connected with his nose. There was an audible crack and blood tricked down his face. He lost his balance and tumbled down the staircase. Rebwar scrambled down to where the man lay unconscious. He took back his wallet, money and driving license and dashed out of the emergency exit. The alarm went off. He was now on Romilly Street. The Coach and Horses pub was opposite. He went around the block to check he wasn't being followed, went in in and ordered a pint of Freedom lager. He sipped it as the emergency services arrived. A little crowd of onlookers gathered. Rebwar watched too.

TEN

Geraldine stayed late at the office. Her other colleagues had all gone to the pub or home to watch TV. Rebwar had passed on what he had found out on his trip to her old neighbourhood. The thought that Richard O'Neill had got away made her uncomfortable. She wasn't getting any sleep and was drinking more than she knew one could excuse as casual. But it calmed her nerves. Avoidance was failing. She had stayed behind to try and find any trace of O'Neil. He'd obviously gotten away, as the police had been looking for a man with a cast.

She accessed the CCTV cameras in the neighbourhood. They were from last year and not many had been saved. She was thinking that she was going to have to go to her corner shop to ask for their video, which was probably even more doubtful. And then she found him. Her palms instantly felt like clay and a shiver travelled down her spine. Breathe in, breathe out she told herself. He looked injured, hobbling along and in pain. Ironically, he ordered an Uber. Of course, she wasn't going to find any info there: tech companies didn't like sharing data with the police. Even court orders didn't work.

Her hands were shaking. He was still alive and hiding somewhere. Now that she had seen him, she was cold. The empty office spooked her. It was quiet apart from a few fans whirring in the background. Low thuds and bumps made her jump. She reassured herself by thinking that there must still be people in the building. O'Neil's cab had driven up to the West End and stopped by Liverpool street. Then her heart sank. Someone different stepped out of the cab. He had switched cabs somewhere.

After an hour of piecing his route together, she identified a few black spots where there would be an opportunity to swap and she made a note of them. She wanted to call Plan B, tell them that their man had got away. But they had to have known. She was angry that they hadn't told her. What had happened at her flat?

Her phone lit up flashing withheld number and she stepped back from it as if it might reach out and grab her. She put her hand to her heart which was pumping away like a techno drum. She took the call.

'Hello?'

'Hey, Sis, It's me. How are you? Still living it up.'

'Hi, Sis…' She let a moment of silence drift by. She wasn't expecting to hear from Rachel, and her sister never called unless she wanted something. Her legs were numb with dread. Whatever Rachel wanted was likely to land her in shit. Whatever she was going to ask, Geraldine decided the answer was no. She slumped in her chair to prepare for the question.

'Are you all right? You don't sound like you're full of beans, Sis. Hey?'

What was the point of trying to hide it? Rachel knew her too well. But No, was still the answer. 'Oh, tough day at work. Still here actually.'

'Come on, Sis, tell me. Are you down? Need a shoulder to cry on? We're not made out of stone, Sis. We are human, aren't we and you're my big Sis. Hey, love you, you know?'

Geraldine's defences were still up. Just waiting for the line - and then no, sorry no. 'Yeah, it's been a long day just need a break. You know?'

'Tell me, I can help. Do you remember when you were doing your exams, your A-levels and I would test you with those cards? Such a laugh! I'd write silly questions and answers just to make you laugh. Dick?'

Geraldine was caught by memory. 'Head.' A little chuckle followed by some laughter from Rachel. She did have an infectious laugh. It rolled like a pop track. Geraldine couldn't help but giggle like she had as a teenager.

'They were good times, hey? So, Zane is getting out.' And there it was, Geraldine's giggle stopped like glass hitting the floor. 'Yeah, fuck me, huh? He's coming out. I don't fucking know what strings or cocks he pulled, but he fucking did. Getting out before me. That f'ing prick. I need your help, Sis. I do.'

There was another silence. Geraldine was still trying to work out what all this meant. 'Ok...'

'No, it's not getting me out, though that would be nice. I need to you to keep an eye on Zane. He's gotten himself with the wrong crowd again. I know it. I can tell you this, Sis... that fucker is going to get himself into more shit than we can all shovel. I don't know why, but he's not capable of keeping a straight life, no. Right Sis? You know that too.'

'No, Rachel,' There! She had said it. Her shoulders

relaxed. 'I can't babysit him. He'll be on parole, they'll be watching him. He's got to report and...'

'Sis, spare me the shit. He's a fucking prick and I love him. I know... I know you don't want to hear it. But I love the fucker and well, that's just how it is.'

Geraldine rubbed her neck and moved her legs trying to get blood back into them. She stood up and tried to stretch but had to hold on to the low partition wall as she looked around the deserted space office. 'Rachel, I can't get involved. You know that. Come on, you know the shitstorm that—'

'Fucking hell, Sis, you can't let me down. I'll... I'll slit my wrists.'

'Rachel, stop being a drama queen.' Cynical laughter filled the earpiece followed by a sniff. Geraldine knew she was being worked on. All the old tricks - but they worked. Rachel, her flesh and blood, knew which of her buttons to press all too well.

'Rachel, I can...' She sighed. 'I can help by keeping an eye out, OK?' Geraldine heard Rachel blow her nose. 'OK, but no more.' Geraldine kicked the paper basket next to her.

'Oh, Sis that would just be ace! I worry so much about him. I miss him so much it hurts. Like acid.'

Geraldine could feel her pain for a moment and it made her well up. She thought of Zara. She still missed her.

'Love you Sis, you know that. I need to go, OK? Hey, you can come round you know, Sis.' Geraldine let the suggestion hang, and Rachel carried on. 'But I understand if not, and I'm sorry about everything. But you know I love you.'

'OK. Yeah, Rach, love you too.'

Rachel hung up. Geraldine collapsed back onto her

chair and it rolled back a little till her legs were straight. Her head slumped forward and she looked down at the dirty carpet covered with breadcrumbs. Her dinner was still laying half-eaten on her desk.

ELEVEN

It wasn't too long before Rebwar spotted Dong and his entourage piling out of the emergency exit, shrieking, screaming and making rude gestures. Rebwar had barely sipped his expensive pint and felt robbed at having to leave it there on one of the benches. He offered it to one of a pair of street guys who were doing their rounds. The first one gave him some abuse for presuming he was an alcoholic, but his mate downed it in one and tried to say thank you while belching.

But he had lost sight of Dong and swore to himself. He set off in search of them past a few busy streets with pubs and crowded pavements and soon found them. Dong was too drunk to walk. He was being held up by one of his boys, the other two looked excited and seemed to be making jokes. Rebwar considered how to confront Dong as he and his group went into Balans restaurant, a late-night munchies venue for clubbers, pub leavers, theatre folk and basically anyone who fancied a burger at 2 am. The security guard waved them in. And a waitress led them to a booth. As rickshaw's ringing their bells and drunken crowds passed by,

Rebwar went over to the security guard who looked him up and down.

'You drunk?'

'Come to have dinner. Just come off a shift.'

After the bouncer waved him in, a smiling waitress asked him if he wanted a table for one.

'I'm meeting up with a friend,' he said and walked over to Dong's booth. The place was opulently decorated with a western saloon feel to it. The wallpaper was busy with swirling geometric patterns, bare bricks, wooden floorboards. When he got to the booth, Rebwar pushed two of Dong's boys along the padded bench. All of them stared, waiting for Dong to take a lead. Rebwar took a deep breath and smiled at them.

'Hello again. We have business to talk.'

'Who are you?' Dong was too drunk to protest at him joining the table.

Rebwar looked Dong in the eyes. 'We have a common friend.'

'Do you want money? Or more...?' Asked one of the boys.

A cocktail of perfumes drifted towards Rebwar. The boys were a little darker skinned than Dong, mocha-coloured and glistening. He thought they might be from the Philippines. One gave a nervous giggle and another stood up suddenly and lunged drunkenly at Rebwar in a karate style move that was difficult to take seriously. Rebwar grabbed his finger and twisted and the boy whimpered in pain. Dong suppressed a smile.

A waiter came up to the table. 'Sir, is there a problem here?'

The boy sat down, holding his finger as if was broken. 'Man up Juan!' Dong turned to the waiter. 'All fine, thank you. Just silly boys' banter. Could you get the gentleman a porn star martini?'

'Very well, sir.' And off he went.

'I need some information,' Rebwar said.

Dong giggled, and the others joined in like teenage girls. 'Oh, I love a man who doesn't waste any time'. Rebwar now understood that Dong was a transexual but had no idea in what stage of transition. Tamar hadn't specified. 'Don't we all. My name is Kim Dong. And who might you be?'

'Rebwar,' One of the boys fanned himself with his hands. The others laughed. 'I'm friends with Tamar. She sends her greetings.'

Dong sipped his frothy yellow cocktail. 'Lovely girl. She did well for me. As you can see, I am now retired. I don't know what I could help you with.'

Rebwar's cocktail arrived. It looked the same as the rest. He raised his glass in acknowledgement to the others and took a sip. It was strong and bittersweet. He looked around and leaned closer to Dong.

'I need to know who brings people in now.'

'Oh! What makes you think I...' Dong looked at the three boys, their attention waning. 'Not my business anymore. It's changed. Brexit. A lot of new business. Chinese still strong. But now eastern bloc, too. Hear that local gangs starting to get interested too. Lots of opportunity.'

'Any names?'

'What? You think I work for free?'

'I think you still owe me money. I'd say I have credit.'

Rebwar turned to the boy who was sitting next to him. 'Tell him.'

'I did nothing! Dong, he lying. He big liar.' Rebwar grabbed his hand and the finger he had twisted before. 'Let go you shit, I...' Rebwar squeezed. 'OK! OK sorry! I did bad thing. Stole his bet.'

'Keep pulling that finger,' said Dong. 'You abused my trust, Milan. I am not an idiot. Don't I pay you enough?' Dong slapped him and a bloody scratch appeared across Milan's cheek, courtesy of Dong's heavy rings. People around them looked over to see what was happening.

'That hurt!' Milan whispered. 'You make me bleed!'

'That's the price, you thief, and you are lucky. Mr Rebwar, I'm sorry for this idiot. I did not realise. I thought you were...' Kim looked at his hand; it had make-up on it and he smeared it on Juan's t-shirt, who thought of protesting but held his stinging cheek instead. 'You should have told me.' Rebwar nodded and smiled, he hadn't exactly been given a chance. 'A hundred and seventy-five pounds...'

Dong's round face smiled and held it, waiting for Rebwar to carry on.

'So how does it work, the smuggling?' Rebwar knew a few smugglers. He himself had come in illegally.

Dong leaned back considering the question. 'How much was the bet?' He eyed Milan who looked away and shrugged. 'Idiot. Oh, been long time since I did it. Trucks is a favourite. If you have money, luxury boat or private plane. But container also good. Some are very creative. Depends on budget.'

'Do you still have friends in the business?'

'Mmm... I can't say. Too dangerous. I am now retired. Want to live long healthy life. No, no, can't say. Sorry.'

'What about Uncle Tam?' said one of the boys, who apparently was paying attention.

Dong threw a glass of water over him. 'You shut up, you little cocksucker.'

'Uncle Tam?' Rebwar wasn't going to let that go.

'Stupid little cocksucker. There is no Tam or uncle.' He looked at Rebwar, who raised his eyebrows. 'How did you get in Mr Rebwar? Truck?'

'Plane from Turkey. Just booked it.'

'Oh, so you are free man, so to speak.'

'Sort of. Is anybody free in this society? Always having to make money for someone.'

'Very true. Sorry, Mr Rebwar, but I can't tell more. Understand I am not a rat.'

Rebwar took out some casino tokens he still had in his pockets and put them down in front of Dong. The security guard hadn't had time to get them off him. Dong took the twenty-pound red and white chip, and two green and white, which were each worth ten pounds.

'Ah, Mr Rebwar, you push a hard bargain... Not, it's worth a lot more than that.'

'I'll find out anyway, Kim. It'll be less painful this way. Otherwise, I'll be turning over stones that you don't want me to. I have no business with you or your old friends. I'm looking for the Gipsy.'

'Who? Look in campsites!' He laughed. 'No one called Gipsy.'

'Uncle Tam?'

Dong drank his drink and ordered another. He moved around in his seat as if he had an itch. Then shook his head.

'I can't. Just say he in jail now. But that is it, OK? I did not say that. No one knows Tam, he is dead, OK?'

Rebwar handed him one of his business cards as he stood up to leave. 'Call me if there is anything.' Dong picked it up and laughed.

'Anything?' He threw Rebwar a kiss and his boys giggled.

TWELVE

Rebwar sat in his car at the end of Swann Walk which led onto the A312. He could just see the tops of boats sailing up and down the river as the sun set. He sipped from the take-away cup, watched his cigarette burn and listened to his CD. Berker had given it to him, Sezen Aksu the Queen of Turkish Pop. The best, he'd said.

———

He picked up his mobile, found the number he was looking for and dialled. He turned the music down.

'Hello?'

'Hi, this is Rebwar, the guy from the pub.'

'What mate? Who?'

'The Six Bells... you gave me your number for a job.'

'Right...' Rebwar heard some muffled background noises. 'Yeah, yeah mate. You need a job?' Rebwar could tell that he was trying to remember, was winging it. 'That's right. A job, yeah.'

'Yes, I lost mine. At Matt's car wash. He was—'

'Yeah, Oh yeah!' The change in tone of voice meant he had actually now remembered who Rebwar was. 'Bad turn, man. Bad fucking shit, actually. Still haven't found the fuckers, have they?'

Rebwar could tell he was still fishing. 'No. Do you have any ideas?'

'Me mate? Na. So what can you do?'

'Drive, wash cars... anything. Just need work.'

'Right, yeah mate, I'll see what I can do, OK? But you'll need to call me later, on another number.' Rebwar wrote down the number on his hand as he wedged the phone between his ear and shoulder. He hung up, finished his cigarette and dropped it out of the car window into the gutter.

'That's littering.'

Rebwar looked up, Geraldine stood on the pavement with her hands in her pockets. He handed her a cigarette and she climbed into the back seat.

'What's the music?'

Rebwar turned it up a little. 'Turkish. New stuff.'

'Interesting... Drive.'

'Where?'

'You know... somewhere with a view.'

Rebar started the car and they rolled quietly off. Geraldine looked out of the window and seemed to be daydreaming.

'What shall we do about O'Neil?' Rebwar said.

'Find him. I want to find him. Any leads?' Geraldine lit her cigarette.

'Nothing. And nothing on the Gipsy. He's either a ghost or a lie.'

'Mmm...' Geraldine stretched in the back. Rebwar

could tell she was more distracted than usual. 'My sister's boyfriend is getting out.'

'Out of where?'

'Prison! Fucking idiot somehow managed to get himself parole, and mug here, agreed to keep an eye on him. Sister twisted my arm.' Rebwar turned the car to drive along the river. Various colourful lights lit up the buildings, bridges and trees. 'I like this route.'

'You could have said no.'

She sighed. She was in a strange mood. 'Do you still have that gun?'

'You don't want that.'

'Don't tell me what I want and don't, right? I want a gun! It's... it's... fuck's sake, just get me the gun, OK?' Rebwar stopped the car and turned around to look at her. She shifted her gaze from out of the window and looked at him. 'What? I... I just want a gun. Is that OK?'

Rebwar shook his head. 'What his name? I'll deal with it. Can you shoot straight?' Geraldine shrugged. He carried on. 'Have you ever killed anything?' She glanced at him and looked away. 'Right, so no, and no. Do you want to learn?' She looked hopeful.

'I can teach you, if ... if you really want. But it changes you.' Rebwar pulled out and drove off again along the snaking river, following the traffic. He changed the subject. 'Do you think he's tailing us?'

'Who?' Geraldine looked behind her.

'O'Neil. He might be trying to find us. Or he's left the country.' Her mind wandered again.

'You know I didn't see Brexit happening. A lot of coppers voted for it, you know that? Just to make their lives easier. Fat chance. As if it's foreigners that are criminals. You see what you want to see, don't you?'

'All my passengers are worried or angry. I think the ones that voted Brexit are quiet. I would like to ask them what it means, exactly.' Rebwar's phone rang. 'Rebwar.'

'Yeah, it's Wayne. Got a job on.'

'What is it?'

'Turn up tomorrow, seven am sharp in front of the Six Bells.'

'OK,' Rebwar said. 'And thank you.' Wayne hung up.

'Got a lead?' asked Geraldine from the back.

Rebwar looked at her through the rear-view mirror. 'Not sure. Still feels like a, how do you say, crazy goose chase?'

She smiled and nodded. 'Wild.' Rebwar frowned.

'It's a *wild* goose chase'.

'Like I said. Anyway, I have a new job with a shady man.'

'Don't talk to me about shady men. Story of my life.' She looked out of the window and disappeared again into her thoughts.

THIRTEEN

Bar Italia was a little late-night coffee bar in Soho. Geraldine had found it a useful alternative to the pub. Instead of buying new clothes, she'd decided to lose some weight. This was something she had tried on repeated occasions. She would typically give up after a few days and take a trip to Primark. This time she was adamant that was not going to happen.

———

She had pulled a favour and got a mobile number for her sister's boyfriend's offender manager. Each time she thought of what a waste of space Zane was, and that her sister just couldn't get him out of her system despite everything he'd done, she shook her head in disbelief almost involuntarily. She also couldn't quite believe she was doing this, but dialled the number.

'Shaun Davies… can I help you?' His voice was smooth and precise, waiting for a question.

'Hi, this is DC Geraldine Smith. How can I say this?'

She squeezed her eyes shut and came out with it. 'I understand you are Zane (second name?) offender manager?' She heard a murmur of confirmation from the other end of the line and ploughed on. 'Well, the thing is, he's my brother-in-law, and as he's just out on parole I thought...' She made a fist with her hand and ground it into her thigh.

'Good evening, DC Smith. That sounds like quite a story. What can I do for you?'

Geraldine leaned back in her chair, stretching her legs out. 'How is he doing?'

Davies drew his breath. 'Well, you know I'm not really supposed to... What the hell, maybe you can help him. We've agreed on a sentence plan, which is a start. He's got some ideas on some courses he wants to do. But I've got to say that since the budget cuts it's quite difficult to keep track of my flock, so to speak. It's me who finds it difficult to keep the meeting times.'

'He's been tagged, right?'

There was a little chuckle. 'Right, sure... and who's paying for that? I've only got one that is being actively tagged. Zane is pretty free, and he knows it. I give him a couple of months, and he'll be back behind bars. Not really motivated to go on the straight and narrow.'

'For Christ's sake, what's the hell is the point then?'

'Hey, don't tell me, Geraldine. It's a waste of time. Most of my colleagues have packed it in, which just makes it worse. And no one is talking about it as usual.'

'Where can I find him?'

'He's usually in The Star or the Beaver Inn in Ashford. That's what I hear, but it won't be long before he's part of some dodgy scheme. He probably already is.'

For a moment, Geraldine wanted to ask him what the point was of having an offender manager, to manage reoffending? 'Fuck, what a fucking mess. Sorry for the language, Shaun. You've been a massive help. Hope things somehow get better. Thanks again.'

'No worries. Have a good day and may God bless you.'

Geraldine said goodbye and cringed, not only at her bad language but the blasphemy too. He was clearly a god-fearing man. She took her coffee mug in both hands as if to find some comfort there and sipped. The thought of having to go to Kent, her old neighbourhood was not a pleasant one. There was a reason why she'd left.

———

Geraldine took the day off and boarded a train to Kent. It was now a fast train along the Eurostar line, then from Ashford International it was a bus ride or a taxi across the M20 to Kennington. She decided to take the bus for old time's sake. It brought back memories of when she was still at school. At that time, she had the hots for Zane, but he ended up with her younger sister. That's when it went wrong. She guessed she was too righteous for him, thank goodness, or she could have ended up on the wrong side of the law. It was a fine line, she thought.

The little Rose Inn was still there. It had been done up but still had the carpets and upholstered benches and pool table. She'd already had breakfast: porridge and blueberries, an attempt at the GI diet. She walked in and saw her old favourite bar. Men stood drinking pints having just finished their respective shifts. She sat at a bar stool and the woman behind the bar turned to see what she wanted.

'What can I do for you love?'

Geraldine looked up at her. She didn't recognise her, though it could have been someone she'd gone to school with as she seemed familiar. 'Pint of bitter please.' Instant regret and pleasure in one.

Two men sitting on the seats close to the window were talking. She listened in. She quickly tuned out as they were talking about the weather.

'Geraldine! Is that you?' A big woman as wide as the industrial deep fat fryers she had in the kitchens came sweeping into the area behind the bar. It was Dotty, the owner of the pub for as long as anyone could remember. 'How have you've been keeping my love? Still a copper?' The men turned and stared at her.

'Hey, Dotty how are you keeping? Like what you've done with the place.'

Dotty's huge frame shook with laughter. 'Nothin' changed then. How's the family?'

Geraldine tried to avoid her gaze, but Dotty moved into her eye line. She too had been a cop but was injured out years ago by a hit and run. But you never lose the instinct. 'Zane's out.' Geraldine said quietly.

'I'll be a Dutchman, you don't say. So what's he up to?'

'Funny, I was going to ask you the same question.'

Dotty pointed her finger at her. 'Oh, I see, already up to no good. Can't say that I've seen him around here. Would have expected him to say hello and have a fry up at least. Are you going to eat something? You've lost weight, you know.'

One of the men at the window seats suddenly got up to leave, as if he was after someone, speed walking to the door, trying hard not to break into a run.

Geraldine nodded in the man's direction. 'Know anything about those two?'

Dotty rolled her eyes. 'Spying on my customers eh? Don't know them from Adam.'

'Ah, pity, hey? How's business?' Good old Dotty, tight-lipped as ever. She did know her customers. From behind her appeared a plate as wide as the waitress's chest. It passed by Geraldine. Fish and Chips. The smell enveloped her.

'I'll let you have some peace.' Dotty turned and went back to the kitchen. Geraldine took a menu from the bar.

———

Instead of taking a bus to Zane's flat, Geraldine decided to walk there, the fish and chips were repeating on her, and now she was regretting her lapse of willpower. Never listen to an empty stomach her mother had told her. His place was a ten-minute walk from the pub. She had been trying to avoid it. The walk there was a depressing one. She remembered it as a clean and vibrant estate with neat bushes and manicured rockeries. Now the pavements were lined with smashed-up bus shelters, discarded rusting white goods, a burned-out car and festering furniture in front gardens. She could smell the rot and decay. Blokes in sports gear hung around smoking and staring. She now wished she had driven down. She pressed Zane's buzzer, Flat 14. After a short wait, the door opened. There was a moment of silence.

'Oh, G? What the fuck?'

'Hi, Zane. You're standing!' He was in a dirty tank top and grey tracksuit bottoms. His greasy hair was combed back; his face a pasty white. His eyes strained to focus on Geraldine.

'Yeah. Doing good, man, yeah.'

'Zane, I'm here because Rachel asked me?'

'Yeah, yeah, Fuck yeah. How is she?'

'Can I come in?'

'Oh, yeah. It's cool.' Zane made an uncoordinated gesture with his arm inviting her in.

'Like what you've done with the place, Zane.' Geraldine said dryly as she looked around. The windows were draped with dirty sheets; black plastic liners filled with clothes and shoes were next to the couch. On the wooden floor beside it was a selection of drugs. Obviously, his offender manager hadn't bothered dropping by.

'Fancy a cuppa?' said Zane.

'You've got tea?

Zane went off to the toilet and left the door open. His phone was on the couch. Geraldine grabbed it and looked through the call history. Zane coughed as he peed. She took a photo of the log just in case she needed some help in finding him. Zane switched a tap on and whistled. Geraldine found a letter lying on the floor, which she picked up and scanned. It was from a recruitment company, Bywater Ltd. There was another crumbled up piece of paper next to it which she slipped in her pocket. Zane walked out of the bathroom with his pants barely back on.

'See you're looking for a job?'

'What? Oh.'

'Zane are you going to flush?'

'Oh yeah. Sorry. Just...' And he went into the toilet.

Geraldine looked at the crumpled up note and she could barely make out his writing. It had a place, date and a time. She made a mental note. The toilet flushed. Zane walked back and flopped onto the couch.

'You going to visit Rachel?'

'Yeah, man, sure.' He grabbed a joint and lit up.

'Fuck, Zane, you're not going to get a job like this. You'll be back inside before you can flush that toilet.'

'I'm OK. Don't worry about me. I'm good, yeah.'

'Zane do you want a job?'

Zane sat up and stared at her. 'Course I do, I just-'

'OK. So can you ask around about someone called the Gipsy?' She knew this was a bad idea, but what else could she do?

'Who?'

'The Gipsy, I need to find him.'

'Oh, right and...' Zane held his hand out. Geraldine gave him three notes. 'Mmm, yeah. Thing is... this ain't going to last me long, G. Prices have gone up while I've been away!'

'On delivery.'

'You expect me to go out there and stick my neck out for you?' Something was wearing off. He was now sitting instead of lying.

'Yes Zane, I do. And I expect you to visit Rachel, OK?'

'What are you, the fun police? Did she send you, huh? Because you can tell her...'

'What?'

'That she can find me some money, right? Leaving me alone here.'

Geraldine could feel her self-control slipping. Nothing had changed. Not that she really expected it would. He'd always had this delusional notion that someone was going bail him out and provide for him, whatever he did. Which was where Rachel came in. Geraldine just wanted to punch him in the face. There was no point carrying on this conversation and she got up to leave. She scribbled her number down on a scrap of paper.

'You know what you need to do, Zane. Try and remember.'

'Yeah, yeah,' He lit his joint and grumbled away. Geraldine left him there.

FOURTEEN

Rebwar arrived at Slade Green Road, not far from Dartford. He'd used a night tube and bus to get there, as he wanted to give the impression that he was an immigrant looking for a job. He walked to the end of the street and checked his watch. It was 5:50 am, the streetlights were still bathing everything in an orange and yellow hue. Just past a warehouse were some red brick units with a bunch of parked vans. It wasn't really what could be called a fleet, as they were in various states of disrepair. Some still had logos on them; others were faded, scratched or bumped.

———

He stood at a closed metal gate looking for a bell. Someone whistled and he looked over. It was Wayne, swaying his arms and flicking his head as he approached. There was a padlock on the gate but Rebwar pushed it anyway. Wayne came over.

'Amir... how's tricks?'

'Sorry?'

'How are you?' Wayne fiddled with a bunch of keys trying to find the right one for the padlock.

'Nice setup. Is there coffee?'

'What? Come on, let's get to work.' Wayne walked off towards a van, while fumbling through his pockets. The van was a faded red or was it rust? The LDV badge hung on to its cracked plastic grill. It wouldn't have been out of place back home in Tehran. After trying a couple of keys, Wayne got into it. The engine turned over with painful metallic noises and he carried on until it fired up. A cloud of black smoke swallowed up the other vans.

'You have a phone with navigation?'

Rebwar nodded.

Wayne unfolded a piece of paper. 'Right mate... here's sixteen addresses. Just drive to each one, ask for the boss, pick up the goods and drive to the next one. Understand? Rebwar took the sheet. 'Straight to the next one, right? No coffee stops or chit chat.' Wayne stepped out of the idling van.

'And drive back here?'

'Once you've picked up the boxes, yeah, and if there are any problems...' Wayne mimicked a phone with his thumb and little finger. 'Call me. Right?'

Rebwar climbed into the driver's seat. 'Fuel?'

'Out of your wages, and any damages.'

For a moment Rebwar was going to ask him about insurance, but he knew the answer to that. Wayne took a call and walked away.

———

His first address was outside of London just by Maidstone in Kent, a scrapyard with mountains of rusting cars, cables, plastic trim, broken windscreens and loose metal parts. He drove into the muddy compound, the van's suspension creaking over the potholes, and parked in front of a caravan. A few men in dirty overalls were working on various parts of cars, some sawing, others shunting them with forklifts. Not one acknowledged him. A man with a limp walked out of a caravan holding a mug of coffee. The smell made Rebwar want one.

'You've come for the parts?'

'Work for Wayne.'

'Who? No idea who that is mate. What do you want?'

Rebwar looked at his piece of paper with the hand-written addresses. He showed it to him. The man shrugged.

'Where is boss? I have pick up.' Rebwar exaggerated his lack of English for effect.

The guy turned and whistled. It was answered with a few shouts and more whistles. A yellow forklift revved up and picked up speed. It bounced over the deep puddles, its metal forks pointed at Rebwar. The machine was either going to stab him or the ground. A few feet before hitting him, it swerved around. A man laughed. His teeth were missing. He had a black beard with the odd white streak in it. He jumped out of the forklift and into a puddle.

'What's the crack, Shaun?' said the man with the limp.

'This fella is talking about a pickup, asked for the boss.'

Shaun brought out a pack of cigarettes; his thick hands were creased with oil and mud. Rebwar noticed the health warnings were in a language other than English.

The man sized up Rebwar and looked at the van as if he wanted to take it apart. 'Must be Wayne's new boy. Give him those the boxes from yesterday.' He turned to Rebwar and said, 'Top of the morning to you fella.'

'Top of?'

Shaun laughed. 'Just not the same with you lot. But you's do an honest day's work. See that fella?' He pointed over to a tall blond man. 'Hasn't taken a day in two years or been late. Call him the Polbot.' He laughed again! 'Fancy working for us? We have lodgings.'

'I have boxes,' said Rebwar.

Shaun and the man with the limp looked at each other. 'Where do you think he gets them? Hey Mick, how does Wayne do it?'

'Fella, what's your name?' Shaun asked Rebwar.

'Amir.'

'Well, you see, Amir... I need people like you. And your man Wayne, he's been greedy. Have you met his boss? Because I'd like to.'

'The Gipsy?' Rebwar threw it in to watch for a reaction.

'Na, I don't think that's his name. Haven't heard of him... And that company, Bywater, what a bunch of crooks, Eh?' And he waited for a moment before laughing. 'I'm only messing with you, like. Go on, Mick, get the man his boxes.'

The man with a limp motioned to Rebwar to follow him, and Shaun went back to his forklift.

'Those,' said the man with the limp and he walked off back to his caravan.

Rebwar saw ten brown boxes of different sizes, all of them with bits of metal in them. He looked closer to see brake discs, suspension parts and other car components. He loaded them into the van.

———

While he was driving, a call came in. It was a woman.

'Could I talk to Amir, please?'

'Speaking,' Rebwar's phone was on the dash, and he mounted the pavement and stopped.

'This is Betty from Bywater Recruitment Services Ltd.'

'Yes.'

'I understand Wayne got you a job? Delivering?'

'Who is this?'

'Betty from Bywater. Wayne works for us, he's the sales manager.'

'And you?'

'Human resources and office manager, as well as anything else they can find to make me do. Amir this is about your job. I just need some more details. Don't worry if you don't have all the bits and bobs. I just need to cross the T's and dot the I's. OK?'

'Yeah, OK.'

'Do you have any paperwork from your last job?'

'What you mean?'

'Like a P45? Or a NI number?'

Rebwar coughed, 'No.' He heard a deep breath followed by hushed up swear word. 'Is that a problem, Wayne promised me a job.'

'Yeah, I bet he did. OK, can you tell me what your full name is?'

'Amir Begani.'

She went on to ask him his age and where he was from. Rebwar came up with a story that he was from Syria. What he thought was a bit strange was that whatever he said, she just believed at once. She didn't ask for anything to back it up. It just didn't make sense.

'Right... Listen... Amir. I'm going to sort this mess. Thanks Wayne.' She muttered. 'Bloody wide boy.' Betty was about to hang up before she added. 'Oh, have you got an address or an email? I'm going to send you a link for an app.' She waited for a reaction.

'You mean like Uber?'

'Yes, like Uber. It's for your jobs. And if Wayne gives you handwritten notes...' She swallowed and sighed. 'Well, tell me. OK? Amir, you need me on your side. You tell me. Understand?'

Rebwar confirmed, said that he did, and then took a moment to think about what had just happened. Rebwar was now Amir Begani, a Syrian from a town he'd made up called Bar. Amir now had a job in London for a company called Bywater Recruitment Services Ltd.

He lit a cigarette in the van and took a deep breath. What was going on? Paperwork was a British pastime. Everything had provenance, and this didn't. It must be some kind of scam. He'd have to ask Raj to look into it, see if he could find out more.

He turned the key to the ignition, and the old engine spluttered. The noise was like listening to someone grinding an old set of false teeth. It took a few tries to find life but as soon as it did, a cloud of black smoke filled his mirrors. He looked at the next address on his list. Brunswick Road in Ashford, Kent. He typed the postcode into his phone.

FIFTEEN

Rebwar was driving to central London with a rattling tea set in the passenger seat. He'd waited for Hourieh to go out to walk Musa to school – something the boy detested but she did it anyway - and then bundled the set into an empty Amazon cardboard box. He'd bought it for her a year or so ago. It had been a compromise for her to stay in the UK and he'd had to use his precious savings to buy a tea set she had been coveting for years. So for Rebwar to take it was a desperate move, and loaded with consequences he couldn't even bear to think about. It had also thrown into question his whole dedication to Plan B. Even though they owned him, as they had repeatedly told Geraldine, he still had the option of running. But it was for Geraldine, he felt he owed her some closure for Zara's murder.

———

He had purposely chosen a pawn shop on Camden High Street, somewhere none of his friends would have gone and that wasn't tied to anyone he knew; he didn't want gossip to travel. He parked the car behind the high street on Pratt Street, just in front of a café and record shop. He took the clinking box out and walked over to My Bond Pawnbrokers. The story he was going to tell Hourieh was that he'd dropped the set and had taken it to be repaired. The shopfront was small and had a window filled with watches and jewellery. Inside was stark, white walls with a locked door at the back. The glass counter had the more precious items such as rings and precious stones. The man standing behind them was medium build with dark hair with a bald patch which shone under the stark strip lights. He had a large pair of steel framed glasses on and reading glasses which hung around his neck His striped shirt was tight around his portly belly. He smiled and looked into the box.

'Need some quick cash?'

'Shopping around see what I can get.'

'That's what they all say.' And pointed at himself 'Jim. Let's see what we've got.' he took out the pieces out and laid them out on the glass counter. 'Tea set. Complete?'

'Yes, the best. Genuine silver and the best craftsmanship. Look at the detail which...'

'Is there a sugar bowl? It does look nice. Receipt?'

Rebwar peered in to the box and realised he'd forgotten to pick up the sugar bowl, the only piece that was allowed to be used in the house. He took the receipt out of his wallet and told Jim he would bring in the bowl.

The man typed some numbers into his calculator, lifted one pair of glasses onto his shiny head and put on the reading glasses. He picked up the silver teapot to inspect it and made masticating sounds like he had gum in his mouth. 'Family heirloom? They all are...' He tapped more numbers into his calculator and showed Rebwar the screen.

Rebwar reached for his cigarettes and took out one out, he needed to think about this. Jim nodded to him and Rebwar went outside and lit up. Two hundred pounds wasn't what he had in mind. But then again, it was something to get him by. He finished his cigarette and went back inside.

———

Later on, he was sitting at the bar of the Sunset Strip in Soho, with Tamar. She was sitting in her bikini, red with white accents. It was a trio of triangles, each one just about covering a respective private part. You would be arrested back home for even owning something like that, Rebwar thought, although from his colleagues he'd heard of some underground bars with such shows. They'd be making all kind of jokes about him if they knew where he was. Tamar swivelled on her stool, long bare legs swinging around, her platform shoes controlling the spin. Different coloured lights flashed to the music. It was quiet, and only a few suited men were drinking in a corner as if they were having a meeting.

Tamar sipped on a glass of prosecco. 'Rebs! How are you, my darling? Been to a funeral?' She could see he was uncomfortable in his black suit and white shirt. A woman next to him smiled. 'Oh, this is Alex, my cam friend.' Rebwar looked at her, trying to work out what she meant exactly.

'Nice to see you. Drink?' Alex said.

'Alex, Rebwar, Rebwar, Alex.' She'd forgotten to state the obvious, which for Rebwar clearly wasn't, and so whispered into his ear. 'She's a he, if you know what I mean.' and she watched him process the information. Alex wiggled in front of him, giggling.

Rebwar looked at her. A beautiful Asian girl in a bikini... and then he looked down involuntarily to see a bulge instead of a neat flat triangle. Alex smiled, her painted lips making her mouth seem huge, her blue eyeliner shaping male Asian eyes. He wasn't too sure what to say or think.

'So, to what do I owe the pleasure?' said Tamar.

'Catching up. Don't see you much since you've been doing that web cam thing.'

'Ah yes,' Tamar said laughing at his discomfort, 'my grown-up YouTube you mean.'

'Yes, that. I don't go on the internet much. Prefer the real world.'

'My, he is old fashioned! I like it!' Alex smiled and touched Rebwar's arm cautiously.

'Are you... you know...' said Rebwar.

'What? Oh, working here? No. Night off. Just keeping the punters warm. And as a favour to the owner.'

An Asian barman put three glasses of prosecco in front of them. For a moment, Rebwar was going to ask for a beer instead, but he knew better, and here he had to let things flow. Alex downed her glass and grabbed the fresh one.

'Cheers,' said Tamar. They both took a swig.

'Any word on the Gipsy?'

'You know Rebs, are you ever off duty? Relax. Enjoy the decor. You know a girl needs a bit of wooing before indulging in the job.' Alex giggled. Rebwar looked around the club. They'd changed the security company since he was last there, so now at least he was allowed in. He wondered if Colin, the weird man who he'd had a run in with last year ever came back. He'd been an early suspect in the organ smuggling case, after Tamar told Rebwar how obsessed he was with the female anatomy. Colin had mapped out her various organs, by outlining them with his finger, as if he was a butcher. It had freaked Tamar out.

Rebwar still didn't like strip clubs, thought it was humiliating and he found no pleasure there. But unlike back in Iran these clubs were totally legal. Mirrors, neon and dark carpets stared back at him. The suited men laughed and jeered at the girls who were all baiting them to get their attention, swooping around them and showing their curves. Tamar had to shoo away a few of the girls who came too close.

'Moody,' Alex said. 'I like you.'

'Where are you from?'

'Philippines. Came over a few years ago. Part of my extended family lived here. Enough about me, how about you gorgeous?'

Rebwar asked for a beer from the bar and smiled at Alex. 'Not my type, sorry.'

'Oh, tough guy? See you're playing the field. Sure you know which side you're on?'

'Stop teasing him, Alex,' said Tamar. 'No one knows a man called the Gipsy. He's not in this neighbourhood, darlin'.' Her puffed-up lips smiled and she turned to talk to a man nearby.

Rebwar turned to Alex, who made a sad face. He felt his frustration rise. Was this pursuit of the Gipsy some kind of test from Plan B? A wild goose chase to keep him busy?

'Want to see a show?' said Alex.

'No thanks. Not my thing. Have you heard of Kim Dong and his boys?

Alex faced the bar. 'Tamar knows him.'

'And what about you?' Rebwar asked.

Alex swivelled back and stared at him for a moment, then nodded.

'How?'

'Got me started in the city of sin.' Alex smiled darkly.

'Human resources, was that his profession?' Rebwar sipped his beer and noticed Alex's leg shake. 'You know him well?' He asked for another round for them all.

'An old story.'

'And his boys?'

'Oh, them? A bunch of leeches. Like little pugs... piss on or fuck any naked leg.'

'I haven't had the pleasure,' said Tamar.

A whoosh of air from the open door announced a group of men who had just walked in. They were in a kind of uniform, jeans and loose, bright coloured shirts covering their bulk. Some of the girls went over to make them welcome. Rebwar was deep in thought as Alex suddenly got up.

'Loo break. You coming my darling?'

For a moment Rebwar thought Alex was talking to him and not Tamar. He watched them walk to the toilet, playing with the men's eyes. He could see it was a drug for them. He went over to the wide-open door, stood outside and lit up. Soho was bustling with life, traffic noise, animated voices, laughter, music and all the smells you could imagine. A strange mix of people wandering through the streets to go to the theatre, some in gowns, some straight from work, and then a few trendy types. Hipsters, he had heard them being called, though he was not too sure what that meant exactly. Everyone seemed to have a label these days. He noticed Tamar and Alex return from the toilet, arm-in-arm for comfort. He stubbed out his cigarette and went back inside.

'Such brutes, what happened to gentlemen?'

Rebwar could see that Alex had taken something. He wasn't as tense and his eyes were darting around. He'd lost some of his coordination and his hips weren't swaying anymore. 'And Uncle Tam?'

Alex giggled and covered his mouth with his hand. A little burp came out. 'Shit that urban myth?' He asked for more bubbles.

'I don't understand?' Said Rebwar.

'That's Kim's cover story. Or shit to make people believe that he was just a victim. Don't tell me he's the boss?'

'Sort of but he's dead, no? Or in jail?'

Alex giggled a little more and slurped from his fluted glass. 'He never existed! He's everything and nothing, whatever he wants to say, really, that yellow shit. He's a nasty man.'

Tamar held him on the chair. 'Come on Alex, maybe we should call it a night.'

'Just getting warmed up. Come on, Tamar. Don't be such a bore.'

'What did he do to you, Kim?' Said Rebwar.

'Rebs, I think we need to call it a night.'

'No, no.' Alex pushed Tamar's hand and leaned in. 'I want to answer the question. Look...' On Alex's arm were some deep scars that had been badly stitched up. 'That's what he did. Fucked me. Like a fucking whore and threw me out like a used tampon. He's not like me... he's a man in a woman's body.'

'Please, Alex.' Tamar tried to reassure the staff that she could control Alex.

'Explain,' said Rebwar

Tamar asked Rebwar to help her. They put a long coat over his small figure, each took an elbow and helped him walk out.

'He's been trying to hide... But they know. Oh, yes. He's going to get his comeuppance.' Alex tapped his nose.

'What's he taken?'

'A cocktail of... I'm not sure. Just need a cab.'

Rebwar waved a black cab and helped both of them to get in. Then Rebwar lit a cigarette and waved them off.

SIXTEEN

Rebwar and Hourieh arrived at the Ramsay Maze restaurant on Hospital Road in Chelsea. He wore a dark blue jacket, and black trousers and had managed to get away with not wearing a tie. She had a dark blue knee length skirt and loose white blouse with a flowery jacket, her hair was tied up in a bun. Rebwar opened the door for his wife and she walked in, he noticed she was smiling, which was unusual. The restaurant was small and had probably been a shop before. A tall wooden bar ran along one side and facing them were red padded benches. It was the same in the back room. It had a French bistro feel to it. This hadn't been his choice. They were here to meet Dr Amir Gul, an old friend from Iran. Gul was a successful plastic surgeon who had helped Rebwar in his last case. He couldn't stand Gul and thought he was an arrogant self-obsessed idiot with a god complex. The perfect surgeon.

It was Hourieh who had set up the dinner. She was still on her mission to get a job. Rebwar had so far managed to forget her demands. When she told him what she'd organised with Dr Gul, that she'd gone behind his back, he'd been furious, but he chose to keep that to himself, smiling and telling her it was a good idea. The food looked rich and expensive: big steaks, pies, fancy side dishes just like the clientele. Hourieh headed for the bar and asked for Dr Gul. Rebwar wondered what she'd been promised. At least he'd been invited. A pretty blonde waitress came over and showed them to their table, which was at the back in a booth. Dr Gul was sitting with a half-empty bottle of wine. His eyes looked a little puffy. Otherwise, he was his usual distinguished, immaculate self: a shiny suit, pressed white shirt and slick black hair.

'Hourieh!' He stood up and shook her hand. 'Glad to see you two. You look beautiful.' He kissed Hourieh on her cheek and turned to shake Rebwar's hand. 'And you've made an effort. So glad you could make it. Drink?'

Rebwar sat down. Dr Gul was already a little tipsy.

'Oh, the pleasure is ours,' said Hourieh. 'Such a beautiful place.'

'My local, I live around the corner...' He picked up the bottle. 'Wine?' They both nodded. He emptied his glass before pouring the rest of the bottle between the three glasses. 'Cheers my dears!'

Rebwar had expected to see Dr Gul's wife. He'd heard she was beautiful, and she might have added a sparkle to this dull and tedious dinner. He was also curious to see how many operations she'd had. She was no doubt a project on which Dr Gul had lavished his skill and time. Rebwar tasted the wine, it was rich and had some berry notes.

'I'm so glad you called, Hourieh, I... I'm glad, yes.'

'Is your wife away?' asked Rebwar, noticing that the Dr didn't seem quite as bullish as usual.

Dr Gul looked away and called out for the waitress.

'How is Myrian?' asked Hourieh. 'Such a lovely woman,

you're so lucky to have her. And so beautiful. I'm sure you've helped her too.'

'Yes, yes'. He dismissed the talk of his wife and handed them both a menu. 'We should order. It's lovely here. It's that famous chef who owns it. The one that shouts a lot. Never watched it but...' He looked for his glasses to read his menu. 'So, is Rebwar looking after you? Must be hard, driving a taxi all day.'

Rebwar was about to reply, but Hourieh said, 'I'm looking for a job, something like a secretary? I need to do something.'

Dr Gul looked over his glasses. 'Aren't you happy being a housewife? Maybe Rebwar needs to get a career.' He laughed and took another large swig of wine.

'Has your wife left you?' said Rebwar.

There was a long moment of silence which turned awkward.

Dr Gul swayed in his chair as his head slumped. 'Yes. She's asking for a divorce.'

Hourieh and Rebwar looked at each other.

'No! I'm so, so sorry to hear that,' said Hourieh. 'That's awful.'

Another bottle arrived on the table. 'Are you ready to order?' The waitress smiled and stood at attention, pad in hand.

Hourieh shook her head. Dr Gul held his forehead as if it to prevent it from falling onto the table. Hourieh got a handkerchief out and passed it on to him. Rebwar looked at the other tables, eyed their plates and discovered he was hungry. He fancied a steak, but the pie looked interesting, with its large bone sticking out of the top.

'Amir, what happened?' said Hourieh.

'She was having an affair with my business partner.

They have left for South America. God, it's...' He gulped down his wine.

For a moment, Rebwar found it funny. He was sure that Gul had had plenty of affairs and he was certainly fond of flirting with the women. Tamar had said he'd asked her how much she charged. She said she'd refused him, but she might also have said that so as not to embarrass Rebwar.

'Who's running the practice?' said Rebwar.

'I am... It's hell. She wants half of it. And, and...'

Rebwar knew that she must have had some dirt on him. Myrian wouldn't have risked having an affair without being assured of a fair chunk of his fortune.

'Oh, Amir, so sorry,' Hourieh said. 'That whore... I knew she was trouble. You know, the first time I saw her... Well, she's beautiful, but that was thanks to you. So you owe her nothing. You made that woman. If you need any help, I'm here. I would invite you over for a tea with my most eligible friends but, my husband damaged my tea service and hasn't got me a replacement!' Her ring-laden hand grasped Dr Gul's.

Rebwar clenched his jaw, picked up his glass and took a large gulp of wine. He was desperate for a cigarette. A change of scene, that's what he needed. But he didn't want to leave them alone. 'When did this happen?' he asked.

'A week ago. I thought it would blow over. We'd been there before. You know, a few rows... but she would usually calm down, see the reality and move on.'

'So you had an affair.' Rebwar couldn't help himself.

'Ah!' Gul coughed. 'Yes, but that was different. She forgave me for that. We moved on.'

'Oh, I'm sure she wasn't the easiest. You're a busy, successful man. You must get all the attention. I mean...'

'You mean?' said Rebwar.

'Well, I'm happily married, whereas Myrian... she was of that type. Well, you know...' She waved her hand around. 'She's just different and... You know. Shall we order?'

'I'm so lost.' Dr Gul cried. 'I don't know what to do. She even cancelled the cleaner.'

Rebwar felt awkward. He'd never seen Dr Gul in such a state. He always had such a veneer about him, and now there was just a shell of a man. But he still didn't trust him. He had always treated Rebwar as a working-class man who served his kind.

'It'll be all right, Amir,' Hourieh said. 'Look, you still have your best years ahead. I mean all my girlfriends think you're the most handsome man... And now you'll be a bachelor.'

'Hourieh, do you think we should go? The doctor's not in a fit state.'

'I'm... I'm all right.' Dr Gul slurred his words. 'Look, let's, let's eat. Yes? I'm OK.' And he sat up straight.

The alcohol had hit his empty stomach. Rebwar tried to get Hourieh's attention.

'Yes, Amir, let's order,' she said. 'So, do you have a job for me?'

'Hourieh, I think—' Rebwar tried to cut in, but it was no use.

'Sure, I need a nice secretary. And a cleaner. Love to have you on board, Hourieh. It'll be fun.'

The waitress asked if they wanted to order.

'Another bottle! Champagne! We are celebrating. Yes. Fuck Myrian, that bitch.'

For a moment, the waitress hesitated then turned to get the champagne. The other guests looked over. Rebwar was now rather enjoying seeing Dr Gul making a spectacle of himself. He felt a hint of glee overtake his hunger.

'Cheers, you're right, Hourieh! That fucking bitch isn't getting anything. Hey Rebwar, what do you think? You know you should be driving my ri-hic, rich clients around.' He carried on hiccuping, his eyelids drooping. Ten minutes later they were both holding Dr Gul upright and walking him home. On the drive back, Hourieh and Rebwar argued.

SEVENTEEN

The first lot of pick ups for Wayne must have gone well, as he'd asked Rebwar back. He drove to his first address of the morning as planes trailed scratch-like marks on the clear blue sky. He drank steaming coffee from a white poly-styrene cup bought at Forest Café, which was opposite Slade Green train station, where he'd picked up the key to the van. It was also the drop-off later on. The coffee was black but tasted bitter and weak, as if it had been filtered down to its most basic element. Which surprised him as the cafe sold Kebabs, but when he'd asked for a Turkish coffee, they looked at him as if he was asking for the key to the safe. He yawned and sipped the piping hot coffee, hoping it would lift his tired eyes. Doing night shifts in his Uber was taking its toll. He'd lost his temper last night with Musa and his frustration had spilled out. Why didn't the boy want his help? It was like talking to a prisoner behind thick glass. It was breaking his heart, he wanted to be there for him. His worry was that he might slip into that dark spiral of drugs. He'd seen it with some of his old friends, none of them had returned.

He lit his cigarette and read the sheet he'd printed out. He didn't trust the app, he needed to see it and feel it. It was all there to be read, no hidden menus or buttons. In black and white. The paper had a letterhead: Bywater Recruitment Ltd. He'd also received an email and had printed that. The letter explained who he was working for and that his paperwork was being processed. Someone was putting a very elaborate front on these jobs. He hadn't really found out anything about them. There was a basic website where you could apply for jobs and some vague description of what their ethos was. He was holding out on telling Geraldine until he'd had time to dig a little deeper.

His first stop was in Essex, a scrap yard close to Southend Airport. He guessed it would be the same scam, recycling old car parts that garages would fit and pass off to their customers as new. Back home, they recycled everything; with the sanctions, they had to. He pulled up at the end of Welton Way at an unmarked metal gate. He wound his window down and called out to a man in dirty blue overalls with slicked back black hair and a smooth face covered in oil marks.

'Come to pick up for Bywater.'

'Yeah, sure. Over behind the Portakabin. Six boxes.'

Rebwar looked over and saw piles of crushed cars. 'Green one?'

'Na, Na, the fucking caravan. Look…' He pointed.

Rebwar saw a small caravan that had once been white. Its wheels had been removed and the body was resting on some bricks.

'Looks like a gipsy caravan.' Rebwar waited for the reaction.

'You mean traveller mate. Can't call 'em gipo's nowadays. Un-fucking PC innit. None round here anyway mate.'

He looked at the caravan, 'pretty sure that thing's seen some travelling though. If you know what I mean.'

'Is it the Gipsy's?'

The man frowned, his black eyes looking for more information. 'If you're looking for real Gipsy travellers, you're in the wrong place, mate! What kind of business do you think this is? Are you's one of Wayne's new recruits?'

Rebwar nodded.

'He's expanding, hey? Heard he's hired some business manager? A girl.'

'Betty?'

'Yeah, her. Making me do some paperwork. I mean, fuck off, right? What's your name?'

'Amir.'

The man laughed. 'Oh yeah, and where you from? Just got off a boat?'

'I just came for the six boxes mate.' Rebwar didn't want any trouble.

'Yeah. Stop wasting my time. Go and get those fucking boxes.'

Rebwar drove over to the caravan. Nearby shrubs had crept closer to the caravan, and were slowly taking over, the door was hanging on one hinge. Inside there were six brown boxes of different sizes, each one open and brimming with greasy, grime-covered parts. The caravan smelled of mould, and he could see daylight creeping in through the holes in the panels. He glanced around. Nothing stood out. Once he'd loaded the boxes and crossed out the address, he inputted the next postcode.

———

Rebwar was on A13 on his way to a garage back in Kent. Some blue lights flashed behind him, followed by a siren. They overtook him and slowed down in front. A stop sign flashed at him. He slowed down and mounted the pavement. The two policemen got out of the car and put their caps on. Rebwar checked himself in the rearview mirror and swore. One of them knocked on the window and he rolled it down.

'Driving license and vehicle papers, please.'

Rebwar hadn't got much with him, and of course he was Amir Begani to Bywater Recruitment whose van this was. 'I only have this new job.' And Rebwar handed them a log book for the van and a letter that Wayne had given him which had some information about Bywater.

The officer looked at the papers. He had a thick moustache and piercing blue eyes. He didn't smile. 'But you have a license?'

Rebwar nodded.

'Any other form of ID. Passport, bank cards?'

'Sorry, no. First job. Call them. They have all my information.' And he pointed at the number on the letter.

'Jim, can you stay with this gentleman. I'm going to make some checks.'

The other police officer looked around the van, checking it. For a moment, Rebwar thought of running. He had no idea where this was going. They hadn't really told him what to do. Why should they? He looked at his phone, thinking of calling Wayne or Betty. He took out a cigarette and offered it to the officer. He refused. Rebwar lit up and slid down the seat. This could take some time. He had no idea what kind of details Betty had made up about him. His phone rang, it was Betty.

'Amir, I'm going to sort this mess out. Are they there?'

'Police? They are outside.'

'OK, now listen carefully. You're going to take the van to the scrapyard, that is what you were doing, OK?' Rebwar was about to ask why. 'I have explained what is going on, that your papers are with me, OK? Don't tell them anything unless they ask. Actually...' She waited for a moment. 'Just don't say anything.' Rebwar could hear her swear in the background. She was stressed. The policeman knocked on the window.

'Sir, please step out of the vehicle and open the back doors.'

Rebwar stepped out. He noticed that passers-by were turning their heads to stare at them. He opened the rusting door.

The officer stepped in and looked into the boxes. 'Where were you going?'

'Scrapyard.'

'Which one?'

Rebwar felt his hand tremble and put his hand in his pocket. 'Maidstone, Bywater Services.'

The officer stepped out and walked around the car, inspecting the tyres and rusting holes. 'Right... Where are you living?'

'London'

'Address?'

The second officer returned and called his colleague over and they had a conversation. Rebwar tried to listen in, he knew they were comparing notes. Classic fact checking. If they were going to get the truth out of him, they would have a job on their hands as he didn't quite know what was going on himself. He had purposely not brought anything with his name on it. The officer with the moustache came over to him.

'This vehicle is not road worthy. It is going to have to be impounded. Now I am going to give you a receipt with a contravention. I understand your paperwork is pending, but you will have to present yourself at the nearest police station in the next five days. Do you understand Mr Begani?'

Rebwar nodded and was made to sign some paperwork. And they pointed to the nearest bus stop, which was a few miles down the dual carriageway.

EIGHTEEN

Geraldine was sitting in a train carriage staring at a crumpled handwritten note that she had found at Zane's. The handwriting was disjointed and misspelt, but she could just about make out a date, possible place and time. There was also a name, but she couldn't make it out. She knew he'd fallen in with the wrong crowd again, but this time she was hoping it would work to her advantage. She was also breaking her promise to her sister Rachel. She was torn between her duties to the job and her family. Maybe she could do both. But things didn't always work out like that.

She arrived at Queensborough train station just after six. She had decided to take public transport as she couldn't get access to a police car. Too many questions would have been asked, and she wasn't in the mood to come up with an elaborate cover story. Plus, she was a terrible liar. But as soon as she got there, she regretted her decision. She hadn't really thought this through. She was so used to London, where you could always get a tube or a bus and nothing was that far away.

This village was on the Thames estuary and seemed

like it had been dragged out of the mud. It was surrounded by boggy flat land and industry. Something about the place immediately felt off; nothing good was going on there. She should have asked Rebwar to come along. But she knew Zane, and he was family, even though he'd changed his number and hadn't told her; nothing new there. Geraldine had no idea what she was getting herself into. She still hadn't found out what or who Zane was involved with. None of her contacts or friends knew anything or were willing to talk. If Rebwar had gone with her, it might have provoked a confrontation, but it would still have been better than being alone. She walked along the seafront where the water was brown with silt and moored boats bobbed up and down. She was in two minds about going into a local pub and asking a few questions. It would definitely attract unwanted attention, and a police badge probably meant the opposite of protection down here.

As she looked out onto the water, she tried to think what Zane could be possibly doing here at 7 pm as the note suggested. It was remote, and he was a city boy. Zane didn't have many skills, certainly none that made him indispensable. Why would they need him somewhere like this? It wasn't his natural habitat. She needed a drink to think. Maybe a pub was a good idea.

The Old House At Home had a pleasant homely feel, something she hadn't been expecting. Not wanting to engage with anyone, she ordered a pint of Guinness, paid and sat down. On her first cool sip, Zane walked in. He spotted her immediately and smiled. But it wasn't warm and sent a small sliver of ice down Geraldine's back. He flicked his finger, which made a little snap, which annoyed her as she swallowed another sip of beer.

'G, what the fuck are you doing here?'

'Could ask you the same question, Zane. What the fuck!' She did her best interpretation of pleasant surprise.

'Did we make an appointment? I probably forgot, hey. Yeah, I'm sure I did.'

'Not at all, I was in the area and popped in for a drink here. What are you here for?'

'Well... just for a quick one.' He called to the barman. 'Stella, mate.' Geraldine nonchalantly checked her phone for any messages, as Zane threw some coins on the bar collected his beer and walked back over to her. 'Mate, I've got a job.'

This time Geraldine's look of surprise was genuine.

'Yeah, some guy from Bywater or something made me legit, and I've got a fucking job, man.'

'Doing what?' Geraldine took a slug of cold Guinness.

'Driving some ferry passengers to London. VIP thing. The bus has air con and a minibar.'

'You've got a bus license?'

'Yeah OK, it's not a bus, bus. Minibus, more like. Van like.'

Geraldine drank another large gulp of beer. She was waiting for the alcohol to do its thing and make her a little more relaxed. So, Zane's meeting was for a real job. 'Ferry passengers?'

'Yeah, G, from somewhere I don't know. Foreign blokes. VIP like. You know?'

'No, which ferry?'

'Oh, just down there. You know I don't get out much. Shit, I'm going to be late.' And he gulped down his Stella. 'Nice seeing you, G, we good, yeah? OK, OK?'

'Yeah Zane, drive safely. Huh?' And he left. Geraldine gulped the rest of her pint and stood up to look at the vehicle he was driving. It was a black Mercedes van, and she made a note of its license plate, got her coat and went out onto the parade. The wind had picked up, and the sun had set. Lights had popped up all around. She spotted a fishing vessel on the other side of the bay. There weren't any others like that around here. This wasn't a fishing village and the other boats were small pleasure craft.

Now she wished she had some binoculars and a car. It was too far to make out. The area looked like an abandoned industrial complex. She was desperate to see what the boat was up to, but she was pretty sure this wasn't anything to do with fishing, and there was no ferry around here. There had been many people caught smuggling; a couple of years before, a big French operation had been taken down. People still paid anything from one to ten thousand Euros to come in. She knew Zane had to be working for a smuggler either consciously or not. And who was Bywater? She carried on watching the fishing boat until a group of about ten people disembarked and walked over to some small metal sheds a bit further inland. A few minutes later the boat was motoring back into the Thames.

She wanted to call it in, but there was more information to be found here. She went back to the pub, ordered another Guinness and watched the crowd in the pub.

'What's that old pier used for across the bay?' she asked the red-nosed landlord.

'That's not used no more. They let it rot ages ago, before my time. Never a soul out there now.'

'Not even a fishing vessel?'

'They anchor in the harbour. Unless they want to stay. I'm no seaman, best ask some of the locals. Why do you want to know?'

'Oh, just curious. Thanks, mate. Nice pint.' And she put a fiver down.

NINETEEN

Rebwar was stuck in crawling London traffic along Gower Street heading into Covent Garden. His passengers were a mother and daughter who were going shopping. He'd tried to make conversation with them, but they were more obsessed with what shops they wanted to see. But at least he could listen to the news on the radio. *An inquiry has been urged concerning the helicopter crash that involved Sir John Merkenstand, the internet billionaire... The pound has slipped further and is in line to reach parity with the Euro... Mrs May is to...*

'Oh, please would you turn off that radio,' said the mother. 'You know it's all a conspiracy and racket for the rich to get richer. Need to get on with it... Brexit means Brexit.'

He turned the volume down and looked for another radio station as they inched their way to New Oxford Street. Suddenly there was a loud rap on the front passenger window. Rebwar could see a warrant card staring at him. That was all he needed: more police trouble.

'Oh my! Is there a terrorist incident?'

He opened the window, and Geraldine's head popped in. She smiled. 'May I come in?' Before he could try and explain that he was working, Geraldine was sitting in the passenger seat. 'Hello, ladies! I'm an old friend of your driver.'

The two women looked at her.

'Geraldine, I'm working.' Rebwar hissed at her. 'I have passengers who actually pay to be driven around.'

'Hey, I'm not going to make a noise, I'm not here. Really, shhh.' She put her index finger to her mouth and smiled.

'Who are you?' said the woman. 'Are you from the police?'

'Geraldine, we can meet later,' Rebwar said quietly. 'I'm dropping them off in Covent Garden.'

'Oh, you're going shopping?' Geraldine turned around. 'How sweet! Mother and daughter going out for an evening shopping. Wish my mum had done that with me. Instead, she took me to the pub to chat up men.'

'Who are you?' the woman said again.

'DC Geraldine Smith. I work with your driver, Rebwar here. I'm just catching up with him, OK? Don't mind me, though. You carry on in the back there chit-chatting about girlie things, whatever you girls chat about.'

'Right. Let us out, please. I'm not having our experience ruined by some woman who thinks she can just do what she wants. I should report you!' She opened the door, narrowingly missing a passing cyclist, who swore loudly at her. 'Come on, Fee. Let's go. We can walk from here.'

There in the middle lane with buses and cars surrounding them. Rebwar had tried to move towards the pavement, but the traffic honked him and he was stuck. He asked the women to wait, but they were off. Rebwar hit the steering wheel in frustration.

'Happy?'

'Hey Rebs, you and me! Just like old times. Come on, let's go to the pub. I'll take you for a beer or whatever it is you drink.'

'You could have called first. And what about my Visa?'

'Are you in a mood? Come for one, Rebs, let's chat in a pub.'

'I'm working. Some of us have to work, you know.' Rebwar followed the traffic with some cars still hooting at him.

———

Eventually Rebwar gave in and they ended up at the Dolphin Tavern in Holborn, a traditional corner pub with little square windows looking out onto the street. It was small inside and everything was fitted around the big wooden bar. The pub was filled with vintage pictures and old nick knacks reminding customers of its antiquity. Rebwar found it stuffy and dirty, but he knew all this decor was what Britain was about, clinging onto their past, a golden age. But it all felt a little sad, like a relic of something that was disappearing. This, he thought, was what Brexit had been about.

He hadn't asked Geraldine if she had voted for Brexit, though he suspected that she had. Geraldine passed him the pint of Kronenburg he'd asked for. He had thought of trying one of those craft ales, but he wanted something refreshing, not a taste experience. Geraldine had gone for a Guinness.

'Cheers.' She sipped the pint and a smile filled her face. 'No, you can't beat it. A good pint in a good pub. None of those shit trendy bars.'

Rebwar looked at her. She fitted in like a worn, well-loved slipper. When Geraldine wanted something, there wasn't really much argument. And she might eventually deliver on her promise of a visa for him and his family. Rebwar knew that she didn't really have the power to make him a legal resident, but she could help. So, he had to keep trying. 'You wanted to talk?'

'Have you found out anything about the Gipsy?'

Rebwar shook his head. 'He's a ghost. No one has heard of him.'

'Well, I did.' She leaned on the bar. 'In Kent.' Which wasn't strictly true, but she thought there was no harm in bringing a bit of healthy competition to their job.

'And?'

'I've got Zane on the case.' She kept it vague.

'Zane? Your ex-criminal brother-in-law?'

'*You forgot* to mention waste of space. But what's interesting is that he actually has a job, working for a company called Bywater Recruitment Services. Though typically it looks like there's some dodgy stuff going on there.'

'Did you say Bywater? Bywater Services? He's working for them?'

They both drank and looked around.

'Yes. Have you heard of them?'

'I'm working for them too! I drive a van and deliver cardboard boxes filled with old car parts. Until the police stopped me.'

'And? What did they do?'

'Nothing really, apart from taking the van and letting me go.'

'Traffic... bunch of idiots.'

'The thing is that I told them my name was Amir Begani.'

'Explain?'

'I didn't want to give my real name when I took the job, but because they have a mobile app, Raj registered me as Amir Begani. Then you get contacted through the app and given jobs. And now I am legal... I think... It makes no sense. But I got a work Visa! I never thought about it, but I must have.' Rebwar lofted his glass. 'Cheers to that!'

'You're shitting me! You've got a work permit? What the hell is going on?' She finished her pint and motioned to the barmaid that they'd like another round. The girl nodded sagely. She didn't seem to have a smile for anyone. They carried on exchanging information about their respective experiences with Bywater Recruitment Services. She about the potential smuggling Zane could be doing, and Rebwar about Wayne and the job, Kim Dong and what happened at Matt's car wash. He still hadn't got any information about the Gipsy, but Geraldine hadn't pushed, so Plan B couldn't have been in that much of a hurry for it. Although some money from them would help. He had spent a lot of time chasing.

'I've pawned Hourieh's beloved tea set for you. Any payment coming?'

Their drinks arrived and Geraldine drank half of hers in one go. She sighed. 'Really? Shit, sorry Rebs...' She looked down and wiped her left eye. 'That bitch, will only pay on delivery. I can't do anything about it. And sorry for ruining your cab journey. Sure, there'll be another one.' She downed more of her drink and nearly stumbled off of her stool.

'Another one.' She slammed the glass down on the bar, just missing the mat. Rebwar looked at her and it was like a passing cloud had touched the sun, her eyes were full of shadows and sadness. He put some money on the bar and got up.

'What are you doing?'

'Going back to work.'

'Please stay here, I...' She grabbed her glass again, her eyes welling up and she sniffed then drank the rest.

'Sorry, I'll be in trouble. You'll be all right.' Her fresh pint of Guinness landed on the bar.

'Oh yeah, sure, I'll be fucking all right. I'm always all right, right.' She looked at Rebwar. A lost look, not knowing what to focus on or say. The drink had taken her over. 'Go on, fuck off. I'll be all right.' Her elbows were propped on the bar, holding her up.

Rebwar hesitated. She wasn't all right, at all. And he knew she was still grieving for Zara. But it was a process.

'Call me if you need me, OK?'

She blinked and nodded. Rebwar felt bad leaving her there, but he had bills to pay and Plan B hadn't coughed up, so he had no choice.

TWENTY

Rebwar was driving back home from his shift at 8:30 pm and he had just turned into Fellowes Road. He was about to call Kamal to tell him where the car was going to be parked so that he could start his shift. The deal had been working well, as it meant that Rebwar didn't have to do sixteen hour shifts to pay back the finance payments on the car. There were times where you would either wait for hours for a job or aimlessly chase a surge around town. This meant Kamal could add another shift that would take them into a small profit.

His side window exploded and showered him with small pellets of glass. A scooter had just passed him. Another window cracked and a metallic thud hit the car. He was surrounded by a gang of scooters. It was dark and their lights were off but he could make out four of them. He swerved into another road and knocked one of the riders off. Wherever he looked, there was a rider. They swarmed around him like flies. One on the pavement. Another one heading straight for him and two behind and probably more.

'*Telhas Teeze*, you little bastards!' He accelerated towards the one in front. He swerved out of his way between two parked cars. Rebwar managed to hit his back tyre, which pushed into one of the cars. Now three were behind him. He took a hard left into another road. A car was driving towards him, there was just about enough room to pass. One of the scooters overtook him and braked hard in front of him. Rebwar didn't flinch and kept his foot down. He spotted the rider's eyes through the visor. His skin wasn't black as he had expected it to be.

The scooter swerved over into the pavement, avoiding Rebwar's car. He saw that they had baseball bats. As another overtook him, he opened his door and the scooter slammed into it. Rebwar grabbed the rider's leather jack and pulled it towards him. The scooter was sliding on the ground, its plastic parts cracking and smashing. The rider's feet scraped along the tarmac. He was trying to say something, but his words were muffled inside his helmet. Rebwar stopped the car and got out.

The remaining scooters drove around him, lashing out with their bats. Some shouted abuse at him but he couldn't make out what they were saying. Rebwar attempted to get the rider's helmet off, but the strap held. A blow hit him on his back. His lungs emptied and he couldn't breathe. The rider next to him stood up and hobbled away. He felt another blow on his arm. The pain was building up. The adrenaline hadn't kicked in. He shielded his head knowing that more baseball bats would be coming his way. Engines revved and they drove off.

He stood up and felt more pain. It was carnage around him. A broken scooter and a baseball bat lay behind him. The leather jacket was in his hand. He threw it into the car and climbed in after it. He had to go before the police came to ask questions he didn't want to answer. He parked the car a few streets away. He looked at the broken windows and dents. Whose idea was this? Was it about taking him off the road so he couldn't make a living? He searched the leather jacket. There was a phone in a leather pouch, some bank cards and a penknife. Looking at the name on the card, Rebwar wasn't too sure if it was the man's jacket. *Darious Onajiel* it said, and the phone needed a passcode.

He remembered the rider's eyes, they had looked Asian. Could it have been the same lot who hit Matt's car wash? But why were they after him? But it must have been some kind of warning, a sign. Rebwar just wanted to know who had sent the message. His phone rang, it was Kamal.

'Hey.' And Rebwar took a breath that hurt like he had fallen off a ladder. 'Yea, yea I'm OK. Listen, someone tried to break into the car and smashed the windows. Do you know someone who can fix it?' Rebwar took another breath. 'Hang on, I have some contacts. Like to try them out.' He thought of using one of those garages that he had delivered those spare parts to. Maybe Kamal might see something or hear something about the gipsy. Maybe he had better luck. Being a Turk he might have more of an in than he had.

———

Rebwar was tapping some plastic sheets over the broken windows when he spotted three hooded kids down the street. He recognised their walk. Swaying from side to side with their arms dancing to their talk. The streetlights created threatening shapes. He reached for the baseball bat that he had got from the scooter gang. The three of them laughed as they pushed each other around. Rebwar relaxed as he heard their voices. He'd met them before.

'Hey man, you got hit?' said one of them in a dark blue Superdry hoodie. 'For real man, that wasn't us, yeah? Before you go and accuse any of my bruvs, yo!' And he laughed.

Rebwar turned to them, their hoodies still hiding their full faces. 'You know who did this?'

'No man, didn't hear any word out there, yo! Bruvs, any word?' The other two kids shook their heads. 'Looks rough man. Right beatin' they gave you.'

'Some Asian kids on scooters. Have you seen them?'

'No man, them scooters are trouble. Even coppers can't catch them.'

'Yeah, even coppers,' another echoed.

'Lucky they weren't carryin' acid. That stuff is fucked up. What you have done to get so much heat on you, man?'

'If you hear who it was, I'll give you a reward. Money?'

'How much? Man, we don't work for nothin', you know what I'm saying? Not gettin' a beatin' like you, man. Not putting my nose in your shit business.'

'Depends on the quality of the information.'

A taller kid whispered into his ear. 'OK, I'll deal with you man. Half up front, you know what I'm saying?'

Rebwar took out the phone that he had found. 'Can you break into this phone?'

The third kid took it off him and had a look. 'Did you forget the code, man? It's a six. Even the law can't break this. Reset or nothin' else man.' And he handed it back to him. 'I can shift it for you.'

Rebwar counted some twenties and handed them over to the one with the Superdry hoodie.

'Nice doing business with you man. I'll bring back some social on who did this. You know what I'm saying?'

The three walked off down the road. Even if he didn't get much out of them it was worth keeping them on his side. Keeping them away from Musa, a price worth paying. Also, they might keep that scooter gang from coming back.

TWENTY-ONE

Geraldine had been busy researching Bywater Recruitment Services Ltd. She'd found that there was a web of companies around them and decided to contact the Ferret to get some direction. This time Geraldine had called the meeting and the place. She was pacing around the viewing deck in the new extension at the Tate Modern. She'd already been waiting for over ten minutes. The view was spectacular, her favourite skyscrapers were there, Walkie Talkie, Shard, Cheesegrater and the Gherkin. She gazed up at them against the blue sky an felt like a child again spotting the different buildings. Cranes competed for space in the new, mushrooming skyline, and the old dependable Thames lay below, the sun sparkling in the wake of the various tour boats cruising up and down the river.

Around were families of curious tourists all looking impressively at the sights. Some held their chests as they saw the fall below them.

'Why did you pick this terrible place?'

Geraldine turned around to see the Ferret, dressed in a grey Burberry mac, black tights and heels. She put down her leather briefcase and tidied her bun. She already looked pissed off, and Geraldine was happy about that.

'Nice view.'

'Not really. Prefer it in pictures. Can we sit anywhere?'

Geraldine looked around her and shook her head.

'I wouldn't call this a meeting place then.'

'Did you get my report?' Geraldine leaned back onto the railings.

'Please, could you not do that.' Geraldine glanced behind her at the drop. 'Yes, I did. Could we go inside?' The Ferret walked inside the glass box that was the atrium to the lifts. 'You've been digging up unnecessary information. I don't see what relevance it has to the Gipsy.'

'But it's a scam. Shouldn't we do something - or pass it to another department? I mean it's clearly human trafficking and also what could be classed as modern day slavery.'

'I asked for information about the Gipsy, not about trafficking gangs. I'm not paying you for that. I gave you specific instructions on what we wanted.'

'You're not paying me at all at the moment.' Geraldine said, partially under her breath but fully intended the Ferret to hear it. 'But I think all this is related. I'm sure the Gipsy is involved somehow. I can feel it.' Geraldine looked around for a non-smoking sign. She needed something to take the edge off. There were three of them. Her mouth was dry.

'Look, can I call you Geraldine? I hate all these code names. Quite frankly they are ridiculous.'

It took Geraldine by surprise, a little flash of humanity and rebelliousness. Maybe she could convince the Ferret to see her point of view. 'Yeah, sure. What can I call you?'

'Charlie.' She smiled. She had applied makeup and

lipstick. Nothing too glamorous, but she did look a little bit more attractive. Less plain.

Geraldine would have never guessed it. Her brown eyes had a bit more life to them. For the first time, Geraldine noticed a wedding ring. Had she caught her off guard? 'Nice to meet you, Charlie.' They shook hands.

'Fancy a coffee? There is a place a few floors down.'

———

Charlie had made herself a bit more comfortable. Beneath her mac she was wearing a dark suit jacket with matching knee-length skirt, Reiss, Geraldine guessed. She had an hourglass figure that suited her clothes. Her red lips sipped her latte.

'I know we're not supposed to talk private lives,' said Geraldine. 'But are you married?'

Charlie looked at her ring and looked at Geraldine. 'Yep. And it Sucks.' She scratched her hair. 'Just about to start going through marriage counselling. Been told to wear it again.'

'Oh, tell me about it. I took mine off whenever I could.'

'Did you make it through?'

Geraldine shook her head and sipped her drink. 'I came out.'

Charlie's eyes widened. 'How did you know?'

Geraldine looked into her eyes, searching for a sign. She hadn't picked up anything from her, apart from the silver cross she wore around her neck and contempt for her beliefs. For sure it was one of the deadly sins that Charlie believed in. Lust, and Geraldine thought of Beckie's skin.

'Are you religious?' Charlie was caught off guard.

'I go to church but... why?'

'Never mind.' Geraldine sipped her tea and tapped the file on the table. 'Anyway, you'll see that Bywater Recruitment Services has been expanding and that it's owned by Chilton, a shell company based on some sunny tropical island. They own a couple of other companies here called Mundus and Heath Solutions. I'm not sure yet what they do, as I can't find anything about them online.'

'If it's some kind of scouting trip to a Caribbean island, you can forget it. Immediately. The brief is clear.' Charlie had reverted back to her officious tone.

Geraldine slid her chair closer to the table and lent forward. 'Look, Rebwar—'

'You mean the Robin?'

'Yes, although now he's going by the name of Amir Begani, since he's been recruited by Bywater' Charlie was about to say something and Geraldine stopped her. 'And guess what?'

Charlie leaned back in her chair and shook her head.

'He's on the books. Officially. P60 and everything. And, as you know, he's still waiting for a Visa from you lot.'

'So, what's your point?'

'Well, how did he get a P60 if he's supposed to be under the radar, huh? And under a false name?'

Charlie took a moment to think and kept looking back at Geraldine.

'Don't you see, there's a massive racket going on here? And looking at their shell companies and records, it's on an industrial scale.'

Charlie snorted. 'If it's legal, I don't see the problem of companies taking over other companies. And I'm sure it was just a clerical error. Maybe there is an Amat Berani.'

'*Amir Begani*. And no, he doesn't exist, Rebwar made him up.'

'Geraldine, a word to the wise... drop it. Focus on the assignment at hand.' Charlie looked into Geraldine's eyes. 'And that's an order.'

'Order? Something has to be done. Profiteering from illegal immigration, is this what Plan B are about? Because that's what I'm getting from this. This Gipsy is just a red herring, isn't it. He's a ghost.'

'Look, Geraldine, I understand you're upset about Zara and O'Neil', Charlie tipped her head to the side in supposed sympathy. 'Maybe you should consider taking some more time off. I'm sure Rebwar can take charge of the assignment'.

'Oh fuck off, don't patronise me and pretend you're all concerned. I'm a police officer. Whatever you think of me or my past, I have a duty to find out what's going on wether you like it or not. And who the fuck are you anyway?' Geraldine stood up and looked around her. Couples and families were looking. As she scanned around and challenged their stares, the eyes looked away and returned to their coffees and cakes. The low murmur and tinkling of crockery returned. She looked at Charlie, who had her mouth open. 'Sorry.' Geraldine mumbled and walked off.

TWENTY-TWO

Rebwar was sitting in a new van and it smelled new, that mix of glues and plastics, something he had never owned. He lit a match and hesitated. Put it out and waited. Back in Iran, some of Hourieh's friends had shown off their new cars to him. He had always made sure he would find a cigar and smoke out of the car. He laughed at the thought of seeing their shocked faces. Drowning out their precious new smell. Some complained, others didn't dare, and maybe they admired his disregard. It was a good test on who you could call on for favours. He lit his cigarette. The van was parked in front of a disused property on Merton Lane. On the gate was a 'for rent' sign. The A2 was just behind a large bush that ran along the road. Trucks and cars whined passed. Dawn was rising and a thin line of light appeared over the horizon like a door opening into the world. The sun had travelled all the way from its homeland and lost all its heat on the journey.

He had been told to wait for a truck from Germany. He had never seen a German truck, probably clean and grey, he thought. Traffic passed, lighting up the surrounding trees.

The younger ones had bloomed, and their vibrant green leaves glowed in the early morning light.

A big truck pulled up, its lights flooding the lay-by like a football field. Rebwar could only see multiple sets of bright lights streaming from the front of the cab. It pulled up alongside him, its engine coming to a loud rumbling stop, then gave a loud hissing sound like an asthmatic sigh. The door opened and a thin man climbed out, in a fleece jacket and jeans. His face was gaunt, but he had a good head of dark hair. Turkish? He came over to Rebwar. 'Amir?'

Rebwar nodded.

'Quick! Come with me and open the back.'

Rebwar followed him. The truck was green with blue and yellow swirling stripes. *Logistics On Time* was written on the bodywork and trailer. It had an address, Friedrich Strasse, Dusseldorf, somewhere Rebwar had never heard of. He could feel the heat of the truck warming his face. It had a fresh oily smell to it and didn't seem as toxic as the ones at home. Rebwar got his keys out and unlocked the back of his white van. It was empty and lined with new wooden panels.

The trucker opened one of the truck's huge back doors. He whistled and shone a torch inside. Rebwar went over to see. Boxes of various size were piled up. One of them popped a lid, and a man came out, followed by others. Rebwar watched the frightened faces as they looked around, trying to understand where they were. There were five women among them and two children. The trucker did hardly anything to help them out. Rebwar stepped forward, but the trucker held his hand out to stop him. It was as if they were contagious.

'They have paid for this,' said the Trucker.

Rebwar watched them help each other. Some of them spoke Arabic, others Turkish. A wave of sweat and piss emerged with them. He could tell they had suffered from the journey, as some limped and others stretched. Their clothes were dirty and crumpled. For a moment Rebwar thought they might have suitcases. But they only had Kaufland and Aldi branded plastic bags with them. Some had water and a few pieces of clothing.

'Get them in your van quick. Quick. No one can see. *Schnell!*'

They ran into the van, piling in. Rebwar closed the doors just before a car passed by. He hadn't heard it coming.

The trucker swore at him in German. 'Get going, you idiot. This is not right, ja?'

Rebwar got back behind the wheel. He could feel his human cargo moving inside, rocking the van. He called Wayne.

'All good?'

'Yes.'

'Good, good.' The truck started its engine and Rebwar closed his window. 'You need to deliver the package to south London. I'm texting you an address. Don't take too long about it. And don't stop for them, just get there. And only once inside do you open that door. Understood?'

'Yes.' And then Rebwar read the text.

TWENTY-THREE

Geraldine was standing in front of the morgue door. Taking deep breaths and trying to calm herself down. Zara's murder came flooding back to her. She had convinced herself that it was only a scar, but now it felt like an open wound, and it hurt. The last time she had been here was with Beckie, who was the forensic that had been processing the body parts that had been discovered around London. Beckie had correctly diagnosed that the killer had to have a surgical background. Geraldine remembered her sweet caramel and vanilla perfume. People in white coats looked at her as they passed by and nausea took hold of her body. They were probably used to people being unwell, and none of them offered to help. Not that she wanted any. She had to deal with this. It was her battle. She couldn't get rid of that image of Zara lying on the bed, and the gaping bloody hole where her heart should have been.

The door was as cold as the sweat spreading over her. She breathed again. Geraldine hated morgues. Normally she would make appointments somewhere outside them. But Beckie had insisted. The thought of her made her feel a little better. She had been so kind. Geraldine pushed the door. There were no surprises in there: three clean stainless-steel tables waiting for bodies, sterile white tiles everywhere and Beckie with her white coat and wavy black hair. Geraldine could smell her sweet perfume through the formaldehyde. The sight of her olive skin made her tingle. All nausea departed.

'Hey, Geraldine. Nice to see you, babes.' It was such an easy, casual greeting.

But not for Geraldine. '...Hi Beckie.' She came over and Geraldine watched her walk towards her, her slim body, her dancing waist, her pert breasts. Beckie knew she was being appreciated and toyed with Geraldine as she always had done. Maybe this had been a bad idea.

'Coffee? Looks like you need one. You look a little down. Are you all right?' She put her warm, soft hand on Geraldine's cheek and then forehead.

It felt so good. It made her tremble a little, and she smiled.

'There you go, a nice smile, something I don't see enough. One sugar and milk? I know it's not a Starbucks, but I needed to talk to you here.' Beckie walked over to her office, which was through another door in the morgue. Geraldine followed her.

'So, as you asked, I did some digging on that fire in your apartment.' She poured out two cups of filter coffee while she talked. 'Whoever worked it was pretty shoddy, or rushed, or something.'

Beckie handed over a mug of coffee to Geraldine, took out a file from her desk and leaned over it. Geraldine could feel the electricity. She breathed in her smell. Focus, focus.

'Are you all right?'

Geraldine sipped her coffee. 'Yes, thanks. You were saying?'

'Yes, I tried to call the pathologist who was on the case but couldn't find him. Someone said he was a freelance, but no one has seen him since. So weird. Then I found this... a photo of the bodies at the crime scene.'

Geraldine studied the picture. She hadn't seen her flat since the fire. It was a ruin, all charred and the windows had burst out from the heat. It was a black shell with all her belongings burned to unrecognisable dark lumps. Beckie pointed at one of the black skeletons.

'This one has a metal implant. Probably from a fractured leg. Not mentioned anywhere in the report. Also, it says that both bodies were of Romanian origin. That's bullshit, no evidence for that anywhere. All I can say is that there were two males. One was about six-three and the other around five-ten. But that's just a guess. The details in the report, or rather lack of them is inexcusable, but as there hasn't been a trial or anything like that...well, it hasn't been questioned. There's no doubt the court would ask for another post mortem.'

'So, would anyone have done a quality check on this report? Don't they get signed off or anything like that? Nice coffee, by the way, it's really helping.'

'Not always. And I got the feeling from talking to the investigating officer that he was just going through the case like a box ticking exercise. He just reeled off what he'd done, there was no critical view on it at all. He'd just taken everything at face value, didn't question anything. But then again, most people just trust that we are doing a good job.'

'Yes, we do.' Geraldine sat down.

Did you ever find out who came in to claim Zara's body?'

Geraldine shook her head and held her thoughts as she had a suspicion that Plan B had dealt with her funeral. She never got an invite or a clue where she had been buried.

'I'm so sorry about Zara. I heard, you know. And I should never have...' Geraldine watched her breathe. '...Hit on you, I was wrong to do that. Sorry.'

'It's fine, really.' Geraldine saw her look at her ring finger. It was bare and with no sign of one having been there. 'I thought you were married.'

'Yeah. It's over now.'

TWENTY-FOUR

Driving along the A20 to London, Rebwar had time to think and feel. His human cargo didn't sit right with him. It wasn't shocking; this happened all the time and all over the world, one of the oldest trades. People trying to find a new life, a better one; he had done it himself. But that had been under his terms. These poor souls were already slaves to someone, probably Wayne and his gang or the company. But his assignment was to find the Gipsy, not ferry illegals. He saw an exit to Green Acres Kemnal Park just by Sidcup. He stopped in front of a closed gate. A car passed behind him along the dual carriageway.

Rebwar stopped the engine and looked around. No one was going to visit the park which was also a cemetery. Shrubs and a green wooden fence kept people out. He contemplated the problem of his cargo. There was a pavement that ran along the road. He was sure they would find a bus stop or tube, but what then? He took out his wallet; he had a few twenties. His other option was to call the cops and make a run for it. He got out of the van and opened the back door. The men and women looked out onto the carriageway. Their eyes scanned for information about where they were. The humid, warm stench enveloped Rebwar. It was how he imagined it would smell if he was ferrying cattle.

'You are free.'

'Where is our contact?' said the oldest looking man.

'What do you mean? You can go. Go and I recommend that you go to the police station and hand yourselves in. But it's your choice. Understand?' Rebwar handed him some money, but he didn't take it. He turned back to face the others. He was a little taller than Rebwar with a thick head of hair and unshaved. 'What are you saying? We paid money to come here. All sorted?'

Rebwar looked around to check if anyone was nearby. 'You are free. Don't you understand? Otherwise, you will be a slave. You need to run and find a new life. Free country, OK? And if you hand yourself in, you might get a good deal.'

'No, mister. No. Take us to what the deal was.' He grabbed Rebwar's shirt. 'OK? Paid good money for this. Wife and me... making new life.'

Two other men got out and ran. They were among the youngest of the group - maybe Syrian. Rebwar didn't really have time to check them. 'Go, go, you are free. You can't work for Wayne, understand? No good. He's a bad man.'

'Take us to this man. Otherwise Gipsy curse will get us.'

'Say that again, Gipsy what?'

'Curse. Man said if we did not do what they said, we will be cursed and die. This country very dangerous but has money.'

Rebwar grabbed the man's shoulders and tried to reason with him. 'Listen... these men are bad and talk lies. Not true. There are no curses here. Who is this Gipsy?'

'Why you do this?' said one of the women in the back. And the man turned to her and said some strong words in his language. She said 'Why you want to help us? You work for them. Is this a trick?'

Rebwar took out a box of cigarettes and offered them out. The woman and man took them. The others stayed there, sitting in the dark of the van. Rebwar hadn't made a headcount. He had no idea who was who or how many were in there. He lit the cigarettes.

'So, what should I do?'

'Mister you do your job. OK?'

'And those two? That have run?'

'We will say they died on way and dumped their bodies. Normal.'

'How many were you? No, don't answer.' Rebwar looked at their faces. He felt even more frustrated. What would he have done? These people knew nothing of this new world, just gossip and dreams. Or maybe they did, but this wasn't the place or the time to discuss it. 'OK, I take you where you want. OK?'

'Take us to man.' said the woman. Rebwar closed the door and got back into the driver's seat.

———

Rebwar arrived at the industrial unit on Meaford Way, just off Penge West train station. There were a couple of units with closed metal shutters and various logos above them. As he approached the sign for the company he'd been sent by text, Gel Glazed Windows Ltd, the shutter slid up to reveal three men inside. A mix of boxes and window frames filled the unit. A man in a denim jacket waved Rebwar in. He drove into the empty space. At the back was a metal staircase that led to an office. It had windows overlooking the grey concrete warehouse. Someone was inside. He guessed it was Wayne, but it was too far to see his face clearly.

The man in the denim jacket waved his hands. 'Quick, quick! We need to get this load out and moving. Park it there and open the doors.'

Rebwar pulled on the handbrake and the man grabbed the keys off him. His cargo walked out. The overhead strip lights lit their faces. They looked scared and huddled together. The man and woman looked at Rebwar. For a moment he thought they were going to say something. He took out his cigarette box again and was about to offer them some. One of the men stopped him and showed him a no smoking sign.

'Outside, if you want to do that.' The man shouted up to the office.

'Wayne, are you going to process them?'

Wayne stepped out of the office, his rolled-up sleeves showing off his snake tattoo. He looked down the steps and said. 'How's the back of the van?'

One of the men went to have a quick look. 'Empty, but fucking filthy. Should I ask them to clean up.'

'That'll be Dental Mike's job.'

'Fuck off, I did it last time! Why's it always me who gets the short straw? What about him?' Dental Mike pointed to Rebwar. 'Motherfucker drove it, he should clean it.'

Wayne looked at the group of men and glanced at his paperwork. 'There's two missing.'

Everyone looked at each other, waiting for an answer. Rebwar was getting his answer ready.

'They die,' said the old man. 'Not make it.'

Wayne walked down the stairs towards them. 'Where?'

Rebwar had a bad feeling about this. He put his hands

in his pockets. The three men moved around like they were ready to pounce on someone.

'In truck, left in big truck.'

'Shit, what?' Wayne thought for a moment. 'Ahh, not our problem lads.'

The three men stood down.

'What do you need me to do?' asked Rebwar.

'Amir my friend.' Wayne put his arm around him and slapped him on the back. 'This wasn't your job. I had to get you last minute. But you did well. I like you, you're a grafter. Now... you can see that this isn't strictly above board.' Wayne turned around to look at the little group of the refugees. 'Boys search them. See if there is anything odd. Don't want fucking terrorists coming in on my watch, do we Amir? Hang on, you're not from some Islamic cult are you? Ha ha!' Wayne laughed at his own joke and moved Rebwar forward.

Rebwar felt his large hand push him towards a room just under the office. He glanced behind to see that the biggest of the other men followed. Once inside, the big man shut the door behind them. The room was bare, with just a few empty metal shelves, a chair and a table.

'Sit, Amir, please. I think you know Dental Mike.'

Dental Mike nodded. Rebwar looked at him: big and tall, cauliflower ears, bald, a flat, broken nose and a mix of gold and black teeth. He folded his meaty arms and stood with his feet wide apart.

'What is this?'

'Nothing to worry about, Amir, just need to ask you a few questions. Routine.'

Rebwar sat down on the wheeled office chair. All of a sudden Wayne grabbed him from behind and held him around the chest. Dental Mike and Wayne each gaffer-taped one of his arms to the chair's armrests. They had done this before; it was quick and efficient, no words exchanged between them.

'Routine?'

'Routine. Now, Amir, what happened to the two men?'

'I'm not sure what you mean.'

The big man slapped his face and it stung like needles.

'What happened?'

'You mean with the German truck? The man opened the back. People came out. People got in. It was dark. No time to count. That's it.'

Wayne shook his head and the man punched Rebwar's face. As his face bounced back, Dental Mike held it tightly. Pain rushed, a different pain, dull and pulsating. Wayne waited.

'Again... how many people came out?'

'It was those people over there. Didn't make a note. I wasn't asked to count.'

'And then?'

'Put them in the back and shut the door. The truck left.'

Rebwar felt another punch this time a little higher. His eye got it. It tingled and his vision blurred for a moment. He'd been here before. A long time ago in the Iraq-Iran war. He had been captured and interrogated. The key was to try and tell them as little as possible and then give them a little nugget, so they thought you had been broken. That was the theory.

'Did you speak to the driver? I need more detail. Hey? Amir, my friend, I won't hurt you if you tell me the truth. Understand?'

The man smashed his face again. It was getting easier, the adrenaline was kicking in.

'He was Turkish but spoke German, I think. Didn't

understand him. He said "quick, quick." That's all. There were no more people coming out. No bodies.'

For a moment Wayne stood back and looked around. Rebwar could taste metal, his blood was dripping from his face onto the floor.

'Mike, give the man a cigarette.' Mike shrugged his shoulders. 'Get them from his jacket pocket.' After some fumbling around he found them and put one in Rebwar's mouth. 'You know we can track that van. I can check your little story and if I find out it doesn't add up... well...'

'I stopped for cigarette break... got lost.'

Wayne lit his cigarette. 'That's all I wanted to know. And you didn't let them out or none of them slipped out?' Wayne stepped closer to him. 'You know I'll find out, right?'

Rebwar sucked the cigarette and it brought a moment's respite from the pounding pain. He was hoping it was enough. Mike smashed his iron fist into his stomach. Rebwar bent over and threw up his stomach contents. It mixed in with the blood. His half-smoked cigarette was somehow still smouldering on the floor.

'Enough Dental, we still need this one. Take him out so the others can see him.'

Dental Mike cut the gaffer tape and helped him to his feet.

'No hard feelings, Amir, but I run a tight ship. All right my friend? Here is a few extras for your pain. You're a good man.' Wayne slipped some cash in his pocket.

'They mentioned the Gipsy curse,' said Rebwar.

Wayne looked at him for a moment. He'd said he hadn't talked to them.

'Oh, that old story.' Wayne laughed. 'Urban myth.'

Rebwar walked out into the main warehouse. Shocked faces stared back briefly but then tried to avoid eye contact.

It would only take one to break and grass on him about the two missing men. Dental Mike opened a side door and guided him out. The door shut behind him. He looked around. Now he had to find his way home. The pain was dulling down to a steady pulse. He could see his reflection in one of the unit windows. They had done a good job. One of his eyes was nearly closed. The cuts on his face would take quite a few days to clear up.

TWENTY-FIVE

Geraldine was in a restaurant called Café Rouge in Dulwich. This was the third time she had changed tables. Now she was in a booth for four people and it felt right for the moment. She looked into the mirror next to the seat. It had been a while since she had put on some makeup and it had taken a few attempts. A large glass of white wine arrived on the table. Geraldine smiled at the waiter and gulped a mouthful down. She was already feeling a little tipsy, but it wasn't alcohol related. Her watch read 7:42 pm. She straightened her shirt and thought for a moment about buttoning it up a little more. You could see a little bit of cleavage.

She swore to herself. Get a grip, G. *You've done this before, and it's only a meeting for fuck's sake,* nothing else. She smiled at the mirror, adjusted the hair that she'd layered with hair spray. She still wasn't too sure if it had worked. She checked her phone again: nothing. She looked around, trying to find other things to occupy her mind: just couples and a few lonely diners. Out here in south London, there were a few theatres and a couple of cinemas left, and it was

Monday, a school night. Most of these people couldn't be bothered to cook, she thought.

'Hi, Geraldine!'

She looked up to see Beckie. She looked stunning. It took a few moments for her to find her breath. She wore a top that was slightly see-through so you could see her lacy bra, below was a short skirt and black heels. There was a little tattoo on her ankle. She bent down and kissed Geraldine on the cheek. Her smell was like a fragrant dish, sweet and musky. The sort of a scent you would find in a forest, that would drift by and you would spend ages looking for it again.

'Hey, I love the top.'

'Thanks, Geraldine. You look nice with make-up. Is that for me?' She smiled.

Geraldine admired her olive skin. She was so jealous. Beckie had no need for make-up; she was naturally beautiful. She wore her wedding ring. Geraldine's heart skipped a beat but she kept calm.

'Drink?'

'Yes! Could murder one. I'll have what you've got. Can I try?'

Geraldine nodded.

Beckie sipped from her glass. Her full red lips left a mark. 'Oh sorry. Not used to wearing lippy.' And she rubbed it away.

'Are they like fingerprints?' Geraldine watched Beckie smile: It made a cute little dimple on her cheek.

'Can be. Not a common use of forensics. Mm nice wine. Bottle?'

The waiter came with the menus which were huge, more of a poster than a menu. Beckie asked for a bottle of the wine.

'So, how are you?'

'I'm good.' Geraldine wanted to grasp her hands. 'You've got your wedding ring back then!' Geraldine instantly regretted saying that. It felt too early. Why couldn't she keep her gob shut?

Beckie looked down at her hand and breathed in. 'To keep blokes away? Habit I guess. I don't know. It's complicated.' Beckie smiled. 'Sorry.' Geraldine said and took hold of her hands. They were soft and warm. Beckie squeezed back. 'Really, it's fine. What did you do with yours?'

'I... I kept it. It's in a box. Although I did have to rescue it from the street a couple of times ... and a toilet. And...' They both laughed. 'I know what you're saying. But I can't wear it anymore. It feels like it's going to burn my skin. I might pawn it...'

The bottle arrived, and Beckie took her hands back. 'Ready to order ladies? We have some romantic dishes for you. Sharing ones.'

'Yeah, thanks, can you give us a moment?' Beckie turned back round to giggle a little at Geraldine. 'Sorry, it's just... I feel like we've been caught.'

'It's all right. I know what you mean. And...' For a moment Geraldine wanted to say everything she was feeling. Then changed her mind. 'Did you find anything?'

'Shop talk already?' Beckie's face changed as if something had prodded her. 'Yes, sorry, sorry, of course, that's why we're here. Not a huge amount really. The DCI, Richard O'Neil...' Geraldine's back straightened and her face flushed. Like a cold chill had blown in. 'He's nowhere to be found. I checked the police files and it's like he didn't exist, record wiped clean. What did they say about him at the time?

Geraldine hesitated before she went on. 'There must be

something out there on him. We just got told he'd left the force and the country for personal reasons. I thought-I hoped he'd died in the fire. Then Rebwar said someone saw him running away from the flat that night.' Geraldine felt like she was about to cry.

'I don't know, G. Can I call you that?'

Geraldine grabbed Beckie's hands again and held them as if they were a lifeline. It had been such a long time since she'd been asked if she minded being called G. It made her feel warm. 'Yes, you can. Go on...'

'Are you all right?'

She felt a hot tear run down her cheek. Memories of Zara and O'Neil flashed back. It made her angry and she wanted to shout. She wiped her eyes roughly, grabbed the wine glass and emptied it. Beckie stared at her. 'It helps, sorry, go on...'

'OK then... I did some more digging. It's quiet at the moment, and I hope I'm not stepping on your patch. You know the body that had a metal implant? Well, it had a serial number, and it was army. They keep a good track of those, unlike the other medical services. You know, if any of their men get pulverised its something that might survive. A little memento for the box. Sorry.'

Geraldine felt a laugh escape. 'You forensic guys... dark, dark.'

'I know. Anyway, he was in the army. Some guy called Patrick McKenzie, a private, he left in 2010. And...' Beckie got her handbag out and took out a picture. She showed it to her.

'Shit, that's... the Squirrel.'

'Who?'

Geraldine breathed in and rubbed her face. 'Plan B. I'm really not supposed to talk about it. But, hey, what the fuck!

I'm supposed to be working for them, but I don't trust them one bit. And yet I have no choice. I fucked up, badly'. She looked around the restaurant and for a moment, she froze and felt she had dived into a river of icy water. 'You really can't say this to anyone. Shit, *I* can't really.' She poured herself another glass, gulped it down and made her decision. 'But, I trust you...'

'G, I know life is full of bad things. I stare at them all day. Things aren't as straightforward as black and white. I know that. And... shit, we've all been bad, right?'

'Yeah, but there's bad and there's bad.'

'What did you...' Beckie looked around to see if anyone was within earshot and with her mouth nearly shut said, 'kill someone?'

'Oh god, no, no, I just went beyond the law. I was going to lose my badge and probably do some time. All because of my sister. Anyway, the point is, Plan B sorted it all out for me, and I've been working for them on cases that aren't... let's say, strictly official ever since'. Beckie was leaning across the table now, her eyes wide. 'But who are Plan B?'

Geraldine looked around again and spoke quietly. 'It's a secret organisation that uses ex-police and crooks to do their dirty work, and the metal implant guy worked for them, I reported to him. But who the other dead guy is, I have no idea... it's fucked up.' She took another large gulp of wine. 'I shouldn't be telling you this. Really, I shouldn't.'

'Are they police or special ops?' Beckie's dark eyes were now looking into hers intently.

'I don't know. I have no idea who they are. They just have code names of animals.' She shook her head, 'fucking idiots'.

'Shit, do you think they have been following you or something?'

It was a good point. She hadn't been too careful in the last weeks, not really knowing where O'Neil was. She should have been on high alert. It was like a slap. Geraldine! She told herself. 'Shit! The fuckers... Maybe it's all smoke screen?'

'What? Are you all right?'

'Oh, it's this Gipsy thing. They've asked my contact to look for a man called the Gipsy. And it's been like a red herring. Fuck, we can't talk about this anymore... Sorry.' Beckie sensed that would be all G would say for now and changed the subject. 'OK. How about some food? Something to share? A platter?'

Geraldine was tired of making choices and decisions. She let Beckie decide while she drank another glass. She was now feeling a little drunk. It was helping her forget and relax. She needed it badly. She sat and watched Beckie's mouth as she talked to her. Like soft gentle strokes in a warm bath, she let the feeling take over her.

TWENTY-SIX

'So he's a ghost too?' said Rebwar.

'You saw O'Neil. I did, too. But, apparently now, he doesn't exist. There is nothing anywhere about him.'

Rebwar stared into the rearview mirror. Geraldine looked rougher than usual, as if she hadn't had enough sleep. Her eyes were puffed up, and her hair was unruly. But she had a glow and a smile. Rebwar pressed for the next track on the car radio. It was an old CD he had found in a suitcase. Black market stuff from back home. Which meant songs that weren't sanctioned by the government. Mostly pre-Khomeini singers. He had confiscated it from some old woman who had reported a burglary. This was in his youth, when he was still fresh-faced and wanting to make an impression. The sergeant gave him a slap for it and told him to keep it. It made him feel guilty. But he listened to it. One of his favourite tracks was *Fereidoon Farrokzad by Aashi-aneh.* Which brought a smile to his face.

'Are we being played?' Geraldine said.

'You know, I had the same thought.'

The car was parked on Frith Street in Soho: and people

passed by singing, joking, laughing, on their way to pubs and theatres.

'We need to prod the nest. Get something out of someone.'

'How's the new job coming along?'

Rebwar pointed at his bruises.

'Looks painful. How did the other guy look?'

It had been the elephant in the room. He'd had to lie to Hourieh that it had been a drunk customer. It had happened before, so she believed it. 'No, I think they were either making an example out of me or it was some sort of initiation. They made me smuggle some people in.'

'You're now officially an undercover cop.'

Rebwar tried to smile, but it hurt. 'And I tried to free them. Two went, and the others preferred to stay as they had paid for the journey. Like it was some kind of service. Should have seen their faces when they saw what had been done to me. But they didn't squeal about the other two.'

'Probably petrified. Any luck with your friend, Raj, and the app?'

'I am going to have to feed him. Yes, thank you for reminding me.' He wrote Raj's name in a little notebook. ' And Betty the HR woman at Bywaters, we need to talk to her. Have you found a company address for her?'

Geraldine shook her head. 'Series of PO boxes they are covering their tracks. But hey, it's only the two of us.' Geraldine lit up and slid the window down. 'So, who were those two immigrants you just casually let loose?'

Rebwar shrugged. 'Just two guys, about mid-thirties?'

'You know they could be terrorists. Then there'll be a world of shit coming down on us.'

'They didn't look like terrorists. I think they were from Syria or Libya.'

'Oh! So you know what a terrorist looks like now? That's all right, then! You need to find them. I don't like the idea of them roaming around. They could be IS, you know?'

'Come on... they were young men looking for a new life. Not everyone comes over to make war.' Rebwar inhaled his cigarette and tried to remember their faces. She did have a point. He should have asked the others if they suspected them.

'I'm going to have to report this. You've got a day to sort this shit out, OK?' Geraldine opened the door then stepped up to his window. 'I know what you were trying to do, but it's the world we live in. We're under attack.'

Rebwar watched her walk away and listened to his music. He hadn't thought that through. He saw Kim Dong's boys run across the road. He couldn't remember who was who, just that there were three of them, all dressed in screaming 80s colours. One of them was trying to listen to his phone. It was as if he was having a seizure. The other two took the phone out of his hands and listened to it. They started to shout something. Maybe in Filipino. All three were trying to speak at once. They seemed to be panicking.

Rebwar stepped out of the car and went over to them. One of them saw him and froze. One of the others rushed over to him. 'We need help. Kim in trouble. Mister, mister, please help.'

All three we now trying to grab him. 'OK, OK. Slow, slow... what is going on?'

'Listen to message, bad.'

One of them started crying. Rebwar listened: Dong was shouting out their names, puffing hard and asking them for help. Rebwar listened to it again. He could hear trees and branches cracking. 'Where is he?' he asked. None of them knew. 'When did you see him last? Here in

Soho?' They all nodded, tears now flooding down their faces, and they hugged each other. 'Where's the closest park?'

'Soho square, just over there,' one of them said, pointing.

Rebwar rushed over and they followed. It was dark and the black metal gates were closed. Rebwar tried to see inside but there was no light. The metal bars had spikes on top of them, but you could climb over. Rebwar chose a corner close to a tree that he could use to help him. He landed on muddy ground and felt his shoes sink. The streetlights in the square threw shadows around him. He pushed through thick bushes until he was on grass. In the middle was the little black and white wooden house he saw almost every day. Not somewhere someone would live. He looked through the window. He could see a ping pong table and some benches. Two of the boys rushed over to him. They had climbed over too.

'Milan has found something. Come, come.'

They took his hand and pulled him. On the bench behind the little house was a man slumped over. It was Dong. Rebwar pulled his head up and tried to find a pulse. His red shirt was ripped, bra showing, skirt covered in blood. His fat body slipped down. And turned as the knife in his back caught the back of the bench. The three boys stared in shock. No one could say anything.

'Stay where you are and no screaming, OK? Understand?' One of them, Juan, was hyperventilating. Rebwar slapped him across the face. His shocked eyes looked into Rebwar's and he grabbed his hand and started to cry.

Rebwar pulled away. 'I need to look for clues.' He had to find as much as he could before the police came, or he would lose any advantage he had. Dong's body was already cold, so the killer would be long gone. He looked through Dong's pockets and found a large silver coin, nothing else.

'We need to find his phone, OK? Quick, quick!'

Rebwar used the torch on his own phone to look around. He spotted two sets of footprints leading to the gate. He took a photo of them and had a quick look at Dong's shoes. He was wearing Nike trainers. The other set had a tread that could have been from a boot. It was also bigger.

'Call his number,' said Rebwar.

Milan dialled it. All of a sudden, a screen lit up in a bush. Rebwar picked up the phone. 'Do you have his code?' Before any of them could answer, he went over to Dong's body and grabbed his hand.

'Wait!' said Milan. The sound of sirens bounced off the buildings. They had to go. 'We can open it.' They rushed over to the gate and climbed over.

———

Rebwar found himself in a bar with them. The music was too loud and men were staring at him. Milan gave the phone to Juan, who pinched his nipple through his t-shirt. Rebwar watched him slip the phone under his t-shirt. He handed it back; it was unlocked. Milan smiled at Rebwar's confused face.

'Can be any body part,' said Juan and they all laughed for a moment, then remembered why they were there, and what had just happened.

Rebwar made a note of the numbers Dong had dialled. He flicked through his photos. They were of all the boys in different stages of undress. He looked through the emails and found nothing of interest. Just marketing messages and promotions for gambling sites.

'Why the coin?' said the third boy.

Rebwar brought out the silver coin. It was larger than any in circulation. It felt light and fake.

'Gipsy curse. A warning?' said Juan.

Milan turned around from checking guys out. 'He had met some men about a job. Very secret. Not want to talk with us. We not like. Trouble.'

'Was he broke or in debt?' Rebwar asked the third boy.

He nodded and began to cry again. Juan held him, but Milan was looking elsewhere. 'What's next for you guys?' All three looked back. Only Milan seemed not to be bothered by his nonchalance.

'Just find the killer, OK? Isn't that your fucking job?' The dramatics were back.

'I need money for that. I don't work for nothing. I had no business with Dong.'

Rebwar was already working for Geraldine for free. That was bad enough.

'You so heartless, mister. So cold.' Juan shook his head and his eyes welled up.

Milan tutted and stood up, looked at the other two. 'Drink?' And he walked off, swinging his skinny little butt like a beacon to anyone who was interested.

'He doesn't seem to be angry about Dong's murder.'

'Oh, he always been an asshole. Dong was having a fight with him.'

'What about?'

'You think he did it?' Juan sniffed.

'Maybe.' Rebwar didn't think so, but he wanted to see if it led to something. Prodding the nest.

'No. Not for money. He was broke, needed cash. No more luck, luck run out at the casino.'

Rebwar watched Milan talk to some men at the bar. He had moved on and was already playing his next cards. Rebwar was intrigued by what the boys would do now. He felt a little sorry for them; they were like lost puppies. But they were survivors. Sure, they would find someone to look after them. Maybe that was what Milan was already sorting. Rebwar handed the phone back to them.

'Keep it safe, and if someone calls it, let it go to answer phone. Then listen to it. I need to rescue my car, OK? Call me if there is any news?' He got his coat and put it on. With Geraldine annoyed with him, things were getting more complicated and he needed her on his side. He needed to find Raj.

TWENTY-SEVEN

Music was bouncing out of their closet-sized kitchen as Rebwar came sleepily down the hallway in his dressing gown. He recognised it as *Hamishe* sung by Sami Beige, a former member of the Black Cats, not a song for a peaceful breakfast. He walked in, looking for his American breakfast. The kitchen seemed more cluttered than usual and he saw that Hourieh had bought a few more pans and other items that he had no idea what they were for. She had discovered a market just down the road and kept coming back with new things. Rebwar had just finished a night shift and needed caffeine. He grabbed a cup from the table.

'That's mine.'

Rebwar hadn't registered that Musa was sitting in the corner having his breakfast. Of course... it was Saturday. 'Since when do you have coffee?'

'Mum said I should try, might wake me up.'

'I think she was joking.' Rebwar took a sip. The sharp, sickly sweetness nearly made him gag. 'How many sugars?' And he gave the mug back to Musa.

'Who's Farouk?'

'What?'

Musa was holding a postcard in his hand. He was wearing one of his usual slogan t-shirts. Rebwar took a moment to read it. *I tried to be normal once.* Then a smaller typeface said, *The worst two minutes of my life.* Rebwar swiped the card off him. A painting of an Indian elephant. He looked closer. It was tied to a small wooden post and eating bamboo. It had two small white tusks with rings on them and a red mat on its back, probably some ceremonial beast for Indian royalty. The striking yellow background made it stand out. He flipped the card. *You should visit India. Lousy food, smelly, diseased and loads of stray animals. You would love it.* It was signed Farouk. *PS the match was fixed.* Rebwar looked at the stamp. It had a date on it. Sent over a month ago from Iran. A message from his prison cell.

'Is he joking? Who is it?'

Rebwar looked for his cigarettes. 'Probably. He's just a former colleague.' Farouk had been Rebwar's partner in the Iranian police force, but his habit of making bad decisions finally landed him in jail.

'Did you see that goal?' Said Musa.

Rebwar sat down, trying to think, what was he trying to say? That he was the elephant, or he was tied to one?

'Dad? Dad?'

'Yeah, did they lose?'

'No Chelsea won on penalties, but Petropolis did 4-1.'

Rebwar pinned the card onto the cork board. Later he would call Bijan and see if there was any more gossip on Farouk. *The match was fixed.* Rebwar got a cigarette out and tapped it on his hand. He was probably referring to the match where they arrested a gang of Pakistani workers at a Petropolis match. They'd had gotten an anonymous tip that the stadium was using an illegal workforce to sell drinks and drugs. The match had already kicked off against Esteghlal and Rebwar's gut feeling was to let it go and look into it later. It was just some gang ratting on another one. But Farouk wanted to go and see Esteghlal play. What was the problem? Seeing his team Petropolis lose was one good reason, but Rebwar agreed. They could just hang around and watch the game.

They drove out to the Azadi stadium a huge sports complex built in the seventies for a failed Olympic bid. It was meant to be a day out, a bogus call out, go have a look, ask some questions, take some notes and watch a game. They should have spotted the Guidance Patrol and the two big buses. There was a bigger presence than normal. The 100.000 seater stadium was close to full. A big game. They flashed their badges and went into the stadium. A huge concrete oval with a wave running through it. Farrouk knew where to go. Rebwar just followed. Petropolis were already losing by one goal. They found a seat and watched. In the twentieth minute, the lights went off. The crowd booed and cheered. But in the mix of the mayhem, gunshots rang out.

Farrouk and Rebwar ran off towards them. It was pitch black, and Farrouk commandeered a torch from someone. It wasn't long before they got lost in the tunnels underneath the stadium. But they came across two bodies riddled with gunshots, non-Iranians, but Pakistani. There was a trail of blood that lead to more. In the end, they found eleven of them. The Guidance Patrol took them all away, including the survivors. They had been tipped off, too. No one was accused of the crime or reported, but internally there had been a witch hunt on who had been behind the whole sordid affair. They both had been interviewed and then suspended. In the end they found some poor retired commissioner to pin it on. People trafficking and drug smuggling. And now Farrouk says it was a match fix. Gambling probably.

Which made sense as there had been a series of international matches where the stadium lights had been cut off mid game. It was all to do with spot bets where if a match was abandoned the bookies would pay out on the final score. And the criminal gangs made sure that they would stop the match when the score was to their advantage. In this case Persepolis being one goal down. He lit up and wondered if Farrouk had to have been involved.

TWENTY-EIGHT

Rebwar hadn't slept much. Dong's slumped dead body had kept his mind awake. Why had he been killed? There were the obvious answers, like gambling debts and revenge. And he said he had retired from people smuggling. One possibility was that an old 'colleague' might have been released. He had a list of numbers to go through from the phone's memory. But there was another idea to test out. Graham, a homeless man who had helped him before. He had found one of the missing parts - a heart. Rebwar had gotten in the way of a courier and in avoiding him crashed. What he didn't know at the time was that in the scooter's cool box was a live human heart being transported. And he was now hoping that Graham had heard some gossip about the murder.

He was back in Soho early, looking for a coffee. The busiest cafe was Bar Italia on Frith Street. It was the local for Soho. There was a small chance that he would be there and if he was, he would be asking for money to feed his habit. The places Rebwar wanted to go were still closed, so he was sat outside Bar Italia by a little round table, sipping his espresso and smoking. Next to him a was a big man with grey hair reading his morning paper. A police car stopped in front of the café.

A man and woman stepped out, both of them wearing high-viz jackets, their radios chattering away. She was taller than him, blonde, and had the look of a wrestler. Rebwar carried on sipping his coffee as they went in. He hadn't gone back to the crime scene, which was just at the end of the road in the little park. He could see a few more police vehicles parked up by the square. It wasn't worth going back there. He might bring a little too much attention to himself. But if his hunch was right, he knew where he could find the man who had followed them. He had done this before, back in Teheran. People like to hang around in the usual places. Random was hard to do. He looked at his Casio watch: 09:21 am. He stubbed out his cigarette, got up, and walked down the street towards Shaftesbury Avenue. It wasn't long before he found the place he was looking for: a betting shop. There were quite a few of them around. He had time.

He walked in and saw only men. One was suited and the other two looked like workmen off a building site. None of them were who he was looking for so he went over to the counter. A short girl was behind the security glass. She must have been in her thirties but had let herself go. She wore baggy clothes and cheap jewellery, she looked like she had given up on life. He read her name badge.

'Hi Mary, I'd like to bet on something. Feeling lucky. Anyone else been here and got lucky today?'

'Can't help you, hon' I just take the bets, don't give out advice.' She said in her monotone voice. 'I'd either be rich or out of business. So, what'll it be?'

Rebwar looked around the TV screens. They were showing horse racing which he didn't know anything about.

'Mary, can you help me out... I'm looking for a friend. He's not doing so well at the moment, if you know what I mean. Been putting on big bets. Anyone like that been here in the last few days?'

Mary looked around and adjusted her loose, branded shirt, her gut competing with her chest. 'Like I said... I'm just taking bets. Can't help you.'

Rebwar slid over two twenty-pound notes. 'OK Mary, take this for a bet. Just give me back a blank slip. We'll call it a system error. Understand?'

She looked down and tapped some keys on her computer terminal then handed him a blank piece of paper back. 'Is it Graham you're looking for? He seems up on his luck recently. Everyone's talking about it. Was in this morning but didn't stay long. Sure if you do the rounds you'll bump into him.' She winked and smiled. Rebwar sensed she hadn't done that for a while.

'How's he looking these days?'

'Pretty grubby and obviously hadn't been to the shelter for a wash in a while judging by the smell. But he did have a new coat on, a dark raincoat. Looked like a football manager.'

'Thanks, Mary. You've been very helpful. Hope you win too.'

'In my dreams, hon.'

Rebwar left the little betting shop, used his phone to check for other betting shops in Soho and walked over to another one. There was a total of seventeen just in Soho. So far Rebwar had been lucky, and if Graham was lying low because of yesterday, it could end up being a long day. Further along on the Chinatown side of Shaftsbury Avenue, was Ladbrokes. His strategy was to try and do a clockwise sweep of Soho, hoping he would bump into this Graham. It was a small Ladbrokes. A few Oriental men were in there betting.

'Has anyone seen Graham? Friend of mine. I have some money for him.'

The men looked at him as if waiting for someone to talk first. The tall thin man spoke at last. 'How he look like?'

'My height, brown hair. Raincoat like a football manager. Been playing recently.' Two of them shook their heads.

'No see here.'

Rebwar noticed some signs written in Chinese around the walls. He guessed this was the border into Chinatown from Soho. Rebwar made his way north, stopping by a couple of William Hill shops, one on Greek Street and the other on Tottenham Court Road. No sign of Graham. He passed a homeless man pushing a supermarket trolley filled with plastic bags. A dog followed him.

'Have you seen Graham?'

The man's suspicious eyes looked away and as his trolley picked up speed it veered off towards the pavement's edge. The small black and white dog barked at Rebwar. Sure, everyone was gossiping about Dong's murder, which was making it harder to find Graham. But he had his vices, and they needed feeding.

Rebwar crossed over Oxford Street and went into a Coral. This betting office had more of a utilitarian feel, it could almost have been selling cleaning or paint products. It was also next to a casino that Dong would have gone to. Rebwar looked around, trying to be inconspicuous. He had already asked too many questions. Two men were watching the screens hoping for bets to come in. Rebwar looked at his phone and his map. There was another bookies close to Oxford Street: a Betfred.

He walked along Oxford Street looking around for Graham. The street was filled with tourists and shoppers and he had to weave around them as their attentions were being taken by men selling cheap perfumes. His nose picked up a heady mix of stinging smells. He looked at his watch, 11:01 am. Rebwar lit another cigarette in front of Betfred. A man walked out and joined him. He offered him a light.

'Been lucky?'

'Not really. Slow day. Waiting for my paycheque so just putting pennies in, sometimes getting them back.'

'You haven't seen a guy called Graham around?'

The man looked at him, suspiciously as if it wasn't right to ask around. 'Boyfriend?'

Rebwar smiled. 'No, I just need to pass on a message.'

'Call him.'

'Has anyone placed any unusual bets recently? Maybe larger than usual?'

'Hey mate, you're creeping me out here. Who are you? A detective or something?' The man laughed and took another drag of his cigarette.

'Yes. I am actually, and I'm looking for a man called Graham. So, I'm just asking if you've seen him. Not too difficult.' Rebwar snapped.

The man finished his cigarette, shook his head in annoyance, and went back inside the shop. Rebwar was losing his patience. He knew he shouldn't have pushed the man that far. But he had to do something; he was prodding, hard, but just wasn't getting anywhere. He saw a homeless man across the street and crossed over. He followed the man till the streets became a little quieter and then approached him.

'Excuse me.'

The man turned around. His face was red and he stank.

Rebwar had to take a moment not to throw up. It reached inside his guts. He offered the man a cigarette and also lit one for himself to make the stink of body odour and excrement bearable.

'Thank you. What's the charity for?'

'Need some information.'

The man held out his dirty hand. 'Directions?'

'No. Looking for a man.'

'What are you? The filth? Not fucking giving you anything. Just come out of the nick, mate. Have you got some drink?'

'I'm looking for Graham.'

'Don't know anyone called Graham.'

Rebwar put a ten-pound note in his hand. 'He's been betting. And he's on a roll.'

'What guy called Graham? Oh do you mean...' And he smiled. His acrid breath crept through Rebwar's smoke.

'Go on...' Rebwar looked at him and gave him another ten-pound note. He still hadn't found the silver sugar bowl that completed Hourieh's beloved tea set that he had pawned. He was going to need it if things carried on like this.

'But he's OK. Done nothing wrong. Just been helping a mate he has.'

'What's your name?'

'Jim and no fucking fix it jokes. Right fucking perverts around here.'

'Sorry? What do you mean?'

Jim looked into Rebwar's eyes, searching for something.

'Jim, who's the friend?'

He looked down at his money as if he was afraid it might disappear. 'He got paid by a man. Good money. Yes, good money.'

'Who gave it to him?'

'Oh, not my problem, man. Look he's... No, I can't rat on him. Look, man, whatever you're into, leave him alone. He was doing good. Yeah, we were cracking it man. You know what I'm saying? And he didn't give me a score. Wanted to make a clean break. I told him that I would help. Leave him alone, right? He's done nothing wrong.'

Rebwar got out a twenty-pound note and held on to it. 'Jim, be reasonable. I can help him, OK? Was he your friend? I only need to ask him a question, nothing else. Just on that job he was doing. It was a job, right?'

Jim nodded. 'Carol, like Christmas Carol. We call him Rol.'

'How would you describe him?' Rebwar gave him another cigarette. 'Tall? Dark hair?'

'Oh, I don't know. He looks like Rol, you know.' And with his hand showed that he was taller than him. 'Curly hair. Always scratches it and a beard.'

Rebwar gave him the twenty-pound note. 'Thanks, Jim. You've been a good man. Go and treat yourself.'

'Nice doing business with you. If you need more answers, I'll have them. Yeah, I have more in here.' He tapped his head. He let him walk off down the road with his oversized trousers dragging along the pavement. Tailing him was tricky though as Jim kept looking over his shoulder suspiciously, as if someone might steal his newly gained wealth.

Rebwar spotted a little shop selling cheap sunglasses and hats, so he ran in and grabbed one of each, paid threw some cash onto the counter and didn't wait for change. He quickly put them on and caught up with Jim, keeping a safe distance. They were heading down a narrow street between a big work site and offices. It was Great Chapel Street and was closed off to cars. At the end was an unassuming NHS walk-in centre. Hanging out in front were some men Jim obviously knew. They too seemed homeless and this was obviously a meeting point for them. There was some laughter and shouting and it echoed off the brick buildings. Rebwar couldn't hear what they were saying. But they exchanged some cigarettes and sachets of junk and left.

Rebwar walked past the Medical Centre, which was clean and had metal bars on the windows. Jim reached the end of the street. Rebwar walked after him making sure no one else was following. After a few more turns they arrived on Golden Square, another one of those small parks in Soho. Jim shouted Rol's name across it. Rol's head popped out of a bin he was looking into and swore back.

'I need to talk to you, pisshead,' Jim said. 'Come here, my legs are killing me. Had to cross the whole of Soho to find you. Come here, shithead.'

'Fuck off.'

Rebwar walked along the pavement with a group of people, making it look like he was with them. Jim and Rol were in the middle of a raised brick and stone square surrounded by grass.

'Hey, there's a guy who wants to talk to you, yeah? He's got money. Easy money. Look...' And Jim showed him some of Rebwar's notes.

'Fuck off Jim! Not supposed to talk to anyone, stupid idiot. Go away.'

Jim grabbed Rol. 'Rol, what did you do?'

Rebwar stopped walking around the square and looked around him. He was expecting to see someone else tailing him. Rol seemed paranoid. He sat down on a bench and put a hat on to try and hide his face. Jim sat beside him. Rebwar waited for a few more minutes to convince himself there was no one else watching them.

'Rol, I need to speak to you.' Rol looked up from his bench. Rebwar could see the fear in his eyes. He passed him a cigarette, one of his last ones.

'Don't smoke. Got something harder?' Rol was shaking.

'This is the man who wants to talk to you,' Jim said. 'Go on, give money.'

'Rol what did you see? Were you there with Kim in Soho square?'

Rol's eyes flashed open like a camera's iris. 'No, no I... I'm not saying anything. Fuck off, man. Not supposed to tell anyone.'

'Yeah man, fuck off leave him alone,' Jim said, seeing that there may not be more money forthcoming. 'Can't you see? Leave Rol alone, he needs alone time.'

'Look, I saw you there. I can call the police and tell them. Understand?'

Rol looked at him and put his head down, looking at the square paving stones.

'Did someone pay you off? Is that why you were gambling? Calling yourself Graham? Tell me, what did you see and who paid you for your silence?' No answer came, so Rebwar pushed further. 'Or maybe you killed Kim?'

'No, no, I didn't, the man did! You got it wrong.' And he stopped himself as some people walked by with takeaway coffees. Rol bit his lip and shuffled on the bench.

'Give him some money, man. Rol needs it.'

'Come on, Rol...' Rebwar said. 'I can see you need to talk. You'll feel better.'

'Man he... he told me to look for some foreign blokes. You know... Jihady dudes from... from where you're from or somewhere.' He tried to focus on Rebwar and folded his arms while he rocked back forth.

'And?'

'Then, I had to call him if I saw them. They were with that fat Chinese girl. I could see they were lost. Asking around for jobs.'

'What's the man's name. Did he have a snake on his arm?'

Rol's eyes widened and he nodded.

'Wayne?'

'Yeah... Yeah.'

And there it was. Rol was talking about the two men that Rebwar had freed from the van. And probably Dong had found them, or someone sent them to him. And Dong was going to help them, but what he didn't know was he was dealing with Wayne's property. Rebwar looked around, now Wayne was most probably after him for releasing two of his smuggled slaves. Now he had to go back to Geraldine and tell her where they were. Though that probably wasn't going to help the two men now.

'Thanks, Rol, take this and look after yourself.' Rebwar shoved some money into his jacket pocket.

'Hey man... and me! I found him for you and made him talk, right mate? Hey, hey!'

Rebwar walked away from them, pondering his next move. He had to watch his back now. He looked at his phone, expecting a message. He dialled Raj's number.

TWENTY-NINE

Rebwar was back at his "office" which was the Shishawi. He'd taken a table at the back of the restaurant. The ones at the front had a mixture of tourists and locals smoking their Shishas. This was something he usually liked to do, but today he needed some privacy as he needed to talk to Raj. Rebwar had already pre-ordered food and drinks with his friend Berker, the Kurdish waiter. He wanted to spoil Raj and guilt him in to working his IT magic to find out more about Bywater, the dodgy company Rebwar had been working for. In the last few weeks, he'd been missing in his boy cave. Rebwar couldn't really pay him what he was worth and what he probably made doing the odd freelance job.

But he could entertain him at least, and a feast was an easy way to get to him. Since this case had started, Rebwar's appetite had gone. It wasn't a pleasure to eat, more a necessity. It had always been like this in the force back in Iran. Other colleagues needed food to think; he needed cigarettes and coffee. This case frustrated him. He needed to take the initiative and Raj could help him do that.

His high-pitched little giggle heralded his arrival at the front of the restaurant, and he was soon waddling towards Rebwar's table. He was even more substantial than Rebwar remembered, his sideways sway filling the spaces between the tables.

'Hey uncle, how's it hanging? Wow, what happened to your face? That looks raw.'

Rebwar got up and gave him a hug, his arms struggling to reach around him. 'Good, Raj, good. Sit down and prepare for a long story. First, I have a feast for you. Beer?'

'Oh yes! Can't wait, I'm starving.' he grimaced. 'Only had a cheeky little cheeseburger on the way down as I walked.' Rebwar couldn't help but raise an eyebrow at the prospect of Raj walking anywhere voluntarily. 'Needed some air.' He giggled again.

'Good, good. Berker has something special lined up for you. Been busy?'

'Always. The internet never stops. Just been trying to crack a new game. Making a plug-in so you can win without having to pay to win. You know... giving something back to those poor players who can't afford to pay out thousands to win a game. Those fucking developers are crooks.'

Rebwar refrained from asking more as Berker arrived with three bottles of Becks. He brushed his thick moustache and adjusted his black waistcoat. 'Hey, Raj nice to see you. You know Rebwar still doesn't know what a computer is.'

'No need to, it's all on the phone now,' Rebwar said. 'I am ahead of the game.'

Raj and Berker laughed. 'Please don't change. So, you ready for a little mezze?'

'Bring it on,' said Raj.

'Any luck with that company?' said Rebwar.

Raj took a large gulp of his beer. 'Yeah about that. Not

easy to crack without being found out. The site sits in the dark web. Clever. Well, Silk Road was, and they paved the way...' Raj giggled at his own joke.

Rebwar was lost.

'Oh Uncle, it's like those dark seedy streets in Soho and London. They have one on the web, Silk Road? The Amazon of drugs?'

Rebwar carried on shaking his head.

'Anyway, the good news is Bywater have a PO box address in London. I've got Betty's mobile, or I think I do.' He took another gulp of beer. 'Classic, just like the Russians...'

Rebwar waited, bemused.

'Doh! It was left in some code. Idiots forgot to delete it. I haven't tried to trace it or call the number. But if I could somehow access their server, I could put in some kind of tracking software, you know?'

'Not really. So, do they actually have an office?'

'It looks like it's all virtual, a piece of software that assigns jobs to a database of workers. You know, a bit like Uber. On a server somewhere.'

'But with Uber you can talk to a helpline, and don't they have an office?'

'Yes, but you don't have to. These guys are obviously on the edge of legality. Maybe they have an accountant some-where. Or something on Companies House but that's not my field.'

Berker came over with a tray full of food, a selection of small plates. As he kept laying them across the table, Raj smelled them and bounced on his seat with excitement. He didn't know where to start. Rebwar offered him some pitta bread. He took one, ripped it and dug into the hummus. Rebwar watched him eat. For a moment, he thought of eating some vine leaves, but wanted a cigarette instead.

'I can visit that PO box?'

'I think so, although a mate of mine uses a PO box service. And basically, it's a company that collects his mail and sends it to him. So you might just be watching another company collect other people's mail.'

'Can't you track all these people using this app thing?' Rebwar held up his phone.

'If I could get in there then, yes. It's not like Uber, Uncle.' Raj took a spoonful of hummus. 'Aren't you hungry? This is delicious.'

'I'm thinking, can't we somehow trap them? You know, send in a fake job?'

'Is Tamar coming? She's so hot. I heard she's doing cams too.' And Raj nudged Rebwar with a wink.

Rebwar nodded. 'Did you find any other names?'

'Like Betty? No, nothing too clear. They've done a good job at keeping it vague. The other companies look more legit but, again, are owned by the same shell company. But I guess they don't do anything illegal, do they?'

Rebwar took another slurp of his beer and tried one of the dips. It was aubergine and it tasted good. 'Ready for the main?'

'Bring it on and another beer. This is great, thanks, Uncle. Sorry I can't be more useful. But if you find me their server or office, I can hack in there. Then, yes.'

'So, they do have an office?'

'Well, maybe. But I think they are going to be using one of those big cloud companies. And they won't really know what they are running. I mean they just hire space out to other companies like Amazon and others.'

'I thought they sold stuff?'

'Lots and lots of stuff. They have huge memory servers that they hire out. Gone over your head? Don't worry. We can't really get into that. That's like super high-end stuff like Tom Cruise in *Mission Impossible*.' Rebwar frowned. 'That's a film by the way.'

'We need to go to that PO box and try the mobile, OK? Could we pretend to be from the company? Do you think...'

Raj's eyes lit up. 'Bluffing them? Worth a try.'

Berker brought over a couple of bigger plates with seared meats. Raj wafted the smell in. 'Speciality of the house, I have a new chef,' Berker said. 'Here is Kebbah Burghul, mixed platter, Zatart and Shish Kebab.'

'Uncle, this is a feast for a king.' Raj dove in.

Rebwar made some notes in his little notebook. He needed to get to Betty. The other person was Wayne, but he was likely to be a much trickier character. 'Could we track someone?'

'What have you in mind?'

'Via his mobile?'

Raj had a few more spoonfuls of rice and meat. His mouth was struggling to retain all the food. 'Not really as we would need access to the mobile company. But the police could.'

'Hey, boys.'

They turned to see Tamar in front of them in her belly dancing outfit, which was a bikini with shiny coins jingling around. She rolled her belly up and down. Raj was captivated.

'Hey, Tamar, nice to see you. Remember Raj?'

She leaned in and kissed Raj on his large cheeks, then rubbed her lipstick off them. 'Hey honey. Looking sexy. I'm sure you know how to spoil a girl. Quite a feast you have. Celebrating something?

THIRTY

Geraldine had been tipped off by her sister Rachel that Zane was on a job in Kent. At their last meeting, Zane had let slip, in a less lucid moment, that he was driving some VIPs up to London. The place was called Littlestone and was on the coast with a long shingle beach running up to a golf course. Geraldine had never been there and had to look it up on the map. She guessed the job had to be another smuggling run. Although, with no quay to dock a ship, she wasn't too sure how this operation was going to go down. She was also in two minds about alerting the local police.

But she worried that they would take over and then would be reluctant to pass on any information. As Rebwar had said, they needed to be on the offensive and this was an opportunity. She had thought of bringing Rebwar along; working alone was not clever, but he was busy taxiing people around. If she had told him what she was doing, he would have dropped everything and come along, but she sort of felt safe with Zane involved: he was family, and this was her promise to Rachel. Which still made no real sense if she thought about it too much, but somehow it did.

This time Geraldine hired a car. A website revealed that Littlestone did have a railway station, but it was one of those small gauge ones that ran steam engines. It was like going back in time. Simple brick bungalows lined all the little streets with a few odd shops and restaurants. This was a little sleepy village on the coast where people came to retire. Which was not the best place to land a boat as no one had much to do here. She was already being stared at by the few locals who were walking around, whereas the vast majority were busy navigating their mobility scooters.

Geraldine looked at her watch: 6:40 pm. They would be landing at night, she thought. She hadn't seen Zane's minivan anywhere, so she carried on driving along the little streets looking out for him. She had decided that they would probably land close to the golf course as there were no houses along that road. She called Zane's mobile. Maybe he would let something slip that might give her an idea of where he could be. On the third ring Zane picked up.

'Hey, G. What's up?'

'Hi Zane. You busy?'

'Na, not really. Just watching some football.'

Geraldine couldn't hear any TV sounds in the background. It sounded like he was in an enclosed space like a car. 'Who's playing?'

'Oh, oh it's some... Euro match. Like, just on, you know? What can I do for you?'

'Just spoke to Rachel and she said you had another job on.'

'Oh me? Yeah, it's going well. But, you know? It's a job, right?'

'Same van?'

'Yeah, why?'

'Oh, just wondering, she said you were in Kent. In Little something or other.'

'Did she? No, she got it wrong. Just a London job. Hey! I've got a mate coming over, can I call you back?'

'Yeah sure, Zane. Sure.' And the phone went dead. Geraldine knew he was lying. He was parked up around here somewhere. This time she had brought some binoculars. The coast road led to the golf course and Geraldine followed it up. Romney Bay House was the last building before the course. She parked the car just past the building. The road further up was empty and desolate. It followed the coast for about a couple of miles and then turned back inland to join the A259. There were some parking spaces up there for walkers who wanted to visit the beach.

Zane was probably up there, but she dared not approach too near in case she was spotted. She needed to know. She could go around the other way, which might be a bit more sheltered. She studied the map on her phone then started the car and drove around to where she thought Zane could be. Geraldine's skills with a manual car failed her as she crunched the gears. By the time she got there, her face was red hot and her back damp. She was feeling anxious.

Geraldine opened the window and felt the salty sea air pour in. It brought back childhood memories of her, her sister and their mum going to the seaside, flying kites and having 99s. It was a long time ago, the age of innocence; before sex and booze. It made her think of Beckie. They had kissed, but she couldn't get Zara out of her head. Her heart pounded like a hammer as her head filled with mixed emotions. Beckie had asked her how she felt, as she put her hand on Geraldine's shirt, near her heart. She stopped in a layby and drifted. But she knew she had to focus on what was happening now.

She stepped out of the car and lit a cigarette, which took her back again to Beckie: those soft lips and delicate tongue searching hers. She stubbed the cigarette out on the ground; it could give her position away. She was going to walk to where she thought Zane was parked, she was convinced he was there, over on the golf course. The full moon would light the way. For a while she star-gazed as she stumbled her way to the beach and found a little mound that overlooked the sea. She squatted behind the marram grass which gave some cover. A black van was parked just by the sea wall. A man was behind the wheel, his face lit by his mobile phone. It was Zane.

Her instinct was telling her to call the police. She needed back up. But she'd had this argument with herself before and decided, no. She looked through her binoculars. There was a boat on the sea, a rib-type, and it was coming to shore. She looked around, half expecting to see someone else. To her left were some bungalows. One or two of them had lights on. Hardly subtle, this smuggling operation, she thought. The boat mounted the shingles and the engine cut. About ten people got out.

It was one of those 'VIP' trips, as Zane had called them. Two men pushed the boat back into the sea and motored off. Zane got out of the van to greet his passengers. Geraldine watched their faces through her binoculars. All were men; a few of them were black, the others eastern-looking. Zane loaded them in the back, got in and drove off. Geraldine had to get back to her car and follow. She spotted some flashing blue lights inland. Had someone called the police or was it an ambulance? She tried to run back but kept stumbling on the rough, uneven ground. It was filled with rabbit holes, and if she wasn't careful she would break an ankle.

Another blue flashing light appeared. No sirens, though. She reached her car and got in, fumbling everything and stalling the engine. The van would have already made its way to the main road, but she kind of knew that it was most probably heading for London. Now she could hear the sirens. One car passed her making its way to the beach. She picked up the van as it took the A259 towards the M20. More police cars passed her. Someone had called it in. She felt like protecting Zane. She called his phone.

'Hello?'

'Hey Zane. Take the back roads.'

'What? Are you following me? G what the fuck? You can't just...' His voice hushed down. 'Listen, leave me alone. Don't stick your nose where it doesn't belong.'

The phone went dead. A car came alongside to hers. At first, she thought it was trying to overtake her, but two men were sitting in the front staring at her. They didn't look like police. One of them was bald and looked like he'd had a fight with a door. The other was smaller and was smiling at her, he had a teardrop tattoo by his left eye. Cock, was her first impression. The side of the car moved closer to hers and she instinctively moved away. Her outside wheel hit the soft verge. In front were headlights heading towards them. The car behind pushed hers. There wasn't anywhere to go except for a grassy bank. Headlights flashed ahead. Geraldine had nowhere to go and the other car made contact. Her own car buckled like a tin can as both ground together like teeth.

She felt her car rise into the air. Motion slowed, and she had time to think. Had Zara suffered? She had never said goodbye. Lumps of muds flew into her windscreen. The car carried on and rolled over onto its roof. Odd, she thought; it was like watching a game. The roof caved in. Glass exploded. The car carried on rolling a couple of turns then came to a stop. The airbag had gone off, but she couldn't hear anything; everything was muffled. Beckie's smile was so heartwarming. Geraldine smelled pungent smoke which brought her back like a smack.

'Are you all right?' She looked up to see a couple watching her anxiously. Both were old and grey haired. 'That car ran you off the road.'

How long had she been there? She felt her senses come back and said woozily, 'Call the police.' And she reeled off the registration to them.

'Can you feel anything?'

All Geraldine could feel was a mounting anger, which was almost outgunning the pain in her body for her attention.

THIRTY-ONE

Rebwar was sitting in his car, it was a beautiful sunny morning with not a cloud in the sky. It was 8:03 am and hopefully early enough to catch a postman delivering some mail. It was his third day at 56 Knowledge Crescent. He'd spent an evening with Raj. They had hacked into the Byways Recruitment Services website and managed to change their mail delivery address from an anonymous PO box to this physical address. The idea being that someone from Byways would have to come to pick up the now redirected mail. And then Rebwar could connect a face to the rogue company. Raj did go into detail on how he got in, but Rebwar had lost him at the back-end of admin login. It was a screen full of commands and numbers. Rebwar didn't mind, he just kept passing pizza slices and fries across like he was in a drive-through. He felt like he was feeding an engine, but it had worked.

Rebwar reclined his seat and felt the sunshine warm his face. Birds sang their calls as they flew around his car. He thought he saw a few sparrows chasing some invisible bugs. He loved their sweet cries. He drew deeply on his cigarette.

Stakeouts were like meditations, letting the environment wash over as if you were watching the sea, listening and looking out for every detail, seeing patterns or a tell. The postman had delivered mail to this address between 9 am and 10 am in the last few days. Raj and Rebwar had picked this residential street for its sleepiness.

He mused on how long it might take before either the sender or Byways would notice something was wrong. But he had to be here from the start. The Crescent was a series of bungalows and houses and in the middle was a large green. This was where the residents would walk their dogs so there were a few red bins dotted around. For the second day's watch, Rebwar had hired a car in order not to be recognised. You just had to alter the pattern a little for people not to notice.

The neighbourhood was a nice one, well-tended and cared for, some of the properties had novelty ornaments in their front gardens, others had extensions and parking spaces. It was a place where Rebwar could see himself living, but he would probably be the only foreigner there. The house they had picked to park outside had an old retired couple living there with a small brown dog. The wife did the morning walk around the green; he guessed she didn't want to ruin their garden. He remembered how Hourieh's father had sworn every time he discovered a yellow patch on his perfectly manicured garden. He kept threatening to shoot his neighbours' dogs and then, one day, actually shot at one of them. But, after a few days, they still kept coming back to pee and shit.

Rebwar's thoughts went back to the mail deliveries and he calculated it would probably be 2-3 days for each of the parties to notice their mail was going astray. He assumed Betty would be the one to come by and pick up the stray mail. At 9:23 am the red Royal Mail van parked up in the close and the mailman did his rounds to each house. Rebwar guessed that about half the houses were occupied by housewives or retired couples. The rest commuted to work and sent their kids to school. Rebwar's phone rang and he looked down to see who it was. Wayne was calling. He had been waiting for this call.

'Hello.'

'Hey! Amir, my friend!'

'Hi, Wayne.' There was a moment of silence.

'You've been good, mate?'

Rebwar could hear some noises of a café in the background. 'Have a job for me?'

'Yeah, that's why I'm... calling. I'll brief you personally. This job needs my personal attention. Meet me tomorrow at the usual van pick up. I'll send you a text. Oh and don't mention it to Betty. Need to keep this under the radar. Get my drift? Understand?'

'OK Wayne. Yes, tomorrow.'

Rebwar stared at his phone. He knew what this was going to be about: the two missing immigrants and why he had lied. The problem had finally called him, and he had to deal with it. Options flooded his mind, and his first instinct was not to go. He wanted to meet under his terms and have some kind of advantage and certainly not get disposed of. Rebwar carried on watching the postman make his delivery. At one house he rang the bell. An old man opened it and smiled. The postman brought out two bundles of post, each one held together by an elastic band. The man took both of them and said a few words to him. Rebwar couldn't hear what was being said but, from the waves and smiles, it seemed pleasant enough.

That second bundle was for Byways, Rebwar was sure

of it. There was something about how the man was holding on to it, which probably meant someone had made contact with them. It was only a matter of time until Betty turned up. She wouldn't trust them to forward them the mail. Rebwar looked at his watch: 9:40 am. He had to move the car and find another observation post. Break the routine, and he might not get noticed. Sure, people would note that he was there, but if it looked like he was waiting for someone or taking a break, they wouldn't call the police. He took out a flask of coffee and poured some. It gave him the kick he was looking for. A supermarket delivery van pulled up next door to the house he was parked in front of. He was going to have to move.

A little red car passed him with a woman driving it. He decided to see where it went. It stopped close to the building he was watching, and the woman stepped out. She had red permed hair that almost matched the car. She looked around for a house number. Rebwar got out another cigarette. She walked up to one of the buildings but it wasn't the right one. Rebwar felt sure this was Betty. From the conversations he had had with her, this is what he had imagined. For a moment, she hesitated to ring the bell. She looked at her phone and turned around.

Rebwar wanted to get closer, but he couldn't without being noticed. He was in the wrong place. He couldn't get his binoculars out, not here. His frustration mounted. She walked along to the pavement to No. 56 and walked up to the front door. A tree obscured the whole scene. She went into the house. As the door closed, Rebwar drove to a better spot. It was a good twenty minutes before she came out with three different sized bundles of mail. He looked around him. It surprised him that she had come alone. She wore high heels, mid-length skirt and a white blouse and lots of glittering jewellery. She had a pretty face, but with lots of make-up.

How had she become involved with Wayne and his crew? She could be working for some bank or insurance. She had such an innocent smile and kindly demeanour. It just didn't make any sense. She sat in her car and adjusted her rearview mirror to add some more makeup. She was making a call. Rebwar took another sip of his coffee and she was off. He let her drive a little distance and then followed.

The traffic was heavy and Rebwar struggled to keep her in sight. Too many vans were in a hurry to get in front of him. She got onto the A412 towards Slough, a dual carriageway, and he followed her up to the roundabout. There were multiple sets of lights and large supermarkets around. It wasn't long till she got away as he was stuck at a red light with two cars in front of him. He tried to guess which direction she had taken.

But he was in the middle of Slough and she could have gone anywhere. There were just too many choices. After fifteen minutes of trying out different routes, hoping to find her, he gave up. He had her car registration number. Geraldine could probably help him find her address, but Rebwar didn't want to ask for favours and she wasn't ready to give them out. Not without grief as there wasn't a clear link to the Gipsy. So he headed back to Knowledge Crescent. He could try and get something from the old couple.

———

Rebwar rang their bell. It had a classical music chime. He waited there, listening for any other sounds. Had they gone? Then he heard some shuffling on a carpet and locks being undone. The old man peered out of the door.

'Yes, can I help you?'

'Hi, I'm here for the mail of Bywater Services?' Then he thought he should have done this earlier. He'd just missed a trick. 'I'm from the PO Box company. Mail Boxes Etc.'

'Sorry, who?' The old man was hunching and cupping his ear. His clothes were a little too big for him.

'Mail Boxes Etc. A client's mail has been forwarded to this address by accident and I have come by to collect it.'

'Yes, yes, she's been by. Sorry.' And he started to push the door closed.

'Who has been? Someone from Mail Boxes Etc?'

'No, no, but it's been dealt with.' He pushed the door a little harder.

'Was it Betty who came by?'

He stopped pushing the door. 'Yes, yes, she did.'

'Oh damn, I'm too late. I needed to talk to her. Do you have her number? The mobile I have doesn't work anymore. She's changed it, you see. I need to call her. Otherwise, you'll be getting her mail again. She needs to sign a piece of paper to authorise the redirecting of the mail.'

'Her number?'

'She came by? It was Betty? Blonde, really short, bubbly and glasses?' The man shook his head. 'So, who picked up the mail?'

'Sorry, Mr...? My wife dealt with it. You need to talk to her, and she's away at the moment.'

'Amir. And you are Mr...?'

The old man shifted his weight from one old slipper to another. 'Blenddom. Come back after 4 pm and my wife can help you.'

'You must have her number, this is urgent. You have given confidential mail to an unknown person. If I can't reach this person, I will have to call the police. And we'd rather not.'

Mr Blenddom stared at Rebwar. He turned around and went into the house. He shuffled back with a notepad and handed it over to him. There were random numbers written on a page with no names. Rebwar looked up at the old man. He just looked back at him shaking slightly and holding onto the door. He obviously didn't know much. Rebwar took a photograph of the page with his phone.

'Thank you very much, Mr Blenddom, and sorry for this disturbance and Mail Boxes Etc apologises for any inconvenience.'

'Have you got a business card?'

Rebwar searched his pockets. 'No, just run out of them. But if there are any more problems, I'll put my number on this pad.'

They said their goodbyes and Rebwar returned to his car. He could see a few curtain nets move in neighbouring houses. It was time to leave.

THIRTY-TWO

Geraldine got off the tube at Hyde Park Corner. Apart from a few tourists, it was quiet. She couldn't remember the last time she had visited Hyde park. She had thought about what she was going to wear. The weather was a little over-cast, and it was meant to rain at some point. It was as if she had to dress for the countryside, outside and exposed to the elements. Instead of her usual bomber jacket, she had on a green parka. She used her phone to find her way to the Serpentine, a little boating lake in the middle of the park. She knew there was a café by the lake and hoped it was where they were going to meet.

The actual meeting point was just off a little pier where a solar boat docked near the statue of Isis. It was an odd choice, but Charlie, The Ferret, was just that: odd, and she still hadn't got the measure of her. But this time she wasn't going to be late. Even though Geraldine had spent time dealing with the cuts and bruises from the crash, her body was feeling stiff and sore. That number plate hadn't yielded anything, another stolen one, but those two staring faces still haunted her. They had smiled before pushing her off the road. It was as if they enjoyed it.

Geraldine walked past the café, which had a few people sitting outside. The view was beautiful and she took a moment to take it in. The lake had a white road bridge that cut the lake into two. Trees surrounded it and people rowed the little boats around on the water. She wondered if she was going to be subjected to that. It was like a little green oasis in the middle of a concrete jungle. She wondered why she didn't escape there more often. Just a tube ride and you could find peace. She snapped out of her reverie and walked over to the bridge. Charlie was feeding some swans at the water's edge.

'On time for a change.'

'Hi, Charlie. You're not supposed to feed them bread.'

'They should be glad that they get fed.'

Geraldine noticed that she had a coffee in a takeaway cup. She wanted one too. She felt a moment of anger that Charlie hadn't bought her one. But she couldn't expect that. Charlie turned to look at her. Geraldine looked back. This time she was wearing a white turtleneck jumper with a small golden crucifix on a chain. She had forgotten that Charlie was religious. Geraldine wanted to sip her coffee. Weren't Christians supposed to be thoughtful to others? Where's *my* fucking coffee? She wanted to say.

'Did you want to get a coffee?'

'No, I'm fine, why did you want to see me?' Anger mounted inside her.

'Are you all right?' Charlie stared at her face.

'Yeah, just some surface scratches. Someone tried to run me off the road.'

'Who?'

'Those Bywater guys. You know, the ones that are

running the immigration racket. Making it look like recruitment. Human trafficking on an industrial scale? Remember?'

'Yeah about that...' Charlie threw her last pieces of bread and a couple of swans and ducks fought over them. 'Lay off the trail, OK?'

'What? But it's linked to the Gipsy. We know it's just a matter of time before he makes an appearance.'

'Well, look elsewhere. That's what we've been told by the zookeepers.' Charlie looked down at the swans and seemed miles away. 'Stupid code names. Winds me up.'

'How's the counselling?' Geraldine hadn't spotted a wedding ring. Charlie looked at her like she had forgotten.

'Oh yes. Great, just splendid.' She stared again at the drifting swans.

'We're getting close. The Robin has made some breakthroughs. We've hacked into their system and managed to change their PO Box address so we can monitor their mail.'

Charlie stood there. Geraldine saw that her face was filled with tears. Geraldine touched her arm. 'Oh, I'm sorry, it's not going well?' Charlie's head dropped down and she started crying. Geraldine looked around self-consciously. Expecting people to take photos. 'Charlie, it'll be OK.' And she put her arms around her. Geraldine thought of Zara. She could smell her and held on tighter. She missed her like a lost jewel. The huge green statue of a swan cast a shadow over them. It looked ugly to her, as if it was reflecting her pain. Charlie moved away awkwardly.

'I'm sorry, sorry, not very professional of me...' Charlie mopped her tears.

'No, I'm sorry... I just know how it feels. I've been... going through stuff too.'

Charlie sniffed and took out a cotton handkerchief to

blow her nose, as if this would put her back on track. 'Geraldine, I've been thinking. We're getting too close, OK? I can't...' More tears flowed.

Geraldine wanted to grab her again. Her eyes were welling up too. Zara was burning inside her. She sniffed and took a deep breath and felt O'Neil's hands around her neck. She massaged her neck and snapped out of it. 'You're right...' Geraldine breathed in deeply. 'Anyway, I was thinking, can we pay the Robin? We'll lose him otherwise. Or at least his enthusiasm will fade.'

Charlie dried her eyes again and motioned Geraldine to walk with her. 'I guess so, expenses and a day rate. What would you say?'

It sounded a bit too business-like. Normally it was brown envelopes with either drugs or a few bundles of cash. 'The going rate? Since when is this all accountable?'

'You're right, it isn't is it? Just not my normal working practice. I'll sort something out. 'A drop', as you call it. Is that right?' Geraldine nodded and they walked on. She wasn't sure where.

'You know I tried to save my sister from jail. That's how they got me. Of course, you know that. It's all in my file.'

Charlie looked at her. 'Did it work?'

'No, she's still inside. Zane, her waste of space husband, just got out. Now I've got a desk job with no hope of promotion. You know that too.'

'You looking for a raise?'

'I'm not too bothered about money anymore, to be honest. I just want to do the job without any hassle.' Geraldine hesitated before asking her next question. 'So, how did they get you?'

Charlie stopped and looked around. Waiting for people to pass them by. 'You got a wire?'

'What?' Geraldine spun around, facing the boating lake.

'G, you know we just can't be too careful.'

Geraldine angrily lifted her top and turned around. 'Here you are. You can pat me down if you want to!' She immediately regretted her outburst, and her rash decision made her blush.

'Sorry G. Sorry. I... And no bra?!' Each of them caught the other's gaze and they burst out laughing.

'Drink?' said Geraldine.

Charlie nodded and they carried on walking, this time with purpose.

'Shit, I need to go to the gym. Don't I?' Geraldine hoped to be persuaded otherwise.

'Well, I would, if I were you!' Charlie poked her in the side and laughed.

'Oh, don't.' Geraldine grimaced and suddenly felt conscious of her body, in a good way.

They arrived at the Lido Bar, a small, single story brick building with white columns out front. On top was a small clock tower that read 3:40 pm. Charlie left Geraldine to sit on one of the wooden benches by the water. She came back with a wine cooler and two glasses. 'Pino Grigio all right?'

Geraldine smiled and there was a comfortable silence while Charlie poured the wine.

So, how did they get you?

'You know I've never slept with a woman. Should I try it?' Charlie looked down at her glass with a smile, avoiding Geraldine's question.

Geraldine lifted her glass. 'Cheers, to... being single?'

'Fuck yes. Glad I'm out of that shit.' And they both clinked their glasses and drank.

Geraldine watched her. She enjoyed her occasional profanity which seemed so out of character.

Charlie put her glass down and looked into Geraldine's eyes. 'Have you heard of HBOS?'

'HBOS? I don't think so.'

'Didn't you hear about it? It was all over the newspapers.' Charlie took another gulp and then a deep breath. 'I still don't know why I did it. Greed, I think, one of the Deadly Sins.' She made a cross and looked up. 'I got involved with a bunch of crooked bankers. I helped them cook the figures and keep the bank in the dark. I'm not proud of myself and they really were scum. But they wanted more and more, and I got deeper and deeper into their corrupt schemes. Officially £245 million deep, but it was a lot more. Fuck!' She shook her head as if she still couldn't believe it had happened.

Geraldine drank more wine, not knowing what to say.

'Yep, when shit goes wrong in banking it goes really wrong. I woke up one day and knew this was not going to end well. My husband had no idea. And when I read what those absolute...' Charlie blushed.

'Cunts you mean?' Geraldine smiled.

'Thank you, yes. What they were up to... Well, it seems I missed out on the real fun. Although parties with hookers is hardly my thing. Give me a Spa and champagne anytime. Maybe with a hunky masseur thrown in.' She giggled.

Geraldine could see that the wine was going to Charlie's head. There was a warm glow on her cheeks. 'How did you get away with it?'

'I didn't, really. One morning a woman invited me for a business lunch. I thought, rather I hoped it was a client and that her business needed some kind of loan. Then a man in a suit joined us at the table. They told me they had an offer I couldn't refuse.'

'Yeah, it starts like that.' Geraldine smiled.

'They had identified me as an asset. They could get me out of the mess I was in - and it was huge – but that I had to work for them. No questions asked. Nothing. Just that I would be a go-between for some agents. Spooked the hell out of me. I couldn't even tell my husband. They said they would officially get me a job in a travel agency. Yes, they still exist.'

'What made you do it?' Charlie cocked her head as if in disbelief.

'Really? Same as you of course. I'd have gone to prison, lost everything. I was terrified. But I guess at least the fact that someone needed me meant it wasn't entirely hopeless.'

Geraldine nodded, she knew how that felt. But still wanted to dig more and find out what Charlie knew about their employers.

'So, who is Plan B, what do you know about them?'

Charlie poured out some more wine. They both looked around. Mothers with prams and tourists surrounded them. But Geraldine knew they couldn't be too careful. They should have moved to another location by now.

'Government? I don't think so. This is a private organisation, though it might be funded by them.'

'Have you looked into it?'

Charlie nodded. 'There were various phone numbers, but they keep changing. Sure, someone with the right contacts could trace them.'

'I thought it was part of the police. But I don't think they would have recruited you or your predecessor. Aside from the annoying animal code names, I think Richard O'Neil was a rogue agent and Plan B tried to dispose of him but failed. He was working for the police, and then just disappeared. You must have heard something.'

Charlie shook her head and adjusted her cross. 'They just post me the info and then call. I don't get to see anyone. Only you at the moment. They did say I was going to have more contacts.' Charlie grabbed her hand.

Geraldine could feel Charlie's loneliness. She squeezed her hand back. 'Look, I know what you said before about backing off, but just give me a week or two more to find the Gipsy. If things are heating up, we must be getting close. I know it.'

'Is that what you detectives do? Operate on gut feelings? I thought you needed a bit more than that.' She drank more wine.

'We are so close. I can feel it, so please at least let me try. Did you ask yourself why we've been asked to cool off?'

'I just follow orders, like you should.'

Geraldine finished the bottle and put it back in the ice bucket. Charlie turned it upside down. They stared at each other. Geraldine looked away. She wasn't going to play this childish game. She and Rebwar would obviously still continue with the investigation; what were Plan B going to do about it? Although, she had seen a little of what they could do on the last case, when they sent Rebwar in to torture someone. But she just didn't care anymore. O'Neil had to be stopped. 'OK, I'll lay off.' She smiled and sipped her wine.

'Thanks. I appreciate it.'

As the sun started to set, she could feel the atmosphere between them cooling off. She listened to the sound of people rowing, laughing, ducks calling, the faint hum of traffic. Charlie finished her glass and opened her make-up mirror. 'Going out on a date?'

'Seeing some friends.' She said abruptly. Like a switch had been flicked.

For a moment, Geraldine saw a cool core. Was Charlie manipulating her?

THIRTY-THREE

Rebwar sipped his Nero takeaway espresso. It tasted bitter and sweet. The caffeine hit made his aches and pains ease for a moment. Hourieh was standing in front of him in the street smoking, waiting for him to answer. He'd forgotten what she'd asked and searched her face for an idea of what it could be. Musa, headphones in and head down, played on his phone. He looked good in his new suit, blue-sheen, white shirt and a red tie. Rebwar could see that he had sneaked a t-shirt underneath with some clever slogan. If he kept the jacket buttoned up, he would get away with it. But there was going to be a scene at some point. Rebwar was surprised Hourieh had missed it, given how much she'd fussed over him before they left the flat.

They had taken the number eleven bus from Sloane Square, then Rebwar had insisted on getting a coffee. A stiff drink is what he really needed. Bijan was getting married.

'So?'

He still couldn't remember. He threw the little cup in the nearest bin to give him more time to think.

'Husband!'

He looked at his watch. 'What time does it start?'

Hourieh rolled her eyes and tutted, that had obviously been her question to him. He studied her for a moment. She was looking beautiful, in a blue silk blouse with a light yellow knee length skirt and some Jimmy Choo heels, a present from Bijan's fiancé, Katarena, on one of their now regular shopping trips. She'd lost a few pounds and the outfit complemented her curves. She wore the family jewellery: pearls and diamond rings. Hourieh caught him staring and got her compact out to add some red lipstick.

The Chelsea registry office was just on King Street, an imposing, sculpted building with four huge columns indicating the entrance. There was an old red double-decker bus marked W*edding Special* parked in front. A set of stone stairs led up to the blue doors. Hourieh gave them all a final check and made Musa take out his headphones.

In the reception room were about a dozen guests, most of whom worked for Bijan. The others were Katarena's friends. They all stared at each other. There were some polite smiles as they all waited for instructions. It had been a bit of a surprise invitation. Bijan hadn't told Rebwar he was getting married. He had only met Katarena once and that was on his way out of Bijan's house. He'd wanted to get Raj to do some background checks on her, but then decided he didn't want to upset Bijan or himself with what he'd find. Bijan was happy, and it felt wrong to risk taking that away from him.

A woman came in dressed in a black trouser outfit. She told the guests that they should follow her. Rebwar recognised Bijan's lawyer and his butler, the others he didn't know. One of them had dirty fingernails and rough, weathered hands; he guessed that must be the gardener. They walked into the next room, huge and imposing: big windows with heavy white curtains lining long dark wooden window frames; a huge fireplace; two chandeliers above them. There was a couple of rows of chairs with a central aisle running up to a pulpit. Bijan was waiting, holding onto his walking stick. His dark pinstriped three-piece fitted him perfectly. He had a red flower on his lapel that matched his tie. His smile said it all. Hourieh grabbed Rebwar's arm.

'You remember when we got married? Oh, I miss my Pada. His face!'

Rebwar remembered her family arguing. 'What were they arguing about?'

'What?'

'You know... at The Jahāz Barān. There was that fight.'

'Oh, don't remember. Doesn't he look magnificent? She's so lucky. Brings a tear to my eye.' And she grabbed Rebwar's hankie from his top pocket and dabbed her eyes. She gave it back with makeup marks.

Rebwar returned it to his pocket. He was sure that the fight had been about her inheritance, although he never found out exactly what that was.

'Will everyone be upstanding for the bride.' announced the woman in black.

Silence filled the room and everyone turned behind them to the door.

Katarena entered in a long white dress that hugged her slim figure and the fabric glowed in the light. The top of the dress was cut to show off a generous decolletage. Her red lips had been further enhanced since he had last seen her. Her long black hair had large curls. Walking with her was a tall curly-blonde woman who was a little taller than her with a strong, angular face and blue eyes. Her body was slim too, and she was wearing a light pink dress that stopped just above her knees.

Hourieh smiled and hugged Rebwar with her left arm. 'Doesn't she look stunning? I chose that dress. Isn't it amazing?'

Classical music filled the room. Everyone was watching Katarena walking up the aisle. As the music stopped Rebwar sneezed, Hourieh told him to shush and squeezed his arm. The celebrant greeted them and told the guests to sit down.

Just as people were settling into their seats, two men in ill-fitting black suits came in. One with a limp, the other a large belly. They approached the bride. 'Are you Katarena Kostova?'

Katarena turned around to face them. 'Yes?'

'Of 21 Westfield gardens, London, E12?'

'Yes.'

'I'm Officer Lark and my colleague is Officer Ferguson. On the authority of Her Majesties Border Patrol. We are arresting you for exceeding your stay here in the UK. As well as having worked without the proper permits.'

'Excuse me? Mr...?'

The officers took out their warrant cards and showed them to Bijan and the registrar.

Bijan held on to his heart. 'You... You can't do this. No...' Katarena held onto Bijan. Charles, his butler, brought over a chair. Officer Ferguson tried to grab Katarena's hands.

'Hey! Get off me. You bad man! You keep away from me. You no right to be here.'

Bijan's lawyer, Camper, went up to Officer Lark. 'Have you got any supporting evidence?'

'Sorry, we are here for Ms Kostova, and we are taking her to the police station. Any questions need to be addressed there. Understand?'

'No!' Katarena screamed out for Bijan, who was sitting on the chair trying to breathe. 'My husband is dying. Call ambulance. Call! Now!' Officer Ferguson was still holding onto her while she struggled.

'Husband!' Hourieh protested, 'husband, do something. You have to do something!'

Rebwar went up to Bijan and knelt down beside him to try to calm him. His butler had undone his tie and asked for water.

'Will you calm down, Ms Kostova,' said the officers. 'You are under arrest. Do you understand?' Officer Ferguson took out his handcuffs and locked them tightly on her wrists. She protested loudly and began swearing in Russian. Her friend tried to reason with Officer Lark, but to no avail. The two border guards marched Katarena back down the aisle which was certainly not the way she had imagined her post-nuptial trip down the aisle would be, and out of the room. Hourieh went up to Bijan to console him. The celebrant told the shocked and bemused guests where the post-ceremony champagne and canapes would be and checked her watch to see how long it was until the next wedding party came in.

THIRTY-FOUR

Rebwar decided to have his coffee at a local called Chamomile on England's Lane, just around the corner from his flat. He had a choice of three cafes and would choose depending on his mood. There was the deli, Black Truffle, which was where he would go if he wanted to treat himself to a pastry or listen to rich kids and their First World problems. Starbucks was on the corner and had nice comfortable seats where he could sit and read his newspaper in peace. Chamomile was more an everyday affair: basic decor with Ikea-type wooden furniture. As if to keep you alert, none of the chairs and tables matched. He would go to the back and sit on a table for two with a view into the garden and think about his day.

On the walls were old movie posters which he would often note down and forget to look up. Facing him today was *The Third Man,* it had always intrigued him. He sipped his espresso and craved a cigarette. Rebwar fidgeted with his phone and sipped his espresso. He was also on full alert for any sign of Wayne or his stooges. He'd deliberately let

Wayne down on his proposed meeting; he wasn't quite ready for that. Wayne had already given Rebwar a brutal taste of what was to come. He was going to make an example of him. Maybe the Gipsy curse was after him again, not something he could report to Plan B. Rebwar knew he should get rid of his phone. If he logged on to the app, they would probably find him. But he could use it to his advantage, too, so he had kept it on his phone, being careful not to stay too long in one location.

Raj had told him to switch it off and take the sim and battery out. They could still track a phone that was switched off. The phone rang. It was Kamal. He was doing a shift in the car.

'*Sobh bekheir*.'[1] Rebwar answered.

'Hey, we have problem.'

Rebwar grabbed his cigarettes from his jacket pocket and made his way to the exit. 'Tell me.'

'I've got your girlfriend in the back of the car. She won't move. She wants you to come down to get her.'

'Geraldine? Has she said what she wants?' Rebwar dragged on his cigarette.

'You, man. She said you haven't you been treating her right?'

Rebwar rubbed his face. 'Tell her I'll meet her for coffee later? Or a pub.'

'Tried that. You've got to come down now. This is costing me, right?'

'Pass the phone to her.'

'No, she wants to talk to you in person.'

'OK. On my way now.' Rebwar dropped the call and went to settle his bill.

———

Kamal had texted his location and Rebwar was about to turn into All Saints Street just off the Caledonian road. The street was lined with a renovated warehouse that housed a mix of expensive flats and office buildings. Rebwar had to walk right to the end before he spotted the Toyota Prius parked on a single yellow. If there were any cameras around he would be getting a ticket. Another expense that wasn't getting reimbursed. Kamal was smoking outside the car. He looked stressed and was shaking his head as Rebwar came over.

'Hey, you need to have a serious talk to your girlfriend. She can't do this, OK? I need to work!'

'Yes, Kamal. Yes, I'll settle this. You take a break. I'll take over this shift. Go home, relax. OK?'

'You owe me, Rebwar.' He pointed his finger at him. 'Otherwise, I'll find another driver to share.'

Rebwar walked over to the car, bending down to try and see Geraldine's face. She was slumped in the back seat with her knees up against the driver's seat looking at her phone. He waited a few seconds before opening the door, lit two cigarettes and handed one over to her. He leant on the open passenger door, smoking. They both looked at each other, waiting for the other to speak. Both hesitating to make the first move. She sniffed and got out of the car. 'Drive or pub?' Geraldine looked at her cigarette and tapped it.

'Drive and then pub,' Rebwar said. 'Get in.' He put the car into gear and drove off. 'So?' He looked at her in the rearview mirror waiting for the inevitable question.

'Did you find the immigrants?'

'They are with Wayne, you know... the guy from Byways Services. So, yes in a way.'

'I guess that's good.'

'Not really, as now he's after me for losing them. He's the one with the Gipsy curses.'

'Well, Plan B aren't interested anymore.' She grabbed a brown envelope from out of her bomber jacket and held it in her hands.

Rebwar looked at it, waiting for her to pass it over. He drove up to the Caledonian Road, checking his mirrors for any suspicious vehicles around them.

'Are we being tailed?' said Geraldine

'Is the Gipsy after me?'

'Do you think it's Wayne?'

'You could tell Plan B that.' He took a right into Mackenzie Road, lined with little shops and two to three storey flats. He glanced behind him.

'Sorry, Rebs. They are fucking us around, and I hate it. Just when we were getting close.'

'What happened to your face?'

Geraldine shifted to look at her reflection in his mirror. 'Oh, little accident.'

He stared at her, waiting for more information.

'Two guys ran me off the road. I'm OK, though thanks.' She looked away.

'A little short guy with a teardrop tattoo and a big toothless man?'

Geraldine stared at him. 'Yes.'

'That's Wayne's crew. The Gipsy curse is after you too. What car did they have?'

'White, false plates.' Geraldine went silent for a moment and Rebwar checked his mirrors. Turning into Arvon Road they parked halfway down by a wooden fence that ran alongside the pavement. He checked his mirrors again.

'Is that my Visa?'

Geraldine snorted and passed over the envelope she had been holding. 'No, but it's some real money.'

Rebwar looked into it and saw a thin stack of notes. He passed it back. 'Paying us off?'

'Fucking take it, Rebs.' They both stared at each other. On the opposite pavement a woman pushing a pram looked across.

Rebwar put the envelope on the passenger seat.

'Sure, there will be other jobs.' Geraldine said. 'And a visa.' She looked out of the window.

'You know I finally found Betty, the secretary of Bywater, well I have a number plate. We should find them. Before they find us.'

'Are you sure they're after us?' Geraldine looked back at Rebwar in the mirror.

'As I heard... is the pope a Catholic?' He smiled. 'We need to get them.'

'Just don't need this shit right now. But your on you own with this, OK? Plan B aren't going to support us.'

'Why?'

'Or just get us arrested.'

'You mean killed, no?'

'Oh, don't... fuck.' She took a deep breath and sighed, then bit her lower lip.

'We have the advantage. Can you find the address for Betty? I have her mobile but want to visit her at home. She knows me as she got me my... I mean Amir's working permit. I can play her. Make her believe that I am Amir and get to her...' Rebwar looked at a nervous Geraldine biting her lower lip. 'Pub?'

Geraldine nodded, and Rebwar drove off.

———

They had ended up in the Lamb on Holloway Road. It had an ox-red and green tiled front and four doors, one of them led to the flats upstairs, the other three to various separate areas inside the pub. It had more of a club atmosphere inside than its' traditional facia would suggest, with black walls and dark wood panelling. The floorboards were original and matched the basic pre-owned furniture. With her hands in her pockets Geraldine studied the beers on offer. Rebwar glanced around at the clientele. He guessed that there was a university close by.

'Pint of Redemption, please. Rebs?'

'Glass of Cognac.'

The bearded barman showed him a bottle, Rebwar nodded. They found a little table in a corner.

'Cheers, Ah, this tastes proper. Nice.' They clinked glasses and Rebwar studied her face. It still looked pretty beaten up.

'Are you all right?'

For a moment, Geraldine seemed to think about it. 'Yeah... no. I still can't sleep like you. Feel like I'm bobbing up and down like a cork in the ocean. Just managing to breathe.'

Rebwar felt the burn of the alcohol down his throat. 'We'll get him.'

She nodded a thank you to him. 'What I don't get is Matt's murder? Why kill your employer?'

'Can you look at what the police have found?'

Geraldine looked at her pint, lost in its bubbles. Rebwar touched her arm and she came out of her trance. 'Sorry, yeah sure, sure. Fuck. Zara... she's still here in me.'

'Can't you take a break? Get away. Fresh air.'

Geraldine laughed. 'Wouldn't know where to start. Don't see myself lying on a beach like a stranded whale or going rock climbing. No, I need to find that fucker. But it's delicate. I think they are watching us.'

THIRTY-FIVE

Rebwar was having his breakfast in his car. Cigarettes and coffee. From Betty's car registration Geraldine had found an address in Chelmsford, Essex, just over an hour out of London towards the South East. One of the shell companies that owned Byways Recruitment Services Ltd paid the rent on the place. Rebwar had driven early that morning to see who was living there. He was a little surprised to find that the address he was now parked opposite was in a residential street populated with modern narrow houses, each with just enough lawn to call a garden. There was no sign of life in the house and the curtains were drawn. Rebwar looked at his watch and checked it with the one on the dash. He tapped the face, as if that would help on a digital watch, then swore, pressed some buttons and shook it. He adjusted it to 9:23 am. He watched as the top window was opened by what looked like a man's hand. He sipped some more coffee.

It was another twenty minutes before Betty appeared opening the curtains. She peered out like she was looking for something. Then a face Rebwar hoped he would never see again looked out of the window. Richard O'Neil. Rebwar swore and held his breath. He reached slowly for his camera and snapped some pictures. Fifteen minutes later O'Neil walked out of the front door wearing a baseball cap low over his face and a dark sports jacket. He half jogged over towards a car. Rebwar felt a chill run down his back, and flipped the sun visor down to hide his face. O'Neil unlocked a car a few places behind him got in and started it. Rebwar sunk down in his seat as the car passed by. He noted the Ford Ka's registration. For a moment he thought of following it, but it was too risky; he needed to stick to the plan. He lit another cigarette and let the adrenaline drain away. He had found the soft underbelly and he smiled. He stubbed out his cigarette, got out of the car, went up to Betty's house and rang the doorbell. A chime of small and large bells echoed in the house. He heard some footsteps approach then Betty opened the door wearing a loose grey top and black leggings

'Can I help you?'

'Amir. Hello, Mrs Betty.'

'Amir?' She stood there waiting for something to click.

'Amir Begani, you got me working permit with Wayne. Yes?'

'Oh Sorry, Amir of course your picture looks different... How did you find me?'

'I found the address.'

Betty stepped back. 'Sorry... Amir... how did you find me?'

'I found your address.'

'How?'

'Some paper or on the app. Yes... the job app.' Rebwar walked in through the door. 'Nice place you have. Tea would be nice.'

'Sorry, Amir, but what do you want?'

'I wanted a chat. Career advice. Job.'

'What? Sorry... we don't do that. Sorry.'

'You married?'

'Look Amir, you need to contact Wayne. He deals with the jobs and all that, all right? I'm busy.' Betty held the door wide open. 'I'm going to call Wayne, OK?'

'You know what you're involved in? Was that your husband? Richard O'Neil?' Rebwar couldn't see a wedding ring on her finger.

'Sorry? But...'

'Mrs Betty, need some advice and you run HR. I have rights, yes?'

'Listen Amir... Do you understand zero hours contracts? I can call you later. I'm busy right now and I can get Wayne to explain.'

'I'm refugee, understand. And not have papers. Need them to rent house.'

Betty looked up the stairs.

'Mrs Betty, please I need advice, understand my family needs a place to stay.' He walked into the large open plan extension at the back of the house. Betty followed and moved around him as if she was trying to protect it. 'I need to protect my family.'

Betty held her forehead and sighed. 'Amir... I understand and...' Betty got her mobile. 'I do and look we can sort all this out.' She dialled.

'You calling police? Mrs Betty I am good worker. Ask Mr Wayne. I...'

'Richard... Yeah all right. Well...' Betty turned around to face the garden and carried on talking into her mobile.

Rebwar looked around the airy extension. One half of it had a three-piece couch set, a lazee boy, a large flat screen

TV, glass coffee table, bookshelf and some prints of paintings.

Betty turned to look at Rebwar. 'Amir is here... Yeah you know, maybe not. He's looking for advice... Yes, he is. OK... Yes, I won't, yes, OK.'

He went up to the framed pictures dotted around the room. Mostly of her and O'Neil. They looked like holiday snaps. One of them was by a lock on a canal.

A couple of loud bangs came from upstairs.

'Sorry but, can you please leave? I'm going to call the police.' She held out her mobile phone.

There followed a couple more bangs.

Betty looked up and stamped her foot down. 'Sorry, hot water... Plumbing's rotten.' She dialled a number. 'Richard! Where are they...? Yes, OK. Quick, yes...'

Rebwar opened the glass door that led into the garden and made his way to a side passage leading to the front of the house. He was halfway to his car when he heard Amir's name being called. He turned and saw Wayne and Dental Mike. Not a sight he had planned or wanted to see. His gun was in the car, in the glove box. They would be on him before he reached it. Time stopped.

'Wayne, I was looking for you. I need advice?'

'Amir, what the fuck are you doing here?' Wayne's phone rang. He checked who it was. Dental Mike was momentarily distracted by the call. Rebwar ran off towards the car and tried to use the remote to open but it was for the passenger door. The two men were now running over to him. He pressed again and the central locking clicked but they got to him before he could get in. Dental Mike slammed him into the car's door.

'I've got a bone to pick with you! You lost some cargo,

didn't you? And I found them with an old queer called Dong.'

Dental Mike laughed and grabbed Rebwar by his shirt.

'Wayne, they escaped from me. And I never heard of Dong.'

Wayne went up to him. 'I had to fix it didn't I? You've cost me money, my friend and now owe me. Understand?' Wayne punched Rebwar's stomach then used his fingers to comb his fair hair back. 'So I own your ass. No more visits to see Mrs B. Understand?'

Rebwar felt sick but managed to nod.

Wayne nodded to Dental Mike who slammed his face into the window. Rebwar felt his jaw hit the glass. He felt a tooth give. Dental Mike grabbed his jaw and with his free hand punched his face.

'Get it Amir. Ten grand that's how much you're going to pay me back and...' Wayne signalled to Dental Mike. 'Let him have half a grand's worth.'

Dental Mike let go of Rebwar who felt himself slide down the side of the car door. He spat some blood and two teeth fell out. About two dozen small plastic pouches landed on his lap. They had white powder in them.

'Sell these and I want interest. By tomorrow and if you don't you'll be missing digits not just teeth. Understand me?'

Rebwar coughed up more blood. He spat it out. Pain was now travelling through his body. He nodded and the two turned and walked away. A few curious neighbours popped their curious heads from behind their blinds. He breathed in deeply and knew what was coming next: Nausea, pain, aches, the shakes. Nothing new.

THIRTY-SIX

Rebwar's face was throbbing still, though luckily the two missing teeth had come from the back of his mouth, so at least he didn't look like some sort of old hag from a kid's fairytale. He had temporarily put the urgency of selling Wayne's drugs and getting the £10k to him on hold to chase up Matt's murder. Geraldine had asked around her contacts to see if there were any useful details about that case. All she could learn was that they had arrested members of a local scooter gang and passed it off as a settling of old scores between rivals. She had given Rebwar Matt's address so he could ask his widow some questions, but he would have to tread softly. They had lived a few streets away from the car wash, a bungalow on Brodie Road in Enfield. He parked the car outside the front gate and went up to the front door.

He pressed a button and a hyperactive electric bell buzzed. It took another two attempts before the door opened and a blend of Indian spices escaped. A little woman stood there, she was thin with dark sunken eyes and dark hair. She was wrapped in a sari and held her arms around herself as if she was in pain. She looked up and

Rebwar introduced himself. She carried on staring at him and Rebwar stared back. From what he recalled, Matt was a local, *born and bred in Enfield*, as he often said, and he sometimes mentioned 'er indoors'. So the petite Indian woman standing in front of him was not at all who Rebwar had expected to see.

Instantly he wanted to know more. 'Mrs Adkins, I'm so sorry for your loss. I am working on your husband's case, I'm a private detective.' Rebwar presented her with a card. She took it and brought it closer to her eyes. 'I would like to ask you a few questions, if that's OK.' She nodded and stood there, holding the door. Clearly, she wasn't going to invite him in voluntarily. 'Perhaps it might be more comfortable if we go inside and sit down? Or we can go for a coffee somewhere?'

'You can ask me questions here.'

'OK, Mrs Adkins.' Rebwar looked around, the neighbourhood was quiet but this was not ideal. 'Do you know anyone who would want to hurt your husband?'

She tutted and re-crossed her arms. 'That's your job to find out isn't it. We are the victims here.' Rebwar was shocked by her anger.

'Is your son in or your daughter?'

'No. Why do you want to speak to them?'

'Mrs Adkins, you must miss your husband, I am just trying to help.'

'What kind of thing is that to say? Who hired you?'

'I used to work for Matt, and I want to find out the truth.'

She still bristled with animosity and Rebwar was close to giving up.

'What qualifies you as a so-called private detective? Let the police do their job.'

'Have they found out who did it?'

'Yes, they have, some little shits from Wembley apparently... and I'd like to see them hang for it.'

'They also said it was a robbery gone wrong, but that's not true. I was there.'

'That's what they said. I believe them.' He could tell she was interested now in what he had to say.

'But there was nothing to steal apart from a couple of hundred quid, which they left behind. I believe it was an execution.'

She stood there looking at him.

'What does your son say?'

'Leave him out of it. How dare you come here and ask questions that are not your business. Are you with those others?'

'Who?'

'Them, the men who called...' She stopped herself from saying any more.

'Mrs Adkins, was your husband being blackmailed?'

'I don't know what you're talking about. Now please leave.'

'Mum, who are you talking to?' A voice called from upstairs to Rebwar's relief.

'No one. Just a salesman.'

'Mum?' A young girl appeared in the hallway, thin, like her mother and dressed in tight jeans and a baggy white top. Each of her fingers had some kind of ring on it. 'Hi.'

'Hi, are you Matt's daughter? You have a brother too?'

'Mum, I heard what he said. He wants to help.'

Mrs Adkins tried to push her daughter away with her hand. And both of them said something in a language that Rebwar didn't know but thought must be Hindi. He watched them argue, each one throwing and pointing their hands in different directions. The girl came back to the front door, while her mother carried on ranting as she stomped into the kitchen.

'Sorry, my mum is still mourning, she's very angry,' the girl said at last. 'Please come in Mr...'

'Call me Rebwar.'

She presented her hand, and Rebwar shook it. It was soft and as delicate as a doll's. Her brown eyes were warm and inviting and she had a perfect white smile. She smelled of rose and candy. Rebwar could see her father's confidence in her.

'I'm Mandy. Come in.'

Her mother's heeled slippers clonked on the linoleum kitchen floor. Rebwar followed Mandy into the living room. Flowers and pictures of Matt were everywhere. The smell was overpowering and nearly made Rebwar sneeze. They were in different states of decay, and he tried not to walk over the fallen petals scattered over the carpet. Rebwar took a moment to look at the pictures. It was like a picture novel story of Matt's life; almost every age was represented by a photo. Rebwar felt a little uncomfortable. The sofa was covered with a transparent plastic wrapping. The TV looked unused and had a huge vase of flowers in front of it. Every available space had a picture frame or more flowers filling it. It was like a chapel of rest.

'Tea?'

'Coffee, please. Black and two sugars. I'm very sorry about your father.'

For a moment, Mandy looked at the pictures. Her big eyes welled up. She sniffed. 'Thank you...' She left the room.

Rebwar had seen Matt at the car wash with his son. He had come to the car wash a few times wanting to talk to his father in private. In the more recent photos covering the room, Matt's face seemed to have taken on the weight of sadness. Rebwar overheard mother and daughter arguing again and the sound of a cup smashing on the floor. He took his cue to see the kitchen. Mandy was squatting on the floor, picking up the broken pieces. The mother looked at Rebwar as if he had stepped over a sacred boundary.

'Is everything OK?'

'Sorry, Rebwar. Just a moment of...' And she sniffed.

'Is your brother around at all Mandy?

'He's back home in Bangalore,' said Mrs Adkins.

'Do you know when he's coming back? Or how could I reach him?'

'No. You can't.' Mrs Adkins glowered at him.

'An email address perhaps?'

'He can't be reached. He's with his relatives in the countryside.'

Mandy poured some hot water from a kettle into a cup, stirred it and handed it to him. 'What have you found out?'

He took the cup and sipped, it was instant coffee, and watery but the sugar helped. 'Thank you. Not too much. But I wanted to talk to your brother, as I saw him at the car wash a couple of times. Did he come to ask your father for money?'

The mother flicked her hands at Rebwar and said something he didn't understand.

'Sorry mother... yes... he was in trouble.' Mandy stared at her mother. 'He had gambled and run up huge debts.'

'With who?'

'Everybody. He was an addict. We struggled with him. He couldn't control himself.'

'Drugs?'

'No, no. At least I don't think so. Just gambling. Dad

tried everything; counselling...' Mandy made herself a cup of tea. The kitchen was small and old. From the seventies with a few new appliances slotted in-between the old yellow units. The sink tap was dripping. He saw that the mother was still house proud. Cloths and plates were neatly laid out and there were a few little statues of a god that Rebwar had never seen except in pictures of India. There was a picture of a sun setting over a yellow river with people washing themselves. This was her little oasis. He was trespassing.

'What have the police said?'

The mother tutted.

Mandy sipped her tea and said, 'Not much, other than they had made some arrests and that it was an ongoing investigation.'

Rebwar took out his little notebook. He had written a few questions down. 'Where were you on the day of the shooting?'

Mandy's eyes looked up into the ceiling. 'Here. Why?'

Rebwar turned to the mother, and her head shook like it sort of agreed with her daughter. 'And your son?'

Mandy breathed in deeply. 'We don't know.'

'He was in Bangalore. On a flight.'

'Mum, no he wasn't. That was two days later.'

'Do you know a man called Wayne, he has a snakeskin tattoo on his arm? Did Matt mention him?'

Both of them shook their heads.

'Can I see your brother's room?'

'Gary didn't have much in there.'

'I assume the police have been here?'

Mandy walked up the stairs and motioned for Rebwar to follow.

'Just to tell us about Dad's murder and to ask a few routine questions like yours.'

'But they have looked for Gary or searched his room?'

'Not that I know of.'

The room was small and had a single bed with a green cover on it. A little white desk in the corner had some old school books on it. Posters of Oasis, Eminem and Dizzee Rascal were stuck to the walls. Rebwar opened the cupboard next to the desk, there were only a few clothes in there and they seemed to have been washed recently; the smell of detergent was strong. There were Adidas and Nike hoodies and a couple of pairs of jeans, which didn't look like they'd been worn as they were still stiff and starchy. He took out a leather jacket that was on a hanger. Went through the pockets and found little pieces of broken glass. They were most probably from a car's shattered window. Rebwar held out his hand with the glass fragments. Mandy just shrugged.

'Has he got a scooter?'

'He sold it.'

The mirror on the inside of the door was cracked as if it had been punched. The sunlight caught the white desk and there was dust on it. Just where the books were piled was a shiny triangular shape. Rebwar lifted the books. He could see a faded rectangular shape about the size of a laptop.

'Do you have his laptop?'

'Sorry?'

'His laptop? He had one. Where is it?'

'Oh, he took it. Yes, he took it with him.' Mandy's whole demeanour had changed from being quite open and friendly, to quiet and nervous. There were a few moments of awkward silence, which Rebwar decided to break.

'How long has he been missing?'

'What? What do you mean?'

'Like I said. How long?'

'He's in India and, like my mother said, he can't be reached.'

'What's his mobile number?'

'Uh I... It doesn't work anymore.' Rebwar noticed her flinch and touch the front pocket of her top. He could see the outline of a phone. Rebwar looked at the window behind her and pushed himself past her. At the same time, he swiped the phone, a cracked smartphone in a worn black case.

'Hey, give me that back!' She tried to grab it.

'It's Gary's phone, isn't it?'

She looked at him, angry at what he'd just done. 'You have no right.'

'Is it broken?' She looked at him with wide eyes that began to fill with tears. Rebwar's voice was gentle now. 'I can help you. I can get someone to have a look at this and find out what happened. We can find Gary. I know he's missing. Why haven't you told the police?'

Mandy scrunched up her face. 'No, he's just missing. He'll come back. He always does. Just laying low, right?'

Rebwar shook his head. 'He's in trouble and there are some bad people around. They wanted something from your father. Gary might have been mixed up in that.' She looked away, he took her by the shoulders and turned her to face him. 'Mandy, are they blackmailing you? You can't keep all this a secret. Your father deserves justice.'

The girl slumped onto the bed, as if someone had let the air out of her. The large duvet nearly swallowed her whole. Her mother shouted up the stairs to her. Rebwar looked around for any more clues before she got upstairs. He could see the room had been thoroughly cleaned. And there was no clutter. Things you might expect a young man to have lying around; spare coins, phone chargers, cables, old bus or train tickets, there was nothing. Mandy sobbed, her thin body convulsing. Her mother walked in and went to console her daughter.

'Leave us alone! You can't undo the past. We have to move on.'

'Your son is missing. Don't you want to find him?'

'I have told you, he's in India with my relatives.'

Rebwar looked at her. It was as if she had convinced herself that this was reality. And if she went there, he would be waiting.

'Why haven't you told the police? Is he guilty of something?'

'Please leave Mr Rebwar. Leave us alone, we have to mourn.'

Rebwar had to admit defeat and leave for now. But he had the boy's phone and would get Raj on the case with that. He got one of his business cards out and placed it on Gary's desk.

'I'm sorry to have upset you. Please call me if anything changes, or Gary gets in touch.' He made his way downstairs still looking around for any clues, but it was as if Gary had never lived there; no school photos or belongings that a boy his age would have owned. Mothers and fathers generally kept sentimental things. Had Matt thrown his own son out?

THIRTY-SEVEN

Geraldine walked into a gastropub in Notting Hill called the Holy Cow. It was one of the original pubs that had embraced the idea that food was now more important than the bar. For pub-goers across the country in the early 90s, that changed everything. Pubs had become restaurants; they were no longer pubs who served a bit of food for a few hours each day. Now you were lucky to find a proper pub. Geraldine felt like a relic of another era, even though this revolution happened before her drinking age. This place served posh fish food. What she really wanted was to lean on a bar, sink a few pints and put the world to rights. Consequently, this would not have been her first choice, but Beckie had suggested it when she called to meet up. Geraldine hadn't seen her since their last dinner when they shared a kiss. It had lingered on her lips for a good week after. Each time she'd think about it, it would tingle. But the memory of Zara was still too present for her to enjoy the feeling too much without guilt kicking in.

She spotted Beckie sitting in a corner at a table for two. Her olive skin was radiant in the candlelight. She wore another revealing lacy top, and a light touch of makeup that brought some contrasting colour to her dark hair and clothes. She smiled. Geraldine smiled back, her stomach fluttering.

'Hey G, nice to see you again.' Beckie stood up, kissed her cheek and hugged her tightly. Geraldine's stomach flipped again.

'Nice to see you, Becks.' They both sat down. 'lovely top...'

'Oh, thanks. Had to buy something. I'm behind on my washing.'

'So, what made you choose to meet here?'

'Don't you like it?'

Geraldine pursed her mouth. 'No, I mean it's nice. Romantic.'

'Oh God, you don't like fish?'

'Oh no, I do, sorry. Just my mind is everywhere. Work's been shit.'

The waitress came over and Geraldine ordered a pint of Kronenberg. Beckie had a glass of white wine. 'Should we have ordered a bottle? Sorry, I'm a little nervous.'

Beckie touched her hand. It was like an electrical circuit had been joined up. Geraldine's worry oozed away. A soft smile appeared, and for the longest moment, they stared into each other's eyes. Beckie's were like dark chocolate pools.

Beckie was the first to come out of the trance and laughed. 'So, yes, sorry... I had a woman come by my office. She didn't want to say who she was. A sort of Whitehall type. Suited and a bit prim.

A chill ran down Geraldine's spine and made her shake. 'Fuck off! What did she say?'

The waitress came back with her pint and asked if they

were ready to order. They weren't. Geraldine hadn't even noticed the large menu sheet.

'I recommend the platter of seafood. Like they are having.' said the waitress pad in hand and flicking her head back at another table.

Geraldine looked over to see a three-tier tower of food. It looked amazing. A spread of everything you could find by the seaside. Beckie nodded and Geraldine ordered it with a bottle of white wine. She had taken control and Beckie had just let her. She hadn't expected that. Beckie was a forensic scientist, someone who was in control, of everything. Geraldine looked at her lingering smile. She still wanted to kiss her.

'And?'

'Well, she told me about Richard O'Neill.' Beckie took a sip of wine and looked up at Geraldine, who looked like she'd seen a ghost.

'Oh shit, sorry to just come out with it like that.'

Geraldine had gone cold and started shaking, she picked up her pint and finished it. 'It's fine really, I just... it's just weird, why would someone come and talk to you about him? What exactly did she say?' Beckie was nervous now, she had to remember her exact words.

'She just said that she wanted to help. That there was more information at the Hendon police academy. And O'Neil had been an undercover officer for over a decade. Also, she said she didn't agree with the direction.'

'Of what? What direction?'

'That was it. She asked me to pass that on to you.'

'Did you get a picture of her?'

Beckie shook her head, her long hair sliding around.

'Fuck, I mean fuck... Did she have mousy brown hair, medium height, a little stiff looking?'

'Uh, yes...'

'Shit!' Geraldine grabbed her hands, she knew it had to be Charlie. 'Go on.' A few strands of Beckie's hair had fallen across her brow as she nodded. Geraldine wanted to brush it back.

Beckie moved closer, as if she was teasing her to touch her. 'That was kind of it. I did offer her a cuppa, but she politely declined and left. I wanted to tell her that she should have talked to you directly. It was as if a ghost had dropped in. No introduction, nothing. So, you know her?'

'Well, I wouldn't say that. I'd question if anyone really knew that woman to be honest.' Beckie cocked her head to the side to encourage more from Geraldine, but she wasn't forthcoming. All she wanted to do was call Charlie and ask her what hell was going on.

'But I did take a day out and visited Hendon academy. I hope that was OK? I was curious.'

'Working my patch again?'

'Do you have one?'

They both laughed. Geraldine blushed a bit. It had been ages since she had been embarrassed about herself. 'You'll have to find out.'

Beckie poured some wine for them both, she took a large gulp of hers and looked away. Geraldine noticed that she wasn't wearing her wedding ring. As it wasn't there, it had taken her a bit longer to notice. Geraldine grabbed her hand.

'I do love your hands. So strong.' Beckie smiled at the compliment. 'So did you find anything there?'

She flicked her dark hair over her ear. 'It was very interesting, So many young innocent faces. Police changes you, doesn't it? How did you look when you were younger?'

Geraldine looked up. 'Like a little girl that still wanted to play with her dolls.'

'I couldn't even imagine that. I thought you would be beating up the boys.'

'That came later. At Hendon.' They both laughed.

Then Beckie remembered something and got a little notebook out of her bag. 'Oh yes. It looks like O'Neil had an alias.' Geraldine nearly choked on her wine. 'It's a Peter Butterworth from Pewsey in Wiltshire. Upper Middle class like Jeremy Corbyn. Enrolled in 1989 and graduated in 1991 from Hendon with a Bachelors. Middle of the class and pretty average in every way, nothing to make him stand out. Perfect undercover material. Just seemed to blend in. It took me ages to find him on those class photos. 'Becks took out her phone and showed her a photo she had taken.

Geraldine looked at the grainy image. There was some resemblance to the O'Neil she remembered, his bony features still there, sticking into her fragile consciousness. She felt her jaw clench.

'What did he do to you?'

Geraldine sniffed. 'He tried to kill me.'

'And now you want him dead? G you shouldn't have to deal with this alone. You should tell the police or Plan B...?'

'They want me to lay off the case, the woman who came to see you, told me I had to obey orders.'

'Well, maybe that's a message, babe.'

'No! O'Neil fucking killed my girlfriend, I'm not letting this go. He can't get away with it. What if he killed you?'

Beckie leaned back and swallowed. 'Are they that out of control? If so, we have to talk to the police.'

'They *are* the police... or at least that's what I think they are. I just don't know who to trust anymore. Shit, shit...'

Geraldine looked down. 'But I do know, he's going to pay for what he did.'

Beckie grabbed her hands again. 'G, who else can help? What about that woman...? She must be on our side. I mean, she just gave us a break.'

Geraldine looked up and breathed in. 'Was there anything else on O'Neil at Hendon or in the files?'

'He made a little stink on the beat in London, and then disappeared as you know. I guess that's when Plan B recruited him. I don't know much about the undercover units.'

'Me neither,' Geraldine looked around like she had been in a daydream and took in the pub. 'Is this place a favourite of yours?'

'My flat's just around the corner. And an old friend used to come here. A special friend who got me into forensics. An old soak called James. He'd retired by the time I met him. He used to come here nearly every day.' Beckie looked around. 'He died last year. We used to bounce cases. Some of his old ones and my current ones.'

'Sounds great.'

'He looked just like an old sea captain. Big guy, white beard, rough skin. I think he had some childhood disease or something... I should have asked what happened, but I was too embarrassed.'

Beckie reached into her handbag to get a tissue out and brought out a small envelope. 'Oh! I totally forgot, this is for you...from the woman who came to see me.'

It was addressed to Geraldine. She opened it and slipped the card out. It had an illustration of two cut halves of an avocado, one half still with its stone in, with outstretched stick arms and legs. The text on the front said

Yey, Let's Avo-Cuddle! And she opened it and read the note *Love Ch X.* In the envelope were a dozen fifty-pound notes.

Geraldine showed her the card. 'I don't suppose you could get any DNA from it?'

Beckie looked at it, turning it over in her hands. And then looked at the envelope. 'Who is she, an ex? Bit weird... does she fancy you? And what about all this money?'

'God no! She's from Plan B, my contact. As for the money... probably to firnly discourage me from doing the job they gave me in the first place. And to stop looking for O'Neil. I think the bitch is playing with me. Why would she come and see you?'

Beckie smiled. 'Maybe she wanted you to know that *she* knows we're looking into O'Neil. Is it some kind of carrot dangling exercise? She thinks if she gives a little bit of info you'll be satisfied with that?'

'She clearly doesn't know me very well if that's what she thinks.' Geraldine knew Charlie wasn't telling her everything. Was she just proving she could get to her friends? But how did she know she could even trust Beckie? Who even *was* Beckie? She'd only met her a few times. She could feel her brow start to ache from frowning and had a sip of wine. The seafood tower arrived on their table, filled with shells: oysters, mussels, cockles and others she couldn't name, all lying on a bed of ice. It looked exotic.

'OK... Been to Paris? This always reminds me of Paris.'

Geraldine shook her head. 'I don't even have a passport.'

'Really? Oh, babe, we need to visit.'

Geraldine let that word swirl inside her. Babe. As if suddenly this was something, they were something, together. 'I would love to.' She took a oyster, put some lemon on it and slurped it down. It was like being by the sea in Kent with her sister and mother. 'I only got to go to the seaside.'

'Did you have a happy childhood?'

'Mixed. Mum was all right. Dad left when I was about eleven. She never remarried. She was great. We were poor and we struggled, but she did what she could.'

'I'm sorry. But you've turned out all right. Lucky me I should say.'

'I'm... I'm not ready yet.' Geraldine looked shocked at her own words. It was as if Zara had just spoken for her.

'Really? You might surprise yourself. I can feel your energy.'

Geraldine finished her glass and ordered another bottle, her brain and pulse in competition for who could race the fastest.

THIRTY-EIGHT

It was around 1am when Rebwar got a call from Geraldine asking him to meet her ASAP at Latimer Road tube station. As he got dressed, Hourieh had huffed and turned over, mumbling about whether or not he was sure Geraldine was a lesbian. She'd had a text from an anonymous number which said that O'Neil was in the area. The text was signed *ChXXXXX*. She was sure the message was from Charlie, but it had a few too many kisses to be comfortable. Rebwar too, was suspicious. So, he had brought his loaded Webley. He'd taken it apart and cleaned it. Twice. It was the middle of June, so the sky was barely dark especially with the flood of city lights. But that night the sky had a haziness to it that was not normal. On Holland Park Avenue traffic had come to a standstill. Something was going on. He managed to take a left onto Royal Crescent and then St Ann Villas. On the horizon in front of him, black smoke was rising. Filled with burning debris, it was like a volcano had erupted.

Cars had stopped along the road and people were getting out to watch the show. Rebwar reversed into a free space, took the gun and left the car. He wasn't too far from the tube station. He tried to call Geraldine but the phone wasn't finding a service. He made his way on foot. The closer he got the thicker the crowds became. More and more emergency vehicles were parked up. Some of them were just abandoned on pavements. People around Rebwar whispered to each other about a tube train being on fire. A major terrorist incident, another said.

The streets were filled with a mish-mash of people. Some in dressing gowns who'd come down from their flats to have a nose, women in full burkas standing with small children on their hips chatting to others, people on their way home from a night out who stopped to watch the drama unfolding in front of their eyes. Rebwar got to a corner where the street turned into Bramley Road. He could see the railway bridge with the entrance to Latimer Road tube station underneath. More flashing blue and red lights filled the streets. Everyone was watching a huge multi-storey building. It was on fire. Thick black smoke rose up. Rebwar stopped and watched for a moment. People around him jostled to get close to the spectacle.

He had to try and get to the tube station. His phone still had no network. Police tape was being rolled out across the road. They were cordoning the area off. What would Geraldine do? He looked around. He had to find a pub. That's where she would be. Even if it was 1:30 am, she would be there trying to get in. He could see one just down the road past the police cordon. He couldn't spot her; it was a little far, and his eyesight wasn't as good as it once was.

Police were pushing people further back. Geraldine could use her badge to stay there. But that didn't help him. He had to go around somehow. Then someone called out his name. Not Rebwar but Amir. He recognized the voice and looked around. No one else had responded to it. He clenched, ready for someone to come at him. He felt the heavy metal gun in his jacket. It wasn't Wayne's slightly high-pitched voice or the deep rumbling tone of Dental Mike. It had to be another one of Wayne's gang who had spotted him. It was a trap. He feared for Geraldine.

Rebwar moved closer to a wall where he could face the crowds. He had to find her. He walked into Bramley Road and then Freston Road, making sure no one else was following him. Three black kids ran past him screaming 'fire' at the top of their voices. They seemed excited by the whole event. He made his way up the street, crossing from one side to the other. The road quietened down once he passed the railway bridge. There was a construction site and what looked like a school at the end of the road. The street turned into a little pedestrian alleyway. He could hear traffic on his left. He missed the safety of crowds, but at least it would be easy to know if anyone was behind him, and there was enough space to fight, space to see his opponent or opponents, space to breathe, space to think.

Before these last few weeks it had been over a year since he and Geraldine had worked together, but he felt strangely responsible for her, as if she were vulnerable. It had never been made official, but they were partners, and you look after your partner. As he walked from streetlight to streetlight further up the alley, he felt lost. The comfort of a mobile phone had gone. He was alone, just him and his wits. Back in Iran that would have been OK. But this was still a foreign land. Sometimes It was like a war zone. Panic was only a few corners away. And tonight there was an acrid smell in the air he recognised. The stench of death.

The path led into the back of a housing estate. Dull grey square boxes built with economy rather than comfort in mind stared back at him. He could see shadows moving around him. He clenched his fists, ready for any jump. Now he was convinced that Wayne and his gang were around. He still hadn't sold the coke they had given him, and soon his time would be up to pay the debt Wayne had demanded of him. His eyes darted from one dark corner to another, looking out for any odd shapes that didn't fit in, like a bad jigsaw puzzle.

He got to Shalfleet Drive, a dead-end road wedged in between two apartment complexes. At the end of the road was Latimer Road tube station, where Geraldine had said to meet, flimsy plastic police tape fluttered around it. Two men ran past him. Rebwar's left hand tightened around the butt of the pistol. He looked around him and breathed in. Sirens still filled the night. He breathed in again and walked quickly towards the tube station entrance. A crowd had formed around it which brought him a bit of comfort from the quiet and shadows, even though it was just as dangerous. Rebwar spotted a pub on the left called the Pig and Whistle which had a late license. It was a concrete black box with some edges missing, more of a bunker than a trendy architectural experiment. People were outside drinking pints and watching the tower burn. As if it was some kind of horrific entertainment spectacle.

Geraldine was there, too.

'Rebs! Fuck you made it!' She looked at her phone. 'How?'

'I walked here. Have you had any more messages?'

She shook her head. 'No, but am I glad to see you.' She stopped for a moment.

'Are you OK?' She nodded and took a gulp of her pint.

'O'Neil. He must be around here somewhere. Why else would the Ferret have sent the message?'

Rebwar looked around him, lit a cigarette for each of them and handed her one. 'So, are we arresting him?'

'I was thinking of something a little more... decisive. Have you got that gun?'

Rebwar nodded. 'Isn't a little bit too hot for an execution? Although the police do have more pressing things to attend to tonight, so they wouldn't be a problem. What about Plan B?'

She looked at him and shifted her weight from side to side, her hair brushing the back of her neck. 'They are the ones who let him go in the first place. He's gotten away with murder. Why can't we? It's what he deserves. He fucking killed my Zara. That fucker needs to be terminated.'

Rebwar looked at the burning tower, which was now lighting the whole area like a giant torch. It was out of control. The heat was radiating out of it like a sun.

'Are you sure it was from her?'

'It was an anonymous number, but the Ferrett's number always comes up unknown.'

'For Allah's sake, it's a trap, no? What did the message say exactly?'

'That O'Neil was in the area and that I'd find what I was looking for at the Grenfell Tower.'

'And?'

'That's it. Just that.'

'And now it's on fire. There's no access, and the police are all over it.'

Geraldine finished her pint. 'Drink?'

Rebwar shook his head. 'How can you drink?' Rebwar now understood how much her rage was consuming her. He was getting worried, about her and the fire. 'OK... We'll have a quick look around the area, but it's not safe.'

Geraldine walked off towards the tube station.

Rebwar stubbed his cigarette out and followed her. 'Should we involve the police?'

'Look, Rebwar, it's up to us now. Just us two.' She pointed at them both. 'We are what's left of justice here, OK?'

For a moment, he wanted to tell her that he wasn't going to follow her into this madness. Last time he had done something on a whim, an innocent child was killed, and he had to leave the country. But there wasn't time to explain. All around them, a slight sense of panic was starting to drift around the streets. Geraldine walked up to the police cordon and flashed her badge to a police guard. She waved to Rebwar to follow her. They walked past the tube station and into a side street. It was deserted, but the sound of sirens and flashing lights flooded the surrounding building walls.

Geraldine and Rebwar looked around them like cats hunting mice. Rebwar was still unsure if this was a trap or a genuine tip-off.

'Have you contacted Zane?' Rebwar had to shout over the noise of generators and fire engine pumps.

'No. I haven't seen him since he took another van full of 'VIP's away, and then I got run off the road by Wayne's goons.'

'Maybe he knows something? He might at least know where Wayne and his crew are, so we can stop worrying about them at least.'

'He's probably high on drugs at this time of night, pathetic twat.' Geraldine called out over the noise. They tried to get as close to the tower as they could, but the whole area was swarming with firemen. A pulsating spaghetti junction of hoses lay in their way. The heat of the fire was like a raging oven. If there was anyone in the tower, they weren't alive anymore. The horror of it hit them. This was bad. People were dying in there. Rebwar grabbed Geraldine's hand to pull her away. They both moved back.

They decided to snake around the tower in the hope they could spot O'Neil, perhaps among the crowds. It was a lot harder than they had thought. The police were evacuating the area and all around the locals were in shock. This was turning from a tragedy to a catastrophe. An air of panic filled the area. Rebwar wasn't sure what they were going to do if they finally did see him. They passed an alley and he spotted Dental Mike. He stopped and looked down the street. Little John was herding a family. Two children were crying and being pushed along. Geraldine looked at Rebwar for more information.

'Wayne's crew.'

Geraldine's face flushed with emotion. 'That's them...' she said craning her neck to see the two men. 'The ones who ran me off the road.'

More people moved around them. They passed the police cordon and were back in with the spectating crowd. They pushed themselves through. It was hard and yet delicate work; too close and they would be spotted; too far back and they would be in danger of losing them. One moment Geraldine had eyes on them and then Rebwar did, and then neither had. As the crowd thinned out, they felt they could breathe again. Rebwar looked down a few side streets. They weren't going fast with the two kids. Through the sirens and roaring fire behind them, Rebwar heard a faint cry. A child crying. He passed another street and spotted a minivan with people being loaded in.

'I think they are in that van.'

'Fuck, you're right. Zane! That's *his* van!'

They both stood wondering what to do. An arrest

without back up? They would just laugh and run.

'Hey, Amir, what the fuck are you doing here?' They both turned around to see Little John, the small man with the teardrop tattoo. 'Come to pay your dues?' He squinted and then his brain processed who Rebwar was with. 'And what the fuck are you doing with that bitch?'

Geraldine clenched her jaw. Rebwar punched Little John straight in the face. His head rocked back and he followed it to the ground. Rebwar went through his pockets and found his wallet and phone. He took them. 'Come on, we need to find another place to watch them.' And they ran off around the corner. Dental Mike was walking off in another direction.

'Let's ask him some questions,' Geraldine said.

'What? He's just the muscle, I've lost teeth to that madman.'

'Come on, Rebs. Never knew you to shy away from a fight.'

'What about Zane?'

But she had gone down the street after Dental Mike. After a few turns, she tapped him on the shoulder.

Rebwar swore to himself. He couldn't take him on. The man turned, and his sheer size seemed to grow in front of them.

'Yeah.'

'Can you tell me what you're doing?' And Geraldine flashed her badge. He didn't know where to look. Rebwar could see his brain telling him Amir was with a police officer and that he had to do something radical.

'What? You're a... None of your business, ma'am.'

'Sir... I need you to evacuate the area.'

'It's him you need to arrest, Amir.' He stabbed a finger in Rebwar's direction.

'Who?'

'Him, he's an illegal, I'm rounding them up. For you lot, right? Check him, he's a dealer.'

Rebwar and Geraldine looked at each other as Dental Mike pulled his arm back ready to launch the inevitable punch. Rebwar stepped back just out of reach of his swing and got ready to draw the pistol. Behind them a police car swung fast into the street the other end from the van. It skidded to a halt, lights flashing, with a loudspeaker telling everyone to leave the area. Dental Mike ran off, Geraldine and Rebwar followed. Police and emergency vehicles were everywhere. Dental Mike turned back to the minivan, having temporarily forgotten his intention of beating Rebwar to a pulp. Suddenly Geraldine froze. She put her hand to her chest and seemed like she couldn't breathe properly. Rebwar looked towards the direction her eyes had fixed upon and followed her gaze. Down at the end of the road near the police car stood Richard O'Neil talking to some officers. Rebwar put his hand on her shoulder to calm her, just as Zane's minivan engine revved up and began to make a hasty three-point turn. Rebwar acted instinctively, he got his flick knife out and ran over to the van.

The van stopped at the curb and its gears crunched. Rebwar stabbed the front tyre and a whoosh of air escaped. The front right corner of the van dropped. Before it could reverse, Rebwar had punctured two more tyres. Dental Mike stepped out of a side door. His size filled the doorway. Before he could grab him, Rebwar ran back to Geraldine, who was walking the other way towards O'Neil.

'No, we can't approach him.'

'Piss off, I'm going! That fucker is mine!'

He tried to grab her jacket, but she kept moving towards O'Neil. 'This is not the time! Geraldine... listen...' Rebwar felt a violent tug to his jacket and he lurched backwards, he could only avoid Dental Mike's attentions for so long.

'Hey G! What the fuck are you doing here?' Zane shouted at her.

Dental Mike, still holding on to Rebwar's jacket, pulled him in a circle. Rebwar slipped out of his jacket, his gun still in the inside pocket. Dental Mike swung the jacket above his head and walked towards Rebwar. The van's passengers were crowding around it. Dental Mike shouted at them to get back in. Rebwar launched himself and with all his strength kicked him in the groin. For the longest moment, nothing happened. He just kept that jacket swinging above his head. And then the jacket slipped out of his grasp and landed on top of the van's roof. Dental Mike dropped to his knees as the pain travelled. Rebwar kicked him in the face and he dropped down.

Rebwar recognised some of the faces around the van. In the mix were the refugees he had taxied over to London.

'Fuck, we've lost him!' said Geraldine scanning the area around where O'Neil had been.

Zane mounted the curb with the van and drove off with the flat tyres, side door wide open. A police car went after it. As the van turned around the corner, Rebwar's jacket slid off the roof. He went after it and slipped it on, relieved to find that his gun was still there. The once empty street was now filling with people as they were being evacuated from the area. Rebwar couldn't see Geraldine.

'Can you help us?' A voice behind him called. He turned to see the man he had tried to release. His wife and child were with him. All around them people were moving away from the burning tower. Where Dental Mike had been slumped was now just a few drops of blood. Rebwar checked his phone again. There was still no reception.

'OK, follow me.' Rebwar retraced his route back to his car. The police weren't interested in them. But each time he passed a checkpoint there was a moment of worry. He could empathise with his new companions. This felt more like being back home. Finally, Rebwar found his parked car. The indicators flashed as he opened it.

'Amir!' Rebwar turned around to see Little John. His nose had swollen up. His voice was hard to make out as his nose was blocked with blood. 'You got sub of by merchandise. You tryin to steal frob be? Stay where you are.' He pulled back his jacket to show Rebwar that he had a gun. 'Don't eben fucking think about it. You three are ubbing with me.' Rebwar stepped back. This wasn't the place to have a shoot-out. His mind went through different scenarios. As Little John passed him, Rebwar grabbed him and Jammed his Webley into his back.

'Two can play at that game.' Rebwar had just missed snatching his gun away but had his head in a lock. Little John was waving his gun around. Rebwar couldn't recognise the model. It looked knocked-off cheap and scratched. The terrified family crouched on the ground beside the car, using it for cover. Rebwar pushed the gun further into Little John's back as a warning.

'Really? You're going to shoob be?'

'Don't push me.' Rebwar hissed into his ear. But he had a point. The bullet would go straight through him. The old vintage gun was probably far too powerful for close quarter combat. But he wasn't sure. Rebwar had a hunch that Little John's gun was a fake or possibly converted. Unlike in Iran, it was harder to get a gun here but easier to convert replicas. Rebwar had to take a decision, as time was running out.

'Go on, shoob, shid head!' Little John waved his gun behind him, trying to find Rebwar. They twisted around. It was like an awkward dance where neither wanted to lead. Then Little John's gun went off. It was much quieter than Rebwar had expected. He couldn't see where the bullet went. Before he could shoot again, Rebwar had grabbed at the gun. Its barrel was hot and it burned his hand. The hammer hit Rebwar's thumb, and Little John kept pulling the trigger. He had also grabbed Rebwar's pistol with his other hand. It was as if they were sliding on ice and holding each other up, each arm wrestling with a gun. Now Rebwar's gun was the loose cannon as he tried not to press the trigger. It waved around as Rebwar's arm struggled in the wrestling match. For a small man, Little John was strong. His little skinny leg hit out. His face was red with rage. Spit and blood dribbled down his face. Then Rebwar's gun went off.

Blood exploded everywhere and the noise rang inside Rebwar's head. It was like he was inside a helmet that had been smashed with a baseball bat. But this was a good sign. It meant he was still alive. No searing pain. No collapsing. No sudden loss of consciousness. He could see ahead of him, which he thought was odd as he was still holding Little John. But his captive had gone limp like a sack. As the smoke cleared he saw that where once the man's head had been, now there was nothing. The bullet had exploded it. Rebwar could taste blood in the air now. He let the body fall to the ground. Blood still pumped out of it.

He looked at the crouching family. Their eyes popped out like they had seen the devil. He looked down. It was as if he'd had a blood bath. He didn't want to think what else was on him. He motioned them to get into the car. The father and son got up but the woman couldn't. Rebwar saw blood staining her clothes. She'd been hit too.

THIRTY-NINE

Rebwar was waiting at Heathrow Terminal 2 at the arrivals. He was holding a board with the name of *Houssein*. A few other minicab drivers had already made a few jokes about the name. Rebwar had brushed them off as he wasn't in the mood. The fire at the tower had ended up as a national scandal and was in all the papers. A few of them had a little column about a gang-related hit in the area. A known gangster had been executed and there was an ongoing investigation. Plan B had given him another job: a taxi pick-up of a family coming in from Frankfurt. It felt like he had been demoted. They had texted him the details. The only bonus was that it was at least a day's wages.

The arrivals hall was a huge modern glass structure with various cafés and shops throughout. At one end were the double doors where passengers filtered out with their trolleys full of luggage. People smiled and waved as they greeted their friends and relatives. A regular occurrence for many, but for Rebwar it was something he missed. Apart from the businessmen, everyone seemed so carefree. He couldn't even remember the last time he had been like that.

Maybe a few summers before when he was on holiday with his family. He looked up at the screens again and they scanned across with new information, the plane that the family he was picking up were on had just landed. He had a coffee in hand but wanted to go outside and have a cigarette.

He continued to watch the arrivals. It was as if people from a wave of countries had landed. Those coming from tropical climes looked the most out of place, wearing shorts and t-shirts with no beach to go to. Rebwar had made an effort and was wearing a white shirt and a suit, a black one from the last funeral he had attended. The other taxi drivers were sizing each other up. Some of them knew each other and were chatting; others were on their smartphones. Apart from the name Hussein and the flight number, he had nothing.

Rebwar hadn't really talked to Geraldine since the night of the Grenfell fire. Certainly not face to face. There had been a brief exchange of words over the phone with her when he took the refugee who had been shot by Little John's stray bullet to the hospital. Then he got a text from her saying she was changing numbers, and he was still waiting for her to contact him. He wondered what was going on with her, he knew she wasn't in a good place but didn't know how to help. The passengers came in waves, and then there was a moment of stillness. His fingers itched for a cigarette as he tried to block out the horror of the last few days. In less than a week it seemed they'd taken two steps forward only to slip 3 steps back. They had located the elusive Richard O'Neil and proven a link with Bywater and Wayne. Yet the identity of the Gipsy was still a mystery, and he was no closer to finding out who killed Matt and if there was a link to Bywater and the people traffickers. Any now they'd been told to back off by the very people who put them up to the job, Plan B. Every time they felt they were getting close to O'Neil he slipped away. His capture was a mission for Geraldine fueled purely on revenge. Rebwar knew from experience that decisions made on an emotional level were never good ones. But who could blame her after what O'Neil had done. It was a mess. And now Wayne was probably on the warpath. They had lost even more of their migrants and he still wanted his 10k. Now he really needed a cigarette, but there was no time.

A few men in business suits came out followed by some women. Dark colours and ties. Then a short stocky woman with two kids appeared, she was looking around anxiously. He guessed that it must be her. The trolley had old worn cases piled on it, which had a familiar feel to them. He guessed she was from Syria or Iraq. He held his sign at chest height for her to read. She looked like she was in her mid-60s. Her clothes were old and worn but she wore them with pride. As she got closer, he could see that she had been crying.

Her eyes were swollen, red, and her face carried years of toil. It was as if she was pushing the world on her trolley. The kids were hanging onto her, looking up at this brave new world. Her eyes picked out the name and she headed towards him. She stopped by the metal barrier.

'Inshallah, hello, Mrs Houssein I am here to drive you to your hotel.'

'Hello, I speak little. Yes, good.'

He ducked underneath the metal bar and took the trolley from her. Mrs Houssein's walk was unsteady and she struggled for breath. For a moment, he thought of getting her a wheelchair, but then her pride wouldn't allow that.

'How was your trip?'

'Yes, long.' A little smile appeared.

'Coffee?'

'No, no, thank you.'

He pushed the trolley to the car park and put the cases in the boot while they made themselves comfortable in the car. By the time he had presented his parking ticket at the barrier, the kids, a girl and a boy were fast asleep leaning against each other in the back seat. Rebwar studied the woman who sat in the passenger seat, but still couldn't place her. It was a recognisable face, one which he had seen back in Iran. But she wasn't from there, as they would have greeted each other very differently. He also thought she might just see him as a taxi driver, a servant. Not that she seemed like an aristocrat or anything, but there was definitely some bitterness and anger in her, as well as the obvious sadness. Rebwar took a risk of upsetting her and said. 'Are you from Syria?'

There was a moment of silence before she replied. 'No. Iraq.'

'Visiting?' Rebwar watched her eyes well up. She took out a handkerchief to dab her her eyes. 'I'm sorry to ask.'

'It's... it's my son. These are his children.' She dabbed more tears.

'Nice children. He works here?' Rebwar was on the M4 on his way to London. He had to drop her off at the Haven Hotel, close to Paddington train station. His sat nav was telling him it was going to take nearly an hour which could be a long one. He switched on the radio. *There were reports of mothers throwing babies from windows as the tower burned, said a witness.*

Mrs Houssein sobbed and Rebwar changed stations to Heart Radio.

'Sorry! Are you OK?'

'My son... my son died in fire.'

Rebwar quickly realised why she was here. 'Oh, I'm so sorry. That's terrible. I saw it. Horrible, horrible.'

'Yes, yes.'

Rebwar wanted to help, but didn't have anything other than cigarettes. He offered one and she took it. Rebwar refrained from smoking one. After a few songs on the radio, he realised that they were going to pass by the tower. He tapped into his sat nav trying to get another route but the traffic had backed up and he was committed on the outside lane. The last exit had just passed and he was going up onto the Westway, the raised dual carriageway that would give them a grandstand view of the burned-out shell of the tower. He could already see the smouldering smoke rising up into the blue sky. He just hoped the smell wouldn't drift by them. He felt awful, as if they were revisiting the scene of a crime. Which it was for her, even though it was probably an accident.

What Rebwar didn't quite understand was why Plan B had given him this job. Where did they fit in? It made no sense. Were they feeling guilty for something?

'Oh my God,' the woman said.

Rebwar's breath was taken away, too. The Tower looked like a giant burnt matchstick. Cars were slowing down to look at the full horror. Her two children woke up to her wailing and crying and looked out. They, too, understood. Rebwar was furious with himself for not thinking. How disrespectful he had been taking her to the scene of her son's death. They had said that there were still some bodies that were unaccounted for inside.

'I'm sorry.' He swore to himself.

The crawl by could have been seen as a sign of respect but for Rebwar, it was the longest quarter of a mile he had ever driven. It was heartbreaking. Every second passed by like it was a minute. He dared not look. Only when he reached the slip-ramp down towards the Edgware Road could he breathe again.

'Do you know if I could see my son?'

'Sorry I'm just the taxi driver. Who organised the trip?'

'Sorry? No understand.'

'Who paid for the trip?' Rebwar rubbed his fingers together.

'Government. They pay.'

For a moment, he tried to think about it. Did she mean her son worked for the government? 'Your son?'

'Yes, they pay for him. Pay everything like blood money.'

After a few turns, he got to the hotel and stopped in front. He helped her to the entrance with her bags.

'Can I pay?'

'It's on the account. No need. Good luck with the stay. And I hope you find peace.'

'Inshallah.'

As he walked back to his car, Rebwar could still feel and taste the horrors of the last few days. It was only also a matter of time before Wayne caught up with him, and for Geraldine to make her next move to locate and destroy Richard O'Neil. But he needed her to contact him. That was his only possible route to Plan B, who he was sure had all the answers. In the meantime, he had to prepare for a Plan B of his own.

FORTY

Rebwar was reading the *Metro*, the free London newspaper he'd found in the hallway. He was still trying to find out what had really happened with the tower block fire. But it was all a political blame game. He'd read that the cladding on the building had caught fire and caused the inferno. His tower had the same problem and tensions were high with the local residents. Hourieh didn't let him smoke in the apartment. He had to go a few streets down to a safe location. It was ridiculous and it annoyed him. Everybody was angry about something.

It was when he was smoking through a window that they announced that they were evacuating the building. They had found alternative accommodation. All the neighbours and residents suddenly started to talk to each other. No one knew what it really meant. Were they moving out for good, or was it temporary and, if so, for how long? Hourieh hurriedly packed a suitcase. Rebwar was sent downstairs to find out more information. There were a few council workers outside the flats and they were being mobbed. He couldn't even hear what was going on, so he took the opportunity to have a smoke. He spotted one of the kids from the Chilcots estate gang. They were watching the mayhem. Everybody was on their phones, either on hold with the council or venting their frustration to an unfortunate friend.

'Cigarette?' The short black kid took one. 'You moving out?' Rebwar asked.

'Man, you've got balls.' The boy tutted and shook his head.

Rebwar looked at him, wondering what he meant.

'Men around looking for a man that sounds like you... goes by the name of Amir. You know him?'

'Who's asking?' Rebwar lit the cigarette for him.

'Two ugly looking dudes, bald with a broken nose and the other with a snakeskin tattoo on his arm. Mean looking and all. Don't wanna mess with them. Y'know.'

'What did you tell them.'

'They wanna pay me and all. But I said, nothin' man. Nothin'. This is my hood, I'm not grassing on my cous.. not that you are and all, but it's the principle, innit.'

Rebwar drew a deep breath. 'Where are they now?'

'Brov' look over that way. By the other tower, man, they went that way. Lookin' for trouble.'

'I think they're trying to muscle in and do some business here.'

'For real? Motherfuckers, yo!' and he snapped his finger. 'Who do they think they are, brov?'

'Trafficking and trouble.' Rebwar stubbed his cigarette on the wall.

'Fuck that. Thanks, brov. I owe you one.' He held out his fist. Rebwar responded by bumping it with his. As soon as he had made his swaggering walk around the corner, Rebwar was back to his flat. He wasn't going to wait to find out if Wayne and his crew were coming to claim their illegal workers or if they were after him. Back at the flat Hourieh was still packing a suitcase.

'We need to go.'

'Husband, we are going. You could help.'

'We need to get out of here. To Bijan's. It's chaos out there and the Council want to put us in a gym hall.'

'But our neighbour is getting a hotel.'

'We're not waiting to find out what we are getting. Where is Musa?'

'He went outside to see some friends.'

Rebwar tried not to swear or look too much in distress. He didn't want to panic anyone. If he told Hourieh what was actually going on, she would have had a fit. This had to be done delicately. Only once they were at Bijan's could he tell her a bit more about the situation. He held her shoulders and looked into her eyes.

'Now my love you know when I can't tell you everything because it's for the family? For the good? Well now is such a moment. I'm going to find Musa and you are going to wait for me in the car park. OK?'

He could see her face was full of questions and fear. But they had been through this drill before. He kissed her and watched her walk off down the stairs; the lifts were too busy with people leaving. Rebwar went back into the flat and got his gun and bullets. He felt bad not taking Hourieh to the car park, but he had to find his son.

The press had arrived and more and more people were crowding around the foot of the tower. Most people were angry at the lack of information. Rebwar tried to think for a moment where Musa might have gone. The danger was around the three towers, that's where Wayne and his gang were. So that was where he must go, to make sure Musa wasn't there. He put on a baseball cap and sunglasses and walked along Fellows Road, the opposite side was lined with trees and large townhouses. He was looking for a minivan like the one Zane had driven.

Geraldine still hadn't called in and Rebwar was starting to worry a little. Since the mayhem, he'd thought she would contact him. She would have heard by now that Little John had lost his head. Surely that wouldn't have escaped her. On the other hand, in the chaos, his body might still be in a morgue waiting to be processed. The death count at the tower was over eighty, they had said.

At the end of the street was a small huddle of people who looked like they all belonged together. They seemed to be moving en mass in a flurry of veils and robes. Rebwar went closer to see where they were going. They were all pulling suitcases along the pavement. He walked on the other side of the road, watching them. He stopped and looked around. More and more people seemed to be walking in the same direction. The Swiss Cottage Leisure Centre was further down the road and he guessed they were heading to the gym, where a makeshift refuge had been created.

He turned around to take out a cigarette and caught a glimpse of someone who looked very much like Wayne at the end of the road. He was dressed in his trademark black sports jacket and white trainers and was busy chatting on the phone. Rebwar couldn't see anyone with him as he jogged along the road to try and get a better look. He didn't have a good feeling about this but had to follow him. Wayne was walking quickly towards one of the middle towers. That's when Rebwar spotted Musa standing with some of his friends taking pictures of the scene directly where Wayne seemed to be heading. Rebwar's heart stopped. Was

Musa their target now? O'Neil had been to his flat and probably seen pictures of his son. It was a wonder he hadn't come for him sooner. They must have finally made the connection between Amir and him.

Wayne was getting closer to Musa, but as he approached, three of the local lads, including the boy Rebwar spoke to earlier, blocked his path. Wayne shouted at them to get out of his way. Rebwar ducked behind the group and ran over to Musa.

'Dad! What's going on?'

'We need to run, son.'

'Why?'

'No time for questions now.' Rebwar grabbed him by the arm and glanced back to see Wayne, who was still being hassled by the three kids. 'There is danger here. Now to the car.'

Wayne hit one of the kids and the other two laid into him. Rebwar saw Wayne's phone spin to the ground, it bounced along the soft play surface. This was an opportunity he couldn't miss, and he dashed over and picked it up, then walked off quickly with Musa into the crowds. The fight with Wayne was getting more attention and provided a good distraction for a getaway. Rebwar kept scanning the people around for Dental Mike or any other dubious characters. Not looking where he was going, he bumped into someone. It was O'Neil. They both stopped dead in their tracks and looked at each other. O'Neil looked puzzled. Last time they had met face to face was in a Mall in north London. He had a cast on his arm and was out to get his revenge. Of course then he was a policeman and now a had switched sides.

'Rebwar. Yes of course...'

Rebwar pushed Musa behind him.

'And this must be your son.' O'Neil leaned over and stared at him.

Rebwar kept glancing behind him. 'O'Neil, what are you doing here? Keeping the peace?'

Before O'Neil could answer, Rebwar turned to leave. 'I'm...I'm in a rush. They are evacuating.' Rebwar felt his hand tremble. With Wayne somewhere around rounding up his illegal work force, it would only be a matter of luck if he didn't bump into them.

'Sure. You heard from Geraldine? Been meaning to catch up with her, if you know what I mean.'

'Who?'

'You know... DS Geraldine Smith. Came for the interview...'

Rebwar shuffled forward a bit. 'No, been busy with Uber jobs. Sorry. Have an appointment.'

O'Neil stepped closer to him. 'Hey, listen, if you do come across her, tell her to contact me. I have some news for her. Actually, something important. You do see her, don't you?'

Rebwar shook his head and took a few more steps away from O'Neil. The crowds moved around them as if they were in the centre of a whirlpool. People were pushing, shouting on phones, pulling luggage. Rebwar tried to move away but they were like balls in a pinball machine. Rebwar watched O'Neil's eyes flipping around, thinking. 'Sorry, in a rush.'

'Hey! Rebwar you're not fooling me. I've got your number. Do you understand?'

'No, but I need to go, DCI O'Neil. Or is it Mr O'Neil?'

O'Neil looked at him with a sideways glance. Looked at his arm where his cast had been. 'You doing OK? Got a job and a family. Are you all legit then?'

Rebwar stepped back pushing on his son.

O'Neil grabbed Rebwar's arm. It was firm like a handcuff. 'Are you...' He laughed. Rebwar tried to pull himself free, but O'Neil held on. 'Rebwar, look after yourself. Give my greetings to Geraldine and your wife. Hourieh isn't it? Is she around?'

'All good. She is waiting for us.'

'Look... I can help you, Rebwar.' O'Neil's knuckles were white with the pressure. 'Do you need a new place to live? I can help with that. Sure your wife wouldn't like to hear me out? I can help. And your son... Musa, right? How old is he? I know the system and can pull some strings, if you know what I mean. Look, you can be safe with me. Hey Musa! Want a place with a PlayStation?'

'If you can find us a house with a garden?' said Musa.

Rebwar stared at Musa, willing him to shut up.

'Sure not a problem. We even have taxis waiting for you. It's all organised for your family. Not a problem. Look over there.'

Rebwar twisted his arm around, which forced O'Neil to let go. 'Thanks, but it's all organised. We have a place.' Rebwar faced Musa. 'We can't keep mother waiting.'

'Dad he's...'

'Listen to your son, Rebwar. We can help.'

Rebwar pushed Musa through the crowds. O'Neil took a few steps after them. 'Keep your head down and move. Don't look back, OK?'

'But he's...'

Rebwar tightened his grip on his son's arm. O'Neil's tall, lanky head bobbed above the crowd behind, trying to fix on him but the crowds got in his way. Rebwar turned into an alleyway which led into the car park and stopped abruptly. Dental Mike was there, pulling two large suitcases and shouting at a crouching family. The alley was blocked by them. Rebwar felt the butt of his pistol. There were three cameras above him and more below. Dental Mike's face tightened, his patched broken nose flaring. He stopped with an angry smile. The young family froze.

Dental Mike reached for his phone. Behind him was the underground car park where Hourieh was waiting for them.

'Dad, what's up?'

'Hey! Wayne's looking for you,' Dental Mike said. 'He's here, and he's got a message.'

Rebwar walked over to him at a rapid pace. He ducked. Rebwar had counted on his slow mass but not his next move. One of the suitcases collided into his stomach. Its weight pushed him back. Rebwar had lost the element of surprise. Now it was brute force versus some rusty techniques. Back in Iran, he could at least keep himself fighting fit at the police gym. Not that he was an avid student. It was more a place to keep your stress and anger at a working level.

The second suitcase swung at Rebwar's head. His hand absorbed much of the blow but he was thrown into the metal railing. The suitcases were like two large anvils, swinging at him. Rebwar rolled down on the ground to avoid them. One of the suitcases slammed into the railing, its momentum stopped. The father pushed his family down the ramp away from the fight. Musa was behind Dental Mike. Rebwar got up and faced him. Dental Mike dropped both suitcases and smiled. 'Revenge is going to be sweet. Was that your work on Little John? I think so. I can see it in your eyes. An eye for an eye. Have you told Wayne?'

Musa ran towards his father. It was the last thing Rebwar could wish for. A thin little teenager running into a wall of fighting muscle. It was a fifty-fifty chance that he would be distracted and Rebwar had a chance to move. 'No, Musa don't!' he shouted.

For an instant, Dental Mike looked back. This was the moment and required all his police skills. It had been a while since he had practiced his hand-to-hand combat but, like the knowledge of riding a bicycle, the moves were still there, rusty but ingrained in his muscle memory. Once he committed, everything just flowed out of him like a predator hunting his prey.

Rebwar punched hard with his left fist to one of Dental Mike's swollen ears. With his right fist, he punched his throat, just where it joined the chest. If it was too hard, Rebwar would kill him; too soft and Mike could still have enough strength to hit back. Dental Mike's hands flailed around in confusion. He struggled and his balance was out. His back hit the metal railings and he tried to support himself. He wheezed and coughed. His knees gave in and he dropped. Rebwar grabbed Musa's hand and pulled him down the ramp, past the stunned family. Their car was just at the end of the garage.

FORTY-ONE

Rebwar and Musa ran to the car in the underground garage. It was empty, no sign of Hourieh. He thumped the car roof in frustration and called out her name.

'Get in son!'

'But where's Mum?'

'No time. We need to go.' Rebwar climbed behind the wheel and started the engine. He passed his phone to Musa. 'Call her.' Before he got the chance a loud tin-like thud resonated off the side door. Rebwar looked around. It was Hourieh. She had thrown a bag at the car to get his attention. She hauled the bag and herself into the back seat, and they drove off. 'Where have you been?' Rebwar said.

'We forgot some things.'

Rebwar shook his head. They passed crowds of people dragging suitcases off somewhere, their plastic wheels bumping and scrapping on the concrete slabs.

'Husband, where are we going?'

'Bijan's. He's going to give us refuge.'

'Have you called him?' Her face was trying to tell him

something he didn't know. 'Have you asked him? We can't just go there. It's rude.'

'It's an emergency.'

'And those men… why are they after you? Are we in danger?'

'Yes, but you have to trust me. We will be safe at Bijan's.'

'We need to go back to the flat.'

'Wife! Trust me, this will blow over.'

'Like the smoke of the tower?'

Bijan's house was a few streets away from Swiss Cottage. With the traffic, it took them twenty minutes. Rebwar pulled up in front of the huge mansion. He did feel a little bad about abusing Bijan's hospitality, but he would understand this was an emergency; his family was in danger. Hourieh had always claimed that she knew Bijan, an old family friend she had always claimed. But it was when Plan B asked him to watch Bijan which is when they became friends. Rebwar now hoped he wasn't bringing them back to his doorstep. 'What happened to Katerena?'

Hourieh shrugged her shoulders.

'Did they?'

'What?'

'Deport her? Maybe this wasn't such a good idea.'

They left the luggage in the car and walked up to the door. Rebwar rang the doorbell. A series of rings followed. They waited for a few anxious moments before the door opened. It was some man that he had never met before.

'Can I help you?' said a man in a monotone voice. He was wearing a suit with a tie. He looked immaculate, manicured hands and shiny skin.

'We are here to see Bijan.'

'Have you an appointment?'

'Just tell him we are here, OK?'

'Mr and Mrs Ghorbani.' said Hourieh.

And the man shut the door on them.

'Who the fuck does he think he is?'

'That's the new man that Katarena employed.'

'And he didn't recognise you?'

'We haven't been introduced.'

The door opened again. 'Come in,' he said with his eyes rolling. 'But be careful with the furniture.'

Rebwar looked up, staring at him as they entered.

'Musa, give me your gum,' said Hourieh.

They walked into the hall. 'Could you please go over to the lounge where he will meet you.'

'Is Katarena around?' said Hourieh.

'No.'

The man opened the doors to a room which Rebwar had never been in. It had an arrangement of groups of white sofas, which made it hard to choose where to sit. It sort of reminded Rebwar of tribal leaders' tents where different groups sat in a hierarchy of importance. He hadn't thought Bijan had any nomadic blood in him. They sat down silently on the group of sofas closest to the door. The room was vast, more of a conference hall than a lounge. The dominant colour was white but gold adorned the corners and ornaments. It was a palace fit for a sultan.

'What if he sends us packing? We should find a ticket back home, you know.'

'Wife, this is not the time.'

Rebwar went over to the large windows. They towered over him. Through them could be seen a perfectly manicured garden in which each bush seemed to have a purpose. The door to the lounge clicked open and Bijan shuffled in.

'My friends, what brings you here?'

'Major, I am sorry to bother you. Do you have time for us? And I'm sorry about...'

'Always, always! Ahh so good to see you, Hourieh and your lovely son too. What a surprise.' Bijan greeted them by kissing their heads. 'Tea?' And they all nodded. 'Sit, sit. Tell me what brings you here. It's not my birthday.' He rang a bell to order the tea.

The all politely smiled and laughed.

'You know what happened at the tower?'

'Terrible, such a scandal. Heads shall roll.' He pointed to the ceiling with his index finger.

'They have evicted us from our tower.'

'You lived there?'

'No, in another one just north of here.'

Bijan nodded as Rebwar continued.

'And there are some men after us. Nothing I can't sort out but, I hate to ask...'

'I told you to keep away from them. What is the matter with this country? People don't respect their elders... it's with free democracy that you get chaos. They need a strong man to restore order. You see all this mess around us arguing about who should decide? They need structure, I tell you. What are they doing with this woman in charge? You can't trust her.'

Hourieh and Rebwar nodded politely. 'So, soldier, do you need my help?'

'We need refuge. It would only be for a few days. Until this mess blows over. I am sorry to ask, it is not my right to do this.'

'My friend, this is the least I can do. Hourieh's father – may he rest in peace - would expect it of me. I am just a miserable old man with bad habits. Rebwar, let's have a drink in my study. Talk old times.'

For a moment, Rebwar wanted to say 'no' and get back out there. But he had to at least give the old man some of his time. He didn't particularly like nostalgia and certainly not Bijan's brand of it, glorifying the war and the old regime. He might have forgotten the horrors, but Rebwar hadn't. They both got up.

'If you need anything Hourieh, just call Charles.' He ushered Rebwar to the door, 'come, come, this way. I have some new things to show you.' He called back to Houreih as they left the room. 'And, you can ask him to bring in your luggage.'

'Is that the butler's name, Charles?' Rebwar said to Bijan.

'Oh, no, no, I call them all Charles, it's easier to remember...'

Hourieh, called after them. 'Thank you, Bijan. Oh how's Katarena? I miss her.'

He stopped mid shuffle in the hall. 'Ah, yes, as they say, it's complicated. She's back in Ukraine with her family. The government flew her out. Like she was some terrorist.'

'I'm sorry to hear. Must be a difficult time.'

Bijan turned around got a silk hankie out of his pocket and blew his nose, before moving off again.

'Musa, say thank you.' said Hourieh nudging her son in the ribs.

'Thank you, sir.' But Bijan and Rebwar had already disappeared into another room.

———

Rebwar sat on one of the three big leather chairs in front of the imposing desk on which was a collection of miniature models of various tanks and a large box of cigarettes. Bijan motioned for him to help himself.

'I'm trying to give up,' Bijan said.

Rebwar got up and stopped for a moment; he wasn't helping the old man.

'Oh, take one, don't worry about me.'

Rebwar took one and used the huge, round lighter. It was set in red marble and had the weight of a hand grenade. 'Thanks for letting us stay here. I owe you one.'

'What are friends for? So, you say you are in trouble?'

'Some crooks that I'm not allowed to investigate or arrest. They are in the human trafficking business. And made it legitimate by buying HR companies. I got a job working for them. Hey, I've even got an alter ego called Amir. Can you imagine? He's got a green card. He can get free health care and everything.'

Bijan took out a packet of gum and chewed one. 'Nicotine gum, *Salām! khasté nabāshee.*[1] So who put you up for this job?'

'Plan B. Same as last time. But this time they've decided not to pay my advance fees. Can you believe it? A criminal organisation that is dictating cost-saving tactics. And I still have no idea who the hell they are.'

'I must say, none of my contacts have heard of them. It's the most secret secret organisation I have come across, and I have seen a few in my time. This can't be run by the government. They are incapable of keeping secrets. It's a gossip station. Coffee?'

Rebwar nodded, hoping for some of the sweets that usually came with such refreshments. Bijan rang the bell.

'What are you going to do?'

'I've been on the back foot throughout this job. Like I'm

chasing ghosts. Although I have finally seen them. I think. People trafficking that's what I've found.'

'A ghost? Hah! You are clutching at straws!'

'And it's the same guy that was behind the organ trafficking. That bent policeman O'Neil he's involved.'

'He likes to trade things, this man. Is he Jewish?'

'Country boy, I think. But he's got an Irish name and uses Gipsy curses to keep his men in check.'

'Look... you need to bring out the enemy. Lure him with something. That's what we did before. Make a trap. You need to take the initiative. Have you got something on him? Family? Something he cares about? That's where it hurts.'

'He has a girlfriend that works with him.'

'Perfect, kill her...'

Rebwar shook his head.

'Too far? ... How about torture? Hell, you could kidnap her?'

'Kidnap?' Rebwar moved forward to the edge of the seat cushion.

'You need to get him to come to you. Take something that he cares for, then you'll have him by his balls.'

The door opened and Charles came in with the coffee and the sweets. Bijan knew Rebwar too well. Charles laid the tray on the desk. Rebwar could see the whole room reflected in the silver coffee pot. Charles lifted it with his white gloves and poured the black hot liquid. As soon as he had tended to Bijan, he excused himself. Before Rebwar could get a sip in or choose a sugary delicacy from the tray, Bijan's bony finger pointed towards a cabinet.

'Get me a whisky.'

Rebwar got up and opened the shiny wooden doors. Inside were six engraved crystal glasses and a couple of decanters with different coloured liquids. He looked back at Bijan.

'The one at the back. It's an Octomore.'

Bijan took out one of the heavy tumblers, removed the glass stopper from the decanter and poured a measure. He could smell the smoky, oily liquid.

'The smokiest whisky in the world. See, I don't need to smoke, just drink this. And, No, I'm not supposed to be doing that either. But a man needs his vices to live. Have one.'

Rebwar poured himself one and brought the two glasses over to the desk. They clinked them. Rebwar tasted it. It was an explosion of fire and smoke. His mouth and nostrils filled with the escaping gasses. Bijan nearly coughed.

'Cask strength. You can't beat that. Like a cleanser.' Bijan sat down in his chair and a smile filled his wrinkled face.

'You've been back to the homeland?' Rebwar asked, his mouth still burning.

Bijan shook his head. 'My daughters went to Turkey to have a holiday there. You can have fun there. I went to join them, or rather, to pay for their shopping. And you?'

'I got a postcard from Farouk. He was in India, or so the postcard said. Have you heard from him?'

'Just rumours that he's working for a syndicate based in Baku the new wild west... You say India? I've heard Chabahar is new trade route for the Indian market.'

'So it's true.' Rebwar took another sip of his drink. He looked at the sweets. His mouth was still processing the storm of alcohol. Farrouk was back to his old ways and a fully fledged gangster. He was now wondering when he'd turn up.

'Take, take!' Bijan waved his hand towards the delicate sweets on the tray.

Rebwar lifted the plate and offered it to Bijan, but he just showed his empty glass. Rebwar went to refill it. 'So I should kidnap his woman? And then what?' And for a moment Rebwar thought of asking about Katarena, who was the elephant in the room, but he preferred to let it stay unobserved.

'Of course. That's why he does what he does. He's a gangster, what he's going to run to the police.' Bijan laughed.

'Betty, she is his MD and the one who got Amir the working permit. Should have asked her to get one for his friend, Rebwar.' He gave a laugh.

'Oh, don't worry about that Visa. I'll buy you one if you are so desperate. But I know you don't want to be indebted to me. I know this about you.'

Rebwar came back with the filled glass and smiled. He took the sweet he had his eye on, a honey and almond one. He let the pleasure sink in before saying yes.

'So, my friend... you need to think like a criminal. It's not that different, you just need to commit the crime and not try to work out how it was done. And you're not trying to get away with it are you?' He suddenly pointed to the desk at the model tanks that covered most of it. 'You like my tanks? I got them made. Just need to colour them in the right unit colours.'

Rebwar picked up a Willy's jeep with an anti-tank gun mounted on it. It brought back memories of the Operation Undeniable Victory where human waves had broken the Iraqi defences. They had used the jeeps to herd people into positions. He still wondered how he had survived that day.

'I'm making a replica of the battle. Come this way.'

FORTY-TWO

It was two in the morning, and Rebwar had relied on the Prius's electric motors to sneak up the driveway to the front of Betty's house. He and Geraldine had been around since 11:00 pm making sure O'Neil didn't come back to stay the night. Initially, he'd wanted to carry out this operation on his own, but Geraldine insisted that it was her job too. It was unfinished business. She'd also been doing some digging around on Betty Gardner. Byways' rented the house for her and she was on their payroll as head of HR, thirty-seven and single. Worked for a few supermarkets and recruitment companies. A pretty clean record that didn't fit in with the rest.

Apart from Grenfell tower, Rebwar had never worked with Geraldine, side-by-side, and this raid had to be slick and professional. Neither of them had kidnapped anybody. If he was alone, at least it was only himself he could blame if it went wrong. Also, she liked to talk things through. There was no time for that. Geraldine wanted revenge but refused to use her warrant card to arrest Betty. This would have made things much simpler, but Geraldine wanted to keep her job, which made Rebwar laugh.

The side gate to the garden was unlocked, and they both sneaked in. The patio door had a simple lock on it, at least it wasn't one of those latches that meant he had to break the window. It took him less than a minute to open it. As they put their black balaclavas over their faces, a wave of hot air escaped from the sliding door. The large room was dark and they shone their torches around inside. It was a large kitchen dining area.

Keeping their torches low to the floor, they made their way upstairs. Rebwar took the lead, walking slowly on the carpet, making sure not to make any noise. The new house still had a few creaking floorboards and the walls seemed thin and flimsy. They made their way up the hallway and came to a door. Rebwar shone his light on it and made eye contact with Geraldine to keep watch behind them. He opened it to find a single bed and a small wardrobe, the guest room he supposed. Geraldine opened the next door while Rebwar kept watch; the hinges squeaked. It was the bathroom. Suddenly a shaft of light appeared from under one of the doors at the far end of the corridor. They had to move fast. Rebwar walked quickly to the door with Geraldine close behind him. He gave her a count of two and burst through the door. Betty was halfway out of her bed when she locked eyes with Rebwar. She froze like a wild animal caught in a car's headlights. And then she screamed. Rebwar got to her quickly and grabbed her mouth, but she bit into his hand. He swore and let go, she'd drawn blood. Geraldine rushed forward and caught Betty with a hard slap around her face. She kept slapping, mainly to shut her up as Rebwar got the gaffer tape out, ripped some off and managed to get it over her mouth. Her face was smeared with his blood.

He pulled her up off the bed, spun her around, and cable tied her hands. Her feet were kicking out at anything. Rebwar pushed her back down and tried to grab her legs. One hit Geraldine in her chest but she managed to grab it. Rebwar caught hold of the other and tied them together. Rebwar turned her over. Her skin was all bloodied. His hand was still bleeding from the bite and he went to the bathroom to find something to patch it up. Betty was still struggling on the bed, her breathing erratic, snot and tears covering her face. Beneath the gag she tried to scream and shout at them. Geraldine took a minute to get her breath back, which seemed to calm Betty down. A couple of deeps thumps reverberated in the house as Rebwar came back to the room. Geraldine looked at him quizzically.

'Plumbing,' said Rebwar. 'I heard it last time I was here.' More dull thuds.

Geraldine walked onto the landing. 'Are you sure?' She said. Rebwar grabbed Betty and made her stand up.

'Hey, over here.' Geraldine stood in front of another door. 'It's locked.'

Rebwar tried to open it. His efforts were followed by another series of knocks coming from inside. After a couple of attempts Rebwar managed to kick down the door. Geraldine flicked the light switch. A young teenage girl was standing by her bed. Her bright red curly hair partly covered her freckled face. Her brown eyes were wide with fear.

Rebwar turned to Betty. 'Who is she?'

Geraldine went over to the girl and talked calmly to her. 'Hey it's OK, we're not going to hurt you.'

'Help me! I've... Please let me go...' The girl cried.

She ran out of the room and down the stairs. They went after her, leaving Betty to hop after them. The girl was dressed only in a thin shirt and shorts and desperately tried to open the locked front door. Rebwar and Geraldine approached her slowly. 'It's OK, we want to help you.' She shouted at them to keep away. From above them came another loud thump. Rebwar signaled to Geraldine to go and see what it was. The girl took her chance and rushed past Rebwar. He caught the sleeve of her shirt, but couldn't keep hold of the material and it slipped from his grasp. She ran towards the kitchen and conservatory area, Rebwar followed her. The room was in darkness aside from the moonlight creating a blue glow around the girl who was in silhouette but was holding something which glinted in the darkness. Rebwar came in, felt around the wall for a switch and the scene was flooded with light. The girl took one of the kitchen knives from the block on the island. It was long and thin, she looked terrified as she waved it towards him.

'Stay away from me!' she said, her hands shaking.

'Please put the knife down.'

'Fuck you! Do you think I'm dumb?'

'No. No, I don't... think about it. We're here to help.' Rebwar thought of taking off his balaclava and dismissed the idea.

'Fuck off! You're one of them. Let me go!'

Rebwar stepped closer, increasing the pressure on her. She probably hadn't stabbed anyone in her life. 'I'm going to take the knife away. And then we can talk. OK?'

'No! Stay back. Back!' Her hands kept shaking. She swiped the knife at Rebwar. She was distracted by looking for an escape route and was feeling around behind her with one hand and struggling to hold on to the knife with the other.

'It's OK, just tell me your name? I'm sure you've never stabbed anyone'

'There's always a first time. Who are you? Why...' She continued to step back, back around the large kitchen island. 'Don't! Stay back! Stay.' But Rebwar kept advancing towards her. Tears ran down her face. 'Please, stay back.'

Rebwar passed the gas stove and took a cloth that was hanging close by. He switched one of the gas rings on and put the flannel over it.

'What are you doing?' Her voice trembled with fear.

The cloth was now alight and Rebwar swung it around as if he was going to do some kind of circus trick. But he was trying to control its burn. 'Let go of the knife.'

'You're... You're crazy. Don't! No. Put it out!'

Rebwar swung around towards her. She screamed. He threw the flannel at her feet and she jumped back and dropped the knife. Rebwar grabbed it and stamped on the burning rag just as the smoke alarm pierced the air. The girl backed into a chair that was behind her and fell onto it shaking uncontrollably. Rebwar dropped the knife and cloth in the sink and grabbed the girl's arm. She pleaded with him to let her go. He moved into the hallway with her as Betty, her feet still tied, hopped down the stairs with Geraldine close behind her. Betty was wearing a dressing gown by now and had stopped trying to scream, she was exhausted from fighting her various restraints. Rebwar took the shivering girl over to one of the sofas and grabbed a throw that was draped over it for her to cover herself. The smoke alarm was still piercing their eardrums. Geraldine and Rebwar looked at each other. Time for phase two of the plan.

FORTY-THREE

Betty and the girl were gagged, tied up and lying across each other on the back seat of the car under a blanket. Rebwar and Geraldine just exchanged quick glances. It was as if each one wanted to say something but was waiting until they got to the safe house. The lit streets were quiet, with the odd taxi or night bus around. At 2:54 am, they arrived at the Green Man pub in Hatfield just off the A1000 by a 1960s residential block and some small shops. The pub was closed and boarded up. Weeds grew through the cracked tiles. Rebwar parked around the back and they both got out and looked around for any sign of movement. It was deserted. They put their balaclava's back on, opened the car door and dragged out their captives, hauling them down the little alley and into the pub's back entrance.

Rebwar and Geraldine had spent some time trying to find a suitable pub that had closed down. There were a few around and they were spoilt for choice. People weren't going out as much as they had before: financial crisis, austerity, Brexit... you could pick any one of them. This pub had very little security, which made it easy to break into and there were no cameras around. They took their captives down into the cellar where the beer kegs had been kept. It was damp and cold. They sat them on chairs and tied them to the frames with zip ties. They closed the door and went upstairs.

The bar was dusty and all around were signs of water damage. The carpets were rotting, and what was left of the furniture was coming apart. They took some stools by the bar. Rebwar switched on an electric lantern. They took off their balaclavas and stared at each other for a moment that seemed to last a lifetime. Neither wanted to start with the awkward question, each waited for the other to break the silence.

'I'm sorry,' Rebwar said. 'I shouldn't have involved you in this stupid plan, and—'

'I agreed to it. And what's wrong? She's a criminal, guilty ... whatever else she's doing.'

'The girl... she's only young.' Rebwar shrugged his shoulders and lit up.

Geraldine gestured for one. 'What the hell was she doing there? Is it their daughter?'

Rebwar handed her a cigarette. 'It's the reason I left Iran. A child was killed in a botched operation...*Kessaftha*'[1]

He looked away, trying to suppress the painful memories. 'I shouldn't have agreed, just as I didn't agree with Farouk. I had a choice...' Rebwar walked away from the bar and let out another series of swear words. 'We should take the girl to Hourieh. Somewhere safe.'

Geraldine shook her head. 'Think about it... we need the whole package, whatever that package is, for O'Neil or whatever that fucker's name is. And this might be the best way to get him. Let's call him.' She walked back down to the cellar.

'Hey! Your balaclava!'

'Oh, she knows who we are. And then she can give the full picture to her cunt of a boyfriend.'

Rebwar could feel his hand shaking, his trauma coming back to him. He clenched his fist and followed Geraldine. A single bare light bulb lit the dark musty cavernous space. Old, dusty and sagging bricks surrounded them. Some old battered beer kegs were lying around. Betty stared at them as they approached as if trying to work out what was going to happen. The girl looked at Betty. The harsh light made their faces look even more gloomy and tired.

Geraldine had taken the liberty of bringing Betty's handbag from the house and now took out a mobile phone from inside. 'Is this your phone? Give me your finger.' Betty's hand instinctively clasped itself into a ball. 'I'll fucking break one if you don't.' The girl mumbled through the gaffer tape. Betty closed her eyes and shook her head. Geraldine ripped off a strip of the gaffer tape they had used to tie them to the chairs, and clamped it over Betty's nose. Her eyes bulged out at the realisation that she now couldn't breathe. 'Give me your finger.' Her hand unclenched and Geraldine took her small, manicured finger and put it on the *home* button of the phone. It opened, and she ripped the tape from Betty's nose, allowing her to take a deep breath.

Geraldine scrolled through the phone. 'Oh, how sweet. Look!'

Rebwar looked at the screen. It said *Honey pots who is going to talk to this shit bag? Xxx.* 'Is that his number,' he said.

'I think you're right. Sure you can paint him a pretty picture, hey? Bitch! And who is she? Geraldine pointed at the girl. 'Call him, OK?' And she ripped the gaffer tape from Betty's pretty soft mouth. A red mark soon appeared on the soft white skin.

'Fucking bitch! He'll kill you both! He'll... He'll beat the living shit out of you.'

'Hey! Who's the girl? And you've got nothing to negotiate with.'

'She's just a bad apple.' Betty gave a fake smile. 'Call him.'

Rebwar dialled the number and a picture of O'Neil's smiling face filled the phone's screen. He held it next to Betty's ear. It rang, and each ring bounced off the dull walls. Just when they all thought she was going to have to leave a message he picked up.

'Hey, babe... What's the crack? Missing me already?' A moment of silence and she breathed in. 'Are you all right?' She swallowed and looked at Geraldine and Rebwar. 'Hey, I, I... Rich I'm in trouble. Can you track my number?' Geraldine and Rebwar looked at each other. It was a valid point. They were going to have to work this scenario quickly. 'Amir and some bitch have kidnapped Daisy...' Betty swallowed. 'And me!'

'Fuck off...' Said O'Neil coughing. 'Get that fucker on the phone.'

Rebwar shook his head.

'He doesn't want to.'

'Well, he should... Who the fuck does he think he is trying to fuck with me. He's...' He coughed harder.

'Are you all right? Get some water.'

'Get him on that fucking phone.'

Geraldine covered the mic on the phone with her hand. 'Tell him we want to meet him.'

'The bitch says that they want to meet.'

'Who's the bitch?'

Betty looked up at Geraldine. Rebwar wondered if she would give the game away. It was a little advantage they had, but he also knew she was filled with anger and revenge. It would make her feel great to give that away.

'Just *the bitch* will do for now.' Said Geraldine.

'Describe her to me?'

'She's a fat bitch with...'

Geraldine slapped her face and Rebwar dropped the call. 'OK, text from now on.' The phone rang again. He was calling back.

'Who is Daisy?' said Rebwar.

'None of your fucking business. Amir, I know about you, and you're going down.'

Rebwar ripped the tape off Daisy's face. She gave a little cry. 'It's the least painful way. Sorry, who are you?'

'Don't tell them anything.' Betty snapped. 'Do you understand? Nothing. They are going to kill you.'

Daisy tossed her head back to flick the red curly hair off her face. 'What's going on? What's going to happen to us? I want to see my daddy?' Her question hung in the damp, stale basement. Betty tried to look away. Daisy's face froze. Betty didn't want to answer her questions.

The phone kept ringing and the text message notification kept buzzing away.

'Switch it off.'

Geraldine grabbed Betty's face to hers. 'Like Amir said, who the fuck is she? Have you been lying to her?'

Rebwar grabbed her cheeks and looked into her eyes. 'Where does O'Neil live?' He squeezed her harder. 'Where?'

'Come on... Amir let's leave her to stew here. And see if Daisy will talk more.' Geraldine undid the tape from her chair and helped her to stand.

'Daisy listen to me... OK? Don't tell them anything.

Rich is going to sort all this out. Be a brave girl, like mummy says, OK? It's all going to be all right. Just don't tell them anything otherwise they will hurt us all.'

Geraldine taped her face again. The three of them left the room and went upstairs.

FORTY-FOUR

The bar had a thick white layer of dust and the carpet-like floor fabric was worn and torn. Geraldine made Daisy sit on one of the sagging benches. She crossed her legs and looked down at the floor.

'Drink?' said Geraldine.

Daisy looked up as if she had asked a stupid question. 'My dad is going to break your necks.'

'And who is he?'

Rebwar lit a cigarette and brought over a chair to sit on. He looked at her face. It had no features that resembled either Betty or O'Neil. He wondered why he hadn't spotted that before.

'And what's his problem?' Daisy said to Geraldine.

'Daisy, who are your parents?' Rebwar said.

'No, I'm not answering either of you. You've kidnapped me and that's a crime.'

'Do you know that Betty and Richard are criminals?' Geraldine said.

Daisy twitched nervously, her eyes not fixing on

anything, just gazing around. Rebwar tapped the ash off his cigarette onto the floor.

'That's disgusting, you should clean it up,' said Daisy.

Rebwar smiled and drew another puff from his cigarette. He blew smoke into her face. She grimaced and made some outraged sounds as if she was in danger of being asphyxiated.

'Daisy, we can help you.' Geraldine said. 'I'm a cop, and we can find your parents.'

For a moment, Daisy studied them. 'Fuck off, and I'm a superhero. My parents will come and save me. Mum and Dad. Only I want to go home and be with them...'

'You call them Mum and Dad?' Rebwar leaned back into his chair.

'Yeah, and call them now.'

'We want to help you.'

Daisy looked at Rebwar like she had been caught out.

'Have they kidnapped you?'

'Piss off! I'm not saying no more.'

Rebwar got up and signalled to Geraldine to follow him to the other side of the pub.

'We need to use her to get to O'Neil. Also we can't stay here too long. What shall we say to him?'

'Can I get one?' Rebwar handed a cigarette to Geraldine. 'Any great ideas.'

Rebwar shook his head. 'We need to work on Betty.'

Rebwar took out his phone and brought up some photos he had taken at their house. He flicked through them. 'You know, not one photo of Daisy at their home. That's why I didn't see this coming. She's like a ghost.' He stopped at a photo of O'Neil and Betty together. He passed it over to Geraldine, who looked at it and shrugged her shoulders. 'What about that boat?'

Geraldine used her fingers to zoom into it. *The Gipsy.* She looked up. 'A canal boat! And you know that's probably his hideout. We need to ask her where it is. Hey, Daisy, have you ever been on a canal boat?'

Daisy looked at them. 'What about them? Smelly things. Damp.'

Rebwar shook his head. 'Let's ask Betty.' And he zip-tied Daisy to the bench.

'Hey, where are you going? No! Untie me now! Hey, fuck, did you hear me? Untie me now! I want to see my mother!'

———

The old door creaked open. Betty's mascara had run down her face. She looked tired and empty. Geraldine went over to her and grabbed her hair. '*The Gipsy?* The canal boat; tell me about it.' And she ripped the tape off Betty's face.

Betty took some deep breaths and looked at her with an air of disgust. 'Where's Daisy?'

'She's not yours.' said Rebwar, who was now walking around her.

'She is! Bring her to me!'

'Where is the boat? Is that where he's hiding? Is that his hideout?'

'You'll never find it, never! He's too clever for you two dumb idiots. Bring Daisy...'

Rebwar and Geraldine shook their heads.

'He's going to fucking find you.' She laughed.

'Did you spend your holidays on that boat. With Daisy?' Betty's eye's searched for Rebwar. 'Like a family? What do you want with her?'

'Like I said she's a rotten apple.'

Geraldine slapped her face. 'Stop lying.'

'Bitch! I'm so going to kick your ugly face. And you Amir... you're never going to see your family ever again.'

'And you think I'm Amir? Betty, Betty you're out of your depth here. You're just a little cog in a huge scam. What are you doing with Daisy? Money? She looks up to you, doesn't she? You've had her for so long that she doesn't know who's who anymore. We can find out who she is and we'll find O'Neil. Or Peter Butterworth, that's his real name.'

'Fuck off! Lies all lies.'

Geraldine rested her left leg on one of the chairs and leaned in. 'I've done some digging, Betty Gardner. Born in Ealing in 1980. Worked in Tesco's, Safeway and other low paid jobs. Ended up in recruitment and slept with her boss and got fired... How I my doing?' Betty looked away. 'Now your boyfriend O'Neil... or Peter.' Geraldine walked around Betty. 'Undercover cop and dismissed for GBH, racist conduct, drunk whilst on service and now involved in human trafficking. Oh... was involved in organ smuggling too.'

Betty laughed. 'You bunch of amateurs. Not scamming me. Go on, call them...'

'Who's them? Byways? Plan B?' Geraldine slapped her again. 'Each time you lie, I'm going to slap you. Where's O'Neil?'

'Fuck off, bitch! Is that all you can do.' Betty spat at her but missed.

'Wayne and Dental Mike?' said Rebwar.

'They are coming here to kick your ugly faces. You better watch your backs.'

Geraldine slapped her again.

'Did you know Wayne killed Kim Dong? Was Kim

about to give the game away? Found some stray Syrians running Soho?'

'That was your beef. Heard you fucked that up, Amir.'

Rebwar stretched his arms above his head. 'So, you knew about that?'

Betty shook her head.

'Where's the boat?' said Geraldine.

Rebwar grabbed one of her fingers and unlocked the phone. Geraldine slapped Betty before she could bite Rebwar. He scrolled through her text messages. 'Just a matter of time till I find it.' Betty looked up at Rebwar her eyes searching him.

'You're wasting your time.' said Betty.

'The Wheatsheaf? It comes up a few times.' said Rebwar reading her text messages.

'Just a local where I live. Daisy, she needs her medicine. She's not well.'

Geraldine slapped her again. 'The King's Lock.'

Betty's eyes locked onto Rebwar.

Rebwar passed the mobile to Geraldine who scrolled through the messages. 'Am I getting close? And this one was sent last week. Sure we can find out where that is. Have you kidnapped her? Where did you meet O'Neil? How long have you gone out with him? Do you love him? Betty, look at me. Listen to me. Concentrate.'

'No! Listen to *me*. Daisy, she needs you, right?' said Rebwar turning her head to him.

Betty's head turned between them, trying to follow their questions. 'Stop, stop. He's, he's...'

'He's not here. Come on, Betty, tell us where he is. Otherwise, we are going to have to harm Daisy and it'll be your fault. She needs medicine, you just said. What kind? What's wrong with her. Come on, tell me. I can help her.'

'Betty, listen to him. He can help you; what's wrong with her?'

'I... I don't know. I don't know.'

'Yes, you do know. Tell us! We can help you. Is O'Neil hitting you? Does he abuse you? He's got previous.' Geraldine slapped her again and grabbed her face. 'Do you like a bit of rough? Is that what you like. Getting talked down to? We can give you more of that. My friend here has tortured many people.

'I... I.' Betty looked down at her feet.

'Listen to us, Betty, we can help you. Help Daisy. Take her home her *real* home. We know she's not yours. Do the right thing.' Rebwar flicked through more of her text messages. 'Is she?'

'No. Stop. She's not.' Betty said. 'I just agreed to help O'Neil. We got her from a foster family. It's O'Neil's... or... so he said...' And she cried.

'How long has this being going on? What does Daisy know?'

Betty looked at Rebwar and took a moment before replying like she was choking on the information. 'It's her dad I think... O'Neil knows him... It was a favour. He's away on some business trip.'

'Who is he?'

'O'Neil's friend? I didn't really want to know. She needs love and a family. It's what we talked about. Planned...' Betty sobbed.

'What would you know about that?' said Geraldine.

Betty's phone rang; with O'Neil's face flashed over its screen, Rebwar passed it to Geraldine. She shrugged her shoulders at him.

'Ask him where we should meet. We can always change

it.' Rebwar ripped off a strip of tape and stuck it over Betty's mouth.

'Yes,' said Geraldine.

'Who's this?'

'Your worst fucking nightmare, dickhead!'

For a moment, Rebwar was about to grab the phone off her. But he didn't want to give his identity away, not just yet. It was still a surprise he wanted to keep. He tried to get Geraldine's attention in an attempt to calm her down.

'And we want to meet.'

'I should have guessed, Geraldine... OK! But I want them both unharmed or I will kill you and that darkie bastard you hang around with.'

'We want money.'

'Of fucking course you do. But you ain't getting any.'

'Million shithead, in two drop offs.'

O'Neil hung up.

Rebwar and Geraldine stared at each other and looked at Betty. 'He doesn't value you much, does he?' Geraldine said.

'He's stalling. We need to find that boat now before they find us.'

Geraldine went over to Betty and unlocked her phone with her index finger. Rebwar watched Geraldine tap and flick away on the screen. 'Here, I've found it. Look.' She showed Rebwar a map. 'When you take a picture, some phones add a GPS tag and link them to a map. These photos in the pub were taken along the Union Canal. I'm sure the boat is along there. We should go there and see it.'

FORTY-FIVE

Geraldine and Rebwar had decided to split up to search for the canal boat. They knew that they had to find something on O'Neil to get an advantage. They couldn't use Betty's phone as there was the possibility that he could track it. It was 5:30 am and they had found a little quiet car park by a towpath close to the village of Boxmoor. Geraldine had trawled some media sites on the drive out. There was a pub called the Three Horseshoes, where a lot of selfies had been taken. Dotted around the area were moorings for Canal boats. It was the best place to start looking. Rebwar had gone on foot and Geraldine had taken the car with the two hostages and went east as far as a little bridge that crossed the canal.

———

She found a drive with a gate leading to a parking place and left the car there. The only sound was the chirping of birds, with a few sparrows shrieking above. The dense bushes and trees hid the car well enough. If someone did drive by they wouldn't take a second glance; it just looked like someone had parked there for the night, or that's what she told herself. The back windows were tinted, so unless someone shone a torch in they wouldn't see Betty or Daisy, who were both tied up. The sun had just risen and its rays were lighting up the trees. It was a beautiful dark blue sky and she could smell the fresh air, a blend of sweet and soothing scents.

Geraldine went over the old stone bridge that crossed the canal and spotted a row of moored boats along the towpath. Past the bridge on the left was an unmarked trail that led to the canal footpath. She went back under the bridge to check out the boats. There were five of them, three on her side of the canal. None of them was the one she was looking for. There was another up by a lock. She walked over to it. In front of her was a straight stretch of the canal with two towpaths flanking it and boats moored on the opposite bank. She tried to read the names and realised it would be easier to cross the canal as not all of the names were displayed in the same place. She used the little gangway over the wooden gate on the lock. In front of her was a large man. She recognised him instantly. It was Dental Mike. He and Little John had run her off the road. He smiled with his few remaining teeth.

Geraldine looked up, he was at least a head taller than her and twice the size. She had been trained to wrestle men down, but this wasn't a fair fight. If she'd had some martial art skills it might have helped, or maybe a mace spray. Better still, a gun. She remembered what Rebwar had done, but her reach wasn't far enough and she would probably miss.

'You're Geraldine, the ugly bitch. Where's Betty? Tell me and I might let you live.'

'And you are? I'm a police officer. We've got... the place crawling with cops.'

His huge frame lifted with his laughter. 'Try another one. Kidnapping? Don't think the cops are in on that. Bent. That's more your style.'

Geraldine stepped back onto the wooden planks. The lock was empty and water was seeping in through some of the gaps in the opposite gate. Dental Mike launched himself at her. She moved back, but he managed to grab her wrist. His hand clasped like a vice. Geraldine turned and pulled back to get away. She lost her balance and tripped. Dental Mike held on to her hand. She fell, missed the thin metal railing and landed flat onto the three wooden planks that formed the walkway. He fell on top of her, blocking her free hand under her back. His ugly face was next to hers. She could smell the sweat and musk.

'What now, bitch? You like it rough?' His weight was overpowering and she struggled to breathe. Still holding her arm out above her, he grabbed her throat with his free hand. He squeezed. 'Fancy a shag?'

She could feel his excitement. His eyes were filled with vicious energy. She tried to roll to free her arm. But he had spread her legs.

She whispered. 'Go on... I dare you.' He leaned in closer to listen to her and she bit his ear with all her force. He screamed and threw his head up cracking his head on the metal railing. Geraldine spat out the mouthful of ear which plopped into the canal.

'You fucking bitch!'

As the blood gushed down his neck, she brought her feet to her chest and with all her force kicked him in the guts. He didn't see it coming, and he fell. A splash, then a moment of silence, a visceral growl, a scream and frantic splashing. Geraldine took deep breaths and filled her lungs. As she looked down, the pleading noise became more and more gurgled. Water splashed everywhere, he was like an animal panicking. She got up and fell again then she saw the lifebuoy a few feet away. She grabbed it off the stand and with all her force threw it into the basin. It hit the stone wall and fell in not far from Dental Mike. But it was too late: his struggle was slowing; his head was well underwater and only his reaching hands showed above the water. The desperate floundering slowed and his body slipped away. For a moment, she looked at the ladder. Should she attempt a rescue? He would have killed her without a thought. And how would she bring him up, he was too huge? She stood there feeling guilt and failure. *Get a grip woman, they are out there to get you!* She looked around. It was calm again: birds singing, lush green trees swaying lazily in the cool wind. And there was no one else around.

She took out her phone and tried to ring Rebwar, her hands shaking with the adrenaline. Her call went to voicemail, and she swore. She looked around, saw nothing obvious that might incriminate her and turned back to the car. She tried to call him again and this time left a message. With the adrenaline slowly wearing off, the only words she could manage were 'call back.' As she turned into the little road, she saw that the car's passenger door was wide open. She ran over. The car was empty. They had gone. She looked frantically around, but they were nowhere to be seen, then she ran over to the road. She stood, pulling her hair back, trying to spot them. 'Shit, shit.' She ran back to the car and started the engine.

In her panic, she chose neutral and then drive, eventually she found reverse and made a few awkward turns until she could drive over the bridge. She drove along the single lane road past some large houses on her right. There were no signs of them. After the third house, she arrived at the main road. Again nothing. They couldn't have got far. What would they do? What would *she* do? Then she turned the car around and went back down the lane. She followed it slowly, glancing in each driveway and little path. Then it dawned on her that they might have had some help. The cut cable ties were lying on the back seat.

FORTY-SIX

Rebwar had followed the canal east towards London. He hadn't come across these waterways before and their beautiful tranquillity made an impression on him. Thick old trees lined the edges of the footpath with a few house gardens backing onto the water. It was a part of the countryside that he had never seen. He had scarcely been out of London. It was like something from a postcard or a magazine. The fresh smell of water was interrupted by the odd puff of fuel being burned. It was coming from some of the boats that were moored across the canal.

He scanned their names and carried on walking until he reached a lock. He quickly grasped the idea of it. Two sets of wooden doors and a basin in the middle. The water on one side was higher than the other. An ingenious way to make a boat descend or climb using the power of gravity. Rebwar knew of the Suez Canal, but that was a major seaway. This, he guessed, was where it was invented like most industrial breakthroughs. He passed the lock and the canal opened up to reveal a wide area where twenty or more barges were moored. Their noses were facing him and behind them was a yard with a few more long, thin barges propped up out of the water.

Rebwar stood there looking at the boats on the water. People were living in some of them. He could hear snoring coming out of the one nearest to him. He scanned the plates on their bows. *Burt the Avenger, Mary, Finders Keepers*. He carried on walking along the path, which took him under a large railway bridge. Past it and around a bend, he came across another long stretch of canal that led to another lock. On the right-hand side, the green bank had opened up and led to the railway tracks. Rebwar could see that canal boating was a leisurely activity and a perfect way to hide off the grid. Apart from a few hippies you weren't too bothered by society. A perfect nomadic life, hidden away in an old forgotten world, like a parallel universe.

No wonder Geraldine hadn't found anything on O'Neil. He moved his hiding place around London with the ease of a swan. Each of the boat names offered something of their eccentric owners' characters, *Happy as a Pig, Rosie Dawn, Nick Nack*. As he got to the lock, one of the boats behind him turned on their engine. A cloud of blue and white smoke drifted over the still water. A train flashed by, its steel wheels making an ear-piercing shriek. By the speed of it, Rebwar could only catch a colourful red stripe. When he looked back at the boat, he froze for a moment. O'Neil was releasing it from its mooring. The boat was called *Fool's Gold*.

Rebwar darted behind some bushes and watched O'Neil. He revved the engine and left the mooring. The boat was going back towards the pub. The lazy noise of the diesel motor thumped away leaving a little wake behind. Rebwar waited for the boat to go round the corner and under the railway bridge before following. He would easily be spotted through binoculars, which O'Neil would surely have on board. Rebwar took out his phone and tried to call Geraldine, it went to voicemail. He called again and then left a message.

Rebwar jogged over to the bridge O'Neil had just navigated. He felt the years of smoking burning his lungs, each breath trying to get in as much oxygen as it could. The churned-up water left an easy trail for him to follow, although there wasn't anywhere he could go except towards the pub. And there was a small, single-track road bridge that could swing out of the way. For a moment, he wondered why O'Neil would be moving his boat? Wouldn't he be trying to find them? Why waste time moving his little home down the canal. It didn't make sense. Was he compromised?

As Rebwar got past the bridge and into the corner, he could see O'Neil in the boat. He had made it to a lock opposite a boatyard. Wayne was there too, helping him with the wooden gates. Rebwar hid behind some moored boats. But they were busy getting the boat through the lock. On the left of the towpath was a little lake. He had to either go forward or back, but he couldn't get around them. So he watched them. Then his phone vibrated in his pocket.

'Where have you been?'

'I've lost Betty and Daisy. And that bastard is dead.'

'What? But I can see O'Neil, and Wayne.' And then he realised what she'd said before that. 'Oh shit.' Rebwar caught a glimpse of Daisy on the boat. 'They are on O'Neil's boat. We need to meet up. Where are you? And who's dead?'

'In the pub car park. Where we parked. And the big ugly guy went for a dip.'

'Ah, OK. Stay put. I'll make my way there.' Rebwar

tapped his phone and brought up a Google satellite map of the area and studied it. Once the boat had cleared the lock, he could get over to the other side and use the map to make his way to the car park.

FORTY-SEVEN

Rebwar had made his way into the quiet gravel car park. It was surrounded by trees and shrubs which backed onto a few houses. And left the Prius across a couple of spaces as though it had been abandoned. Rebwar approached it and saw Geraldine sitting behind the wheel. She looked stunned. Rebwar opened the door. 'Are you all right?' She stared back at him blankly and a moment later turned around and put her feet out onto the gravel. She breathed heavily with each movement. 'What happened?'

She shook her head. 'They got away.'

'How? they...'

She looked up, angry again. 'I bumped into that shit-head. You know the ugly bloke.' She looked away.

'Dental Mike?'

Geraldine nodded.

'Did he free them?'

'No, no. He fell into the canal and drowned.' Rebwar came level with her. 'OK, I pushed him in... after I bit his ear off. But he was going to rape me. Why would he do that?'

'Geraldine you're in shock. Should we call the police?'

'I *am* the fucking police. That's what I told him, but it made no difference.'

'Yes, well, we've found O'Neil and Wayne now. We should call it in.'

'What? And let them get away with it. He'll just smooth talk himself out of it again, and we'll end up in the shit. Even Plan B didn't manage to get him did they?'

Rebwar stepped back and turned, looking around, waiting for something to come to him. Of course, she wanted revenge, it was all she wanted. 'Where's Betty?'

'They got away...'

And for a moment Rebwar felt a chill that made his breath stop. He opened the car's bottom glove box and took out the old Webley.

'Shit! That was—'

'Careless...'

He took out a handkerchief from his pocket and cleaned the barrel. Small dark red spots came off onto the white fabric. He split the gun to look into the revolving chambers. It had five rounds.

'Hey, Rebs,' whispered Geraldine.

Rebwar tensed.

'Just behind you - about five o'clock...' He turned his head around slowly and squinted towards some bushes. He shook his head at Geraldine.

'I think I saw Betty.' She said.

'The railway is behind? Yes?'

'Rebs, you go towards the road and I'll go over towards where I saw her. Casual - like we haven't seen her, yeah? Oh and don't lock the car door.'

He followed her instructions. He slipped the gun into his waistband and zipped up his jacket, his eyes darting around, looking for any movement. As he walked onto the road, he could see on his left the Three Horseshoes pub with its swing bridge and, on the right, a bridge with a narrow tunnel running under the train tracks. He went right and took the dirt track that ran behind the car park and beside a steep grassy embankment that led to the tracks. Geraldine appeared at the end of the track and shook her head. Rebwar backtracked and spotted Betty. She was opening the driver's door to his car. He took out his gun.

Geraldine hobbled back from the other side. Betty was inside the car opening all the storage compartments she could find then feeling above the sun visor obviously hoping to find some keys. Rebwar stood in front of the car, holding his gun. He motioned her to get out. Her eyes were mesmerised by his gun and followed it as a cat would a toy.

Geraldine lunged and grabbed her collar. 'Not a word. OK? Or...' She pointed at Rebwar's gun. 'He's trigger happy, as Wayne's man, Little John, found out.'

Betty's eyes darted between the two of them.

'Just nod or shake your head, right?'

Betty nodded.

'Are you alone?'

She nodded again.

Rebwar looked around him. Wondering what was going on that canal boat and why they weren't looking for Betty. And he and Geraldine. 'Did they release you?'

Betty shook her head.

'She ran away from me... and then I got lost.' said Betty, her eyes streaming.

Rebwar thought for a moment. 'So, it's either the police or we finish this ourselves.' His watch said it was 6:36 am. They had to do something soon, otherwise they would lose them, and someone would call the police. 'Can we trust her?'

'Do we have a choice?'

'I want O'Neil's head. He's a sick fuck,' said Betty.

Both of them looked at her in amazement. Rebwar studied her face wondering what had happened. Just a minute ago she was trying to run away. 'Who is Daisy?'

Betty's head dropped. 'Sir Merkenstand's little girl. He never came clean about it. Kept telling me that it was a need to know basis. Poor Daisy, she doesn't even know what happened to her father. He's...' She sighed. 'He was in a helicopter crash.'

'Who is Sir Merkenstand?' said Rebwar.

'Some big billionaire businessman that O'Neil knows. He's like... Was... an Uncle to him.'

'What happened?'

'OK enough of the sentimental stuff...' Geraldine said. 'We're running out of time... Let's get that fucker, OK?'

'What's in that boat?'

'It's his home. Nothing, really. You know the usual stuff.' Betty shrugged her shoulders.

'Guns?'

Betty shook her head. 'Drugs maybe.'

'OK,' said Geraldine. 'Let's go to the pub and confront them. Right?'

FORTY-EIGHT

Rebwar really wanted a few moments to think out the situation, but there wasn't time. Geraldine wanted her revenge, regardless of the cost. He wanted to stop her, let that rage calm down, let her think. Gut impulses didn't make sense and got you into situations. All three cautiously walked down the road towards the pub. It was a beautiful mild morning with not a cloud in the sky. Birds flying, feeding on the floating insects. Rebwar listened for any unusual sounds that would warn Wayne or O'Neil. He could just about hear the dull thud of a diesel engine. Apart from the odd train passing by behind them, nothing had come around. As they approached the bridge he told Geraldine and Betty to wait.

The bridge had been swung open, a section was across their path. Rebwar made his way past the barrier. On his right was the pub and on the left was a wooden fence and a bush. He poked his head out and saw O'Neil standing the at back of the boat, alone. He had cast off and was revving the engine to go past the bridge. Rebwar wanted to stay and see where the rest of them were. The boat came towards him, and he was going to be seen, so he turned back to the car park where Betty and Geraldine were waiting behind a tree.

'They're about to pass.' Rebwar took out his gun, grabbed Betty, swung her around and put the gun next to her head.

Her body tensed. 'Wait, what are you...?'

The boat slid past the bridge. O'Neil's face caught the scene and his gaze fixed on them. Geraldine hadn't followed and was waiting behind, out of sight. She had a plan of her own in mind, but hadn't shared it with her partner. O'Neil slammed the engine into reverse and the boat came slowly to a stop.

'Fuck me sideways, Ghorbani? I should have fucking guessed that you would be involved in this.' Betty turned her head and looked confused at hearing his name. Rebwar pressed the gun into her neck, and she shook with fear. 'And where's that bitch Geraldine?'

'Where's Daisy?' Rebwar countered, but O'Neil ignored the question.

'What's this all about? Money? Plan B?'

Rebwar looked around, trying to spot Wayne or any other henchman that he might have brought along. 'Hand over the girl.' Betty squirmed as he pressed the gun harder into her flesh.

The diesel engine slowly ticked over as O'Neil watched them. 'You're bluffing.' He scoffed, but Rebwar could see he was rattled. 'Who else is with you?'

'Richard, do as he says!' Betty shouted.

'Oh yeah? You wouldn't dare say anything, you're up to your neck in it. I'm not buying it.'

'Daisy!' shouted Rebwar. 'We've come to get you.'

O'Neil shook his head with a sardonic laugh. 'I think

you've miscalculated the situation. Put the gun down, OK? So, who's Amir?'

'It's him.' said Betty who was still shaking. 'He's Amir, he infiltrated the network. Betty's head dropped and she sobbed.

Rebwar now realised he was in more danger, even though Dental Mike was out of the way, he still hadn't accounted for Wayne. He slipped behind Betty and used her as a shield. O'Neil was most probably armed. 'You're a man down.' said Rebwar and shouted out towards the boat. 'Daisy, Daisy.'

Daisy popped her head out of the hatch and O'Neil grabbed her. She cried out in fear.

'Daisy! It's OK. We've come to get you.' Rebwar tried to reassure the girl.

O'Neil laughed. Rebwar saw Daisy's frightened eyes. She hit out and tried to get away from him. But he grabbed her throat and squeezed.

'Daisy! Listen to him. It's for the best. Please, Richard let her go.' Betty said.

'Calm the fuck down.' O'Neil's grip tightened and Daisy gave in. 'You know I don't really know what you've got to negotiate with here,' O'Neil said. 'Who sent you? It was Plan B wasn't it?'

'Richard my love, he's with that woman, Geraldine.'

O'Neil laughed harder and shook his head. 'I knew it.' He brought a pistol from his waist. Rebwar recognised it as a SIG P938, a favourite, 9mm and very easy to conceal. 'What are you going to do now?'

'Give me Daisy, and you can have your girl back.'

O'Neil smiled and pointed the gun at him. 'Or I could just shoot you? You think you're fast enough?'

'Do you want to risk that?'

'Look, she's more valuable than Betty, so I'm not ready to trade her.'

Rebwar watched O'Neil's face as he weighed up the situation. He could sense Betty's fear. 'It's not a time to bluff.'

Out of nowhere, Geraldine jumped onto the front of the boat. She had sneaked around behind the pub. O'Neil pointed the gun at her. The narrowboat had two access doors with a sunken platform at the bow. She crouched for cover.

'DS Smith! Glad you could join us for the cruise,' O'Neil said.

All of a sudden there was a loud crack. Like a whip, it jolted everyone's attention and was quickly followed by another. Rebwar felt Betty flop into him. He felt something warm and sticky in his right hand. He looked at her face. Her eyes were wide open and staring into the distance, empty and devoid of life. He struggled to keep her standing, but her lifeless body slid to the ground. He'd been lucky, the bullet had gone through her and missed him. A rifle, he thought - from behind the boat.

'Betty!' screamed Daisy. 'Oh my god, oh my god! She's been shot!'

Another crack and some wood splintered at the front of the boat. Rebwar guessed it had to be Wayne shooting at them. He rolled off the road and dropped below the swing bridge. There was a little ledge which was the foundation of the pivot. He was under the bridge and could see the side of the boat. He heard O'Neil shout to Wayne to stop firing. Daisy was hysterical, crying and shouting. From the boat came loud thuds, swiftly followed by the sound of a wooden door giving way. He guessed that Geraldine had made her way into the cabin through the front door. O'Neil revved the engine.

Rebwar stood up and saw O'Neil staring at Betty's body. He was clearly in shock and standing alone in the cockpit, not paying any attention to where the boat was heading. Wayne stood on the other side of the towpath, bent over, out of breath and holding a rifle. A tear ran down O'Neil's face, he turned to Wayne, pointed his pistol and emptied a clip. Wayne's body stumbled back as each bullet impacted, as if he was being punched into the ropes. He disappeared into the bushes behind him. The boat hit the wooden jetty just past the pub. The force pushed O'Neil over and he fell into the cockpit.

Rebwar lifted himself onto the road where Betty's lifeless body was lying. In a mad panic, Geraldine rushed out of the forward hatch with Daisy and both jumped ashore into a nearby garden. She shouted to take cover and dragged Daisy with her up the garden. Rebwar could sense her panic; he knew something was coming, but wasn't sure what. O'Neil stood up and looked into the boat's hatch. Rebwar turned around and ran over to the pub. He got to the corner and then was hit by a massive shockwave. It pushed his right shoulder around, made him trip and fall to the ground. O'Neil's body flew down the canal. The blast had thrown him past the bridge. The noise hit Rebwar like a hammer. Wooden splinters flew past him like aimless arrows. Pieces of boat bounced along the canal path.

Then there was silence. Like the sound had been turned off. Rebwar's ears rang as if an electrical speaker was malfunctioning. Of course, he knew all this, and what was coming next. He'd been in plenty of blasts back in the war in Iran. He tried to get himself up. He wanted to get to Geraldine. He fought to raise his body. It took a few tries, he kept falling back down as if a heavy sack of grain had been laid on his back, no pain, just a dullness. He was pretty sure he was OK. He managed to get to his knees and look behind him. Only burning wood and smoke was left. The boat had sunk. He stumbled towards the bridge and saw O'Neil's body face down in the canal.

Rebwar felt a hand grab his shoulder. He turned, ready to strike. It was Geraldine. Her mouth was moving but he still couldn't hear. Daisy was next to her, looking at the scene. Geraldine grabbed his hand and pulled him. They had to go. They made their way to the car park. People had come out to see what had happened. They must have looked like ghosts, with their dusty faces and spatters of blood and dirt. As they walked to the parked car, Rebwar's hearing was slowly coming back, but everything echoed like he was inside a glass bottle. Geraldine got behind the wheel and Rebwar helped Daisy into the back and swung himself into the front passenger seat.

FORTY-NINE

Rebwar waited for his hearing to recover. The pain of the blast started to catch up with his body. Geraldine drove quickly away from the scene, the car catching branches and hitting the verge. In their mirrors, they could see the thick black cloud rise above the trees. It had an eerie mushroom shape. She drove through the narrow lanes, avoiding the zombie-like people. Captivated by the sights, they ignored the passing car. At each gap between the bushes was an entrance to a house. The once deserted lane was busy with its residents. Geraldine carried on driving around them.

They joined the main road, and the sirens became louder and louder. A series of emergency vehicles passed them at high speed. Fire engines, ambulances, and police. They watched silently. Rebwar wondered if Daisy was about to scream or jump out, but she just stared at them, and they passed by. Geraldine's eyes danced around, looking at the mirrors. She kept driving, somewhere. Anywhere just to get away from the scene. To regroup.

The flow of sirens and flashing vehicles died down.

Rebwar's breath returned and he was about to ask where they were going.

'I think we're being followed,' Geraldine said.

He turned around to look and instantly felt pain. He took a deep breath.

'The black BMW.'

He leaned forward to look into the side mirror. At a roundabout, Geraldine took the first exit into a residential estate and followed a road that ended up looping back onto the one they had left. The BMW was still on their tail.

'Can you see its registration?' Geraldine asked.

'Too far,' said Rebwar.

'Daisy, do you recognise it?'

She shook her head. Geraldine carried on driving along the road till she came to a junction and took a right onto Cherry Tree Lane. The BMW followed them. Rebwar had a bad feeling they should have stayed on the main road. Geraldine realised her mistake and tried to make a turn at the next clearing. In front of them was a high metal gate. The BMW flashed its lights. Geraldine gave out a little sigh.

'Friends of yours?'

She shrugged her shoulders and stopped the car. Charlie and a young man in a dark suit stepped out of the car. He was tall, tanned and had dark, short cropped hair. Rebwar got out of the car too and saw that the man also had a gun. His piercing blue eyes studied both of them. Rebwar felt the Webley's wooden stock that protruded from his belt.

'Where's the girl?' said the tall man.

'Charlie, what's going on?'

'Plan B business my dear, strictly need to know.' Smiled Charlie tapping her nose.

'Who is she?' Geraldine nodded to Daisy.

'Like the lady said. Need to know. Bring her to me.' He

took some cable ties out of his pocket and handed them to Geraldine.

'Give me the girl and no smart moves.'

Rebwar looked around. Daisy cowered on the back seat, her red curly hair covering most of her face. He took out a pack of cigarettes and offered one to the man. He declined.

'Daisy...' Geraldine spoke quietly to her. 'I'm sorry. They are going to take care of you. And take you home.' She held Charlie's gaze. 'Isn't that right Charlie, she's going home?' There was no reaction and the man kept pointing the gun at them.

'We are unarmed,' said Rebwar.

The man went over to him, frisked him and took his gun. He smiled. 'You are now. Stand over there.' He pointed to a place close to the metal gate a few metres away from the car.

'Daisy, we need you to put these on.' Geraldine said. Daisy panicked and shuffled to the other end of the seat and tried to open the door. The child lock was on. 'I promise it'll be all right. We all work for the same people.' She turned to Charlie again. 'Can you stop with the shit James Bond routine and tell us what's going on.' Again, Charlie said nothing, but nodded to the man.

'Put your hands on the car and spread them.' The man frisked Geraldine and put his gun back into his shoulder holster.

Rebwar stood by smoking his cigarette, powerless to intervene. Daisy silently decided to get out of the car and let Geraldine put the zip ties around her hands.

'Ow! That hurts.'

'Sorry, old habits. Where are you taking her? At least tell me that.'

The man grabbed Daisy by the shoulder and put her

into the back of the BMW. He shut the door and came back over to them.

Charlie turned to Geraldine. 'What happened at the canal?'

Geraldine looked at Rebwar. 'Tell us what you're doing with the girl.'

'Taking her back into Plan B's custody and then where she belongs.'

'Richard O'Neil seemed to think she belonged to him.'

'Never heard of him.'

She tried the name Beckie had found. 'What about Peter Butterworth?'

The man tensed. 'That fucker? Where is he?'

'Lying face down in the canal with his cronies.'

'Should have happened years ago.'

'Why did he have the girl?' said Rebwar.

'Enough...' said Charlie.

'And Sir John Merkenstand? How does he fit into the picture?' Geraldine wasn't going to let it go.

The man approached Rebwar. 'May I?' He took a cigarette and Geraldine took one, too. 'In Northern Ireland Butterworth and I did some covert jobs during the troubles. Still, I never knew who he was really working for. As for Sir Merkenstand...' He shrugged.

'That would explain the pile of weapons I found on his boat, The Gipsy.' said Geraldine.

'And all the smoke back there. What was Butterworth up to?' The man dragged on his cigarette.

Geraldine paused for a moment. 'Well, nothing now. But he was running an HR business. In that all his resources were humans, trafficked into the country. A modern-day slaver you could say.' She looked over at Charlie. 'Like I told you.'

Charlie laughed. 'Ah, an entrepreneur. What can I say? Crooks always look for the next opportunity. Crime is booming. Keeps us in business. Right chaps, we need to deliver the package. Thank you for your assistance. I'll be expecting a report from you ASAP.' Charlie pointed at Geraldine as they walked towards the car.

'Hey! Look after her, right?' said Geraldine. 'She's just a teenager. She'll need help. Think she's got Stockholm syndrome... Seen some awful things.'

They got into the car, reversed out of the lane and drove off back to the main road.

'Fancy a drink?' said Geraldine.

Rebwar looked at his watch, it was 10 am. He nodded.

———

Rebwar was sitting in the hotel bar at the Holiday Inn in Hemel Hempstead. It was one of those places where you could get a drink without too many questions being asked, although they had been made to wait until 11 am for the bar to open. Rebwar had drunk a few coffees by then, and both had used the facilities to tidy themselves up, as if they'd had a hard day on a building site. Geraldine put two pints on their little table. Both gulped down a third of it. Stella. It tasted good and washed the dust and horror off the day.

'What about the girl? Stockholm syndrome...'

'Yeah... Rebs, we have to let it go. We got that fucker.'

'Do you feel better?'

Geraldine pushed her chair back with her feet and looked at the ceiling. 'Not really. Still hurts. But I feel like justice has been done. We were lucky.'

Rebwar raised an eyebrow. 'Yeah, I know, stop looking at me like that. It was stupid, but I was angry. Still am.'

'It'll fade. Time slowly passes like grains of sand. We were lucky.' He took another sip of his beer. 'And my Visa?'

Geraldine laughed. 'You don't give up, do you? I'll ask.' And she looked at him. 'OK, I don't know for sure, but you're doing OK, right? We did good. We solved a crime. Sure, you'll get paid. We found what they were looking for. I mean, we found the Gipsy. What carnage!' She looked at her scratched hands and took another sip of her drink.

'What now?'

'We wait for them to call us in. See where the dust settles. Sure, Zane will go back to his cell. Won't be missed, stupid waste of space. Break my sister's heart, though, and she'll probably blame me for not helping. Bitch.'

'Family!' Rebwar finished his pint. 'Same again?'

FIFTY

Rebwar was standing in front of Matt's house. He finished his cigarette and crushed it with his shoe. He straightened his black jacket and shirt, then smoothed his fingers through his hair. He walked up to the door and rang the bell, waited for a moment until someone shuffled up to the door. It was Mrs Adkins with her sunken eyes staring at him.

'Hello, Mrs Adkins. I need to talk to you and your daughter.' She pushed the door, trying to close it and Rebwar pushed back with his hand. 'I have some important information, Mrs Adkins. Please give me a moment of your time. It's important, and it concerns your son.'

'Mum! Who is it?'

'It's that foreign idiot from your Dad's garage. Thinks he knows everything. Please go away and leaves us alone. I am a grieving widow, don't you know? I'll call the police, do you understand?'

'Please, Mrs Adkins.'

'Mum, mum!' It was Mandy, Matt's daughter. 'Hi, it's Rebwar isn't it?'

'Yes, I have information about your brother, Gary.'

'Let him in, Mum. See what he has to say.'

Her mum opened the door just enough for him to come in. She tutted and went into the living room. The various bouquets of sympathy flowers were now sagging, petals scattered the carpet.

'Mum, you making a cup of tea?'

'He has to earn it. No.' She leaned back on the plastic-covered sofa.

'It's OK. I'm fine. Please sit down.' Rebwar found himself a chair to sit on. 'I know what your son did, and you need to listen to me.'

Mrs Adkins crossed her arms and took a deep breath.

'Gary was involved in the murder, and I know you know this.'

'How dare you accuse him...'

'Please, Mrs Adkins.'

Mandy looked at him with her head slightly twisted to the side.

'I heard them having arguments. He wanted your husband to develop the land, to sell it. But Matt didn't want to. And Gary had debts. And, by the way, the police probably know a lot of this. They are building a case. So just stop protecting him. Those boys on scooters were his old friends, weren't they? Got on the wrong side of the law. He was involved with the gang. I found glass fragments in his leather jacket, which were from my car when I was mugged by the scooter gang. Did he promise them money?'

Both of them were quiet.

'I know Matt didn't want to sell and probably you two disagreed with him too. It wasn't making much money. Perhaps he should have retired or at least planned for it. So where are you hiding Gary? He's not in Pakistan, is he?'

'How do you know all this?'

'Emails,' lied Rebwar.

'India, Mr Rebwar. That's where he is,' said Mrs Adkins.

'India, OK, well I'm just going to give you some advice. I'm not going to go to the police as I have no evidence, but you should, otherwise you two will be spending most of your time in the near future at the police station. Hand him in. Or convince him that he needs to give himself up. Look... any one of those boys from the gang will grass on him in a heartbeat. They probably already have. And the police will easily play them off against each other. They're young kids. You understand?'

'Mum.'

Mrs Adkins raised her hand at Mandy.

'Mr Rebwar, this is no help. He will go to prison, and my son is not guilty. Those kids murdered my husband. My child is innocent.'

'Have you asked him? Have asked him to swear to tell you the truth, on his father's grave? Have you looked into his eyes and been convinced that he's not lying?'

Mrs Adkins looked away and at the ceiling. 'I tell you my son was not involved.'

'I heard your son lie to his father. He set him up. Asked him to be there on that day. Wasn't Matt supposed to be at the pub with his mates? Every Friday afternoon, it was the betting shop and then to the pub. He was never at the car wash on a Friday afternoon when I was working there, but on that day...'

'It was those men who asked for those foreign workers. Not my son.'

'Yes, that was a convenient excuse. Clever on his part to take the opportunity of making everybody think it was a gang muscling in. But they were only interested in putting their own workforce in the car wash. It made no sense to kill him. They're not going to make money out of a dead man, are they?'

'Mr Rebwar, we don't believe you.'

Rebwar got up. 'Just ask your son what he has done, and then convince him to give himself up. The police will find him and arrest him soon, and you, unless you turn him in. Or you could all go to prison for accessory to murder. Mandy you have your whole future in front of you. Please don't throw it all away.'

Mandy looked at him, her eyes welling up. 'He didn't do it. No! Why would he?'

Rebwar hated to see the young girl so distraught. 'Money. You know your brother had bad debts. Matt had enough of bailing him out. You know this, Mrs Adkins. I am now going to leave you both and hope you do the right thing.' He left the two women looking shocked and broken, staring at the living room floor, strewn with faded petals. He closed the front door and walked down the road.

———

On the following Sunday Rebwar took the day off. He usually liked to work on Sunday as it was a happier, chattier crowd but the previous few days had taken their toll. He needed some rest and was going to listen to a football game on the radio. He preferred that to the TV, he could sometimes imagine that he was back in Iran, and Musa and Hourieh were probably going to go out. They hated the sound of the commentary; they both wanted music that they could chat over. He had told them what he was going to do but they were still there having tea with only fifteen minutes till the match started.

'Not going out?'

Rebwar glanced over to see Musa's black t-shirt. *I'm not always sarcastic, sometimes I'm asleep* was written on it in white type.

'It's raining again.' Hourieh said. 'This country is just wet, wet. Musa, why don't you listen to the match with your father.' Musa looked at them both like he had just been told to clean the bathroom. ' And have you got any washing? Like that t-shirt, that joke has worn thin.' He looked down at it and spotted a few stains, took it off and handed it to her. He went back to his room. 'Well, that'll be that for today. Might see him this evening for his dinner. Husband, give me that top. And is that tea set fixed?'

Rebwar took his tank top off and went to his bedroom for a clean one. In a new outfit, he sat on the living room couch and switched on the little portable digital radio. He lit a cigarette and choose an old copy of *Abrar-e Varzeshi*, Iran's sports paper. The radio bleeped to 3 pm and the news came on.

'David Davis, the Brexit secretary, has announced that the repeal bill will also "end the supremacy" of EU law in the UK, "delivering" on the result of last year's referendum. He went on to say that the UK is planning on scrapping all EU laws. In further news, police have arrested three members of a family in Enfield, east London relating to the murder of Mr Matthew Adkins, who was found dead at his car wash a few weeks ago.'

Musa walked into the room with a new t-shirt which said *I put the 'I' in anxiety*; he said to Rebwar,' You mind if I listen to the match?'

'Sit. Sit, here.' Rebwar got up and cleared the sofa of old newspapers. 'You want anything? Beer?'

'Really?'

'Just a few sips as it's Arsenal vs Tottenham. Who are you supporting now?' Rebwar went into the kitchen to get the beers, as his son settled on the sofa.

———

DID YOU ENJOY THE BOOK?

Thank you for reading my book and hope you enjoyed as much I did writing it. If you could find a moment to leave a review for which I would be eternally grateful for. This helps other readers to find this book and share the buzz. It only has to be a few words, a rating or even a helpful vote on a reviewer's comments. It all helps us indie authors to get the word out.

The Contact

Sign up at www.olsschaber.com and get your free novella.

A prequel to the Rebwar series where we meet his first contact Clive. A dramatic inciting incident sets off a chain of events where Rebwar is left to pick up the pieces.

Rebwar - The Missing Parts

(Book 1)

Ex-Iranian police detective Rebwar hides from his past behind the wheel of his London Uber. But when an enigmatic organisation threatens to expose his identity, he has no choice but to lend them his skills. And when his missing persons assignment leads only to a severed foot, he'll have to connect it to a body to prevent being deported.

When he finds his quarry's wife in bed with another man, Rebwar is forced to revive his old interrogation methods to extract a confession. But when the case is closed despite body parts still appearing, he's convinced there is more to the murder than his superiors want known. Determined to learn the truth, his private investigation uncovers a conspiracy that could see him torn to pieces

Rebwar - Plan B

(Book 3)

Iranian ex-detective Rebwar still struggles to gain his footing in

London. Barely making ends meet driving an Uber, he can't keep his marriage from fraying. And when the shadowy agency blackmailing him orders an investigation into one of their own, he's caught between domestic stress and clandestine murder.

In over his head when a key political figure is killed, Rebwar walks a knife's edge of danger pursuing the truth. But when his main informant disappears, he exposes a plot for him to take a fatal fall.

Can Rebwar finally unmask his sinister employers before he loses his family... and his life?

When I started writing the series, I put my main character Rebwar in a council tower block in Chalk Farm London. It's called the Chalcots estate and is a typical 60s development that are dotted across London and the rest of the UK. I picked the Dorney building to put his family in, which is one of the four towers in that estate. When I started to write the second book, the Grenfell tragedy happened and a few weeks afterwards the government took the decision to evacuate all the buildings with the same cladding.

And that it the reason that I have included Grenfell in the story and is my small tribute to the disaster. My books are fiction and there to entertain but also hold grains of reality. You can read more about the disaster with these links below. Also, if you feel like contributing a donation to all these people that suffered this terrible tragedy, I am also putting a link to some charities. I certainly have. Thanks Ols

Charities
Grenfell Foundation - www.grenfellfoundation.org.uk
They support the survivors in the community.

British Red Cross - www.redcross.org.uk
One the of the key foundations that dealt with the immediate aftermath and are still helping.

Ols Schaber, The Missing Parts: Rebwar. Kindle Edition & print.

ACKNOWLEDGMENTS

I must thank the people around me that have made this series possible. I feel so lucky to have them there and they encourage me to keep going. It's quite an undertaking writing a good yarn and even more to self publish. I couldn't have done it without them. My amazing wife Tracey who helped edit this book as well as my editor Ed Handyside, my brother Fred, and so many other great friends. You know who you are.

NOTES

Chapter 34

1. . Good morning.

Chapter 41

1. .. Don't be so tired. Saying when someone's been working hard.

Chapter 43

1. .. Filth